The Och

By Euan Stewart McIver

Copyright

Dedicated to :

Hector and Eileen who always believed I would finish this.

Alexanderina for inspiring the idea long ago while recording tombstone inscriptions and for showing me many of the places mentioned in this book.

And Rick for his faith in this work and without whose encouragement it would never have been finished.

Preface :

Many years ago, in a graveyard in Edinburgh, the idea for this story was born. It became a short story which was then developed into a fully blown narrative, using real places and (mostly) real people. It is set in a time of great change and activity in Scottish history. Using old maps, historical data and Parish Records this story has its roots in fact.

The Ochil Eye stone does exist and two examples of this semi precious agate sat on my desk during most of the writing and rewriting of this work.

Some ends are left open – for a sequel, when time allows.

THE OCHIL EYE - ...being the Memoirs of the Reverend William Lindsay, M.A. sometime Episcopal minister of the Paroch of Avay in the Shire of Stirling and later Keeper of the King's Papers at the Jacobite Court at Rome 1681 — 1747.

This is his story, arranged in chapters and set forth for the first time

 "Ilka thing hath its time

An' sae had Kings o' the Stewart line."

Old Scots Saying.

CONTENTS : <u>PART ONE</u>

<u>The Rev. William Lindsay's Narrative 1681 - 1685</u>

<u>PART TWO</u>

<u>A Tale Told by the Fire 1681 - 1685</u>

<u>PART THREE</u>

<u>The Rev. William Lindsay Continues his Narrative 1686 - 1747</u>

<u>PART ONE.</u>

<u>The Rev. William Lindsay's Narrative 1681-85.</u>

<u>I Come to Avay.</u>

I well remember my entry into the kirk and manse of Avay. The bright, April morning sunshine was glinting on the rocky face of Craigleith, where the Stirling Castel fowlers catch their falcons, as my horse splashed through the waters of Kaverkie Burn and I found myself within the bounds of the parish, that was to be the scene of my ministerial labours till destiny caught me up in her political web.

Times were troubled then and feelings ran high on matters of religion. But two years before, that saintly man, James Sharp, ArchBishop of St. Andrews, had been dragged from his coach by those who supported the Covenants and cruelly murdered on wild Magus Muir before the very eyes of his bairn.

Not long after, the Duke of Monmouth, defeated those same wry-necked Presbyterians at Bothwell Brig. I mind the prisoners being brought into Edinburgh, for I chanced at that time to be visiting a cousin who was finishing his studies at the college.

Even then Davie Lindsay showed his Presbyterian leanings and I was, therefore, not surprised when he suggested we should watch the entry of the captive Covenanters. Douce housewives and canny tradesmen thronged the Grassmarket to see the hillfolk marched in by the dragoons.

A greasy 'prentice loon next me in the crowd gave me a dunt that sent my "Horace", a volume that I prized much, flying from out under my oxter into the gutter.

"Fourteen hunner hillmen," he exclaimed, greatly excited, "an' they're gaun tae herd them a' like nowt intae the Greyfriar's kirkyaird."

"Blessed are ye when men shall revile ye and persecute ye for My sake," piously interjected an elderly grey-haired man, who had overheard the lad's remark. And I thought I heard Cousin Davie add "Amen" as I bent down to pick up my treasured volume.

Troth to tell, though I could not in all conscience agree with their unnatural rebellion against the government of God's annointed King, I was, in no small measure, moved by their courage and tenacity of purpose, but I would not have said so to Cousin Davie, who was all too ready to convert me to his way of thinking. And so it was that my ain faith, Episcopacy, was riding the rigging of church polity, when Sir Charles Erskine,the Laird of Avay, presented me, William Lindsay, master of Arts of the University of Sanct Androis, to his kirk on the twentieth day of April in the year 1681.

I had just attained my twenty first year and though my person was of small interest to myself, my friends considered me a well set-up young man. In stature I was close on five feet and eight inches. My own hair was reddish brown but I favoured a black wig falling fully over my shoulders. Both my parents were dead and I was their only child. From my schoolmaster father's mother, who had married late in life, I inherited my grey eyes: from my paternal grandfather, a Highland tailor, I had gotten my voice, soft in tone, yet sounding clear from the pulpit. But enough of these personal vanities.

When I came to the bridge at the mill burn I reined in my horse and looked about me. The cottar houses were neatly kept but showed no signs of much prosperity. I observed that the thatch was in poor order.

Yet, in contrast, on my right lay a tidy, two-storied house with a rig of arable land before it. Some hens scraped in the midden at the door. A young staig was tethered to a tree. _From the byre came the lowing of a cow. Altogether the place had the appearance of being a croft of some importance. Later I learnt it was the Butterha' of Avay, belonging to James Alexander, a feuar of some standing in the village.

Across the burn the smith was busy, hammering a horse shoe into shape. Great beads of sweat stood out on his face as he thrust the bar of iron into the furnace and then beat the glowing metal to his satisfaction. I watched until the whole operation was perfected for the skill of those who work with their hands has always fascinated me.

Then this heir to the craft of Tubal Cain looked up, caught sight of me and shouted:

"Are ye for the toun or the Strude, Sir?"

"Neither," I replied. "It's the kirk and the manse I'm seeking."

"Haud straucht up the brae, Sir."

Giving me a searching look, he added, hesitantly,

"Micht ye be Mr. William Lindsay, oor new meenister?"

"That I am," I replied.

Whereupon the smith came forward to the bridge end.

"I'm John Paterson, Sir, an' this is my smiddy. Folk ca' it the Island fur the hill burn rins on ae side an' the mill lade on the ither as ye can see. I'll be weel pleased tae help ye at ony time. The session aye gies me the kirk wark - repairin' the gate locks an' mendin' the bell. I pit on a new half wheel tae the bell but sax months syne, an' a puckle o' nails I ca'd intae the timmer o' the ruif.

Weel, Sir, I wish ye a' happiness in Avay. We're sair needin' a meenister. Mr. Forbes, man, lay lang ill or he deed an', as ye ken, the kirk's standit vacant a gey while "

Having expressed my thanks to the smith for his kindly greetings I urged my horse forward. The way to the manse lay through a long avenue of chestnut trees that were then beautiful in bud. On the rising ground to the left I spied a small clachan which I took to be that part of the village, called the Strude. According to our Scottish historians a great battle was fought there in Pictish times, but for my own part I know not what to believe concerning the matter.

Certainly, in my time at Avay, John Marshall, whose croft was the biggest in the Strude, unearthed a skeleton when digging beside a great rock. The body had been buried in a curious fashion, for the knees were bent so that the corpse lay in a crouching position, which the Laird assured me was the custom in Pictish times. Moreover, there is the great pillar of stone standing in the field that borders the road leading from the kirk itself to the Strude. Strange lettering covers the face of this stone which I believe to resemble that "idolatrous monument" (as the sour Presbyterians dubbed it) at Ruthwell kirk, which the General Assembly in my father's time ordered to be cast down.

Howbeit I must not digress over much for I write, not of the ancient past, but of the past that once was my youth — Eheu fugaces!

My first glimpse of the manse of Avay was indeed disappointing. It was altogether ruinous. The eastern gable was bulging outwards and great holes gaped cruelly in the northern wall. The thatch was mouldy. The windows needed glazing. As I pushed open the front door it sagged drunkenly and I saw that the crooks and bands needed the attention of John Patterson, the Smith.

A fustit smell filled my nostrils. There were two firerooms below and one above. The south laigh room was pavemented but green with damp. The walls had been roughly cast with lime. Above was little better for the deals of the floor were showing signs of rot. I went outside to observe the office houses -a barn, byre, stable, brew house and coal fold. These were no better than the house itself; if possible they were worse. Yet I noticed that some attempt had been made to prepare against my incoming. In the house, floors had been swept, and outside, a supply of coals and peats had been got.

At my induction the kirk was thronged, not with parishioners alone but with folks from neighbouring villages. The service was conducted by Mr. Humphry Galbraith, minister of Dollar, who read the letters of collation and institution from Andrew, Lord Bishop of Dunkeld.

Thereafter Mr. Galbraith handed me the Holy Bible, the keys of the church door, and the bell cord: and in the grounds of the manse and glebe, I was given symbols of earth and stone.

Mr. Galbraith, having given me the right hand of fellowship, the elders of the parish took me heartily by the hand, thus signifying their readiness and willingness to adopt me for their minister. wherein I rejoiced greatly and thanked my Maker.

My induction took place on a Wednesday and the following Sabbath I preached from the Psalms:

"I will lift up mine eyes unto the hills, from whence cometh my help."

I considered this appropriate as the parish nestled at the Hillfoots of the Ochils. After divine service that Sabbath I met with the session in the kirk, for we had no session house, to enquire into several matters anent the government of the kirk and the conduct of the parish.

William Smith, in addition to being the schoolmaster of Avay and precentor in the kirk, was also the session clerk. He was a tall, lantern-jawed man of forty years of age, scholarly enough considering the meanness of the parish and the smallness of his salary, but without method in the keeping of the church records as you shall see presently.

Before I proceeded to my examination Mr. Smith asked at me about making appointments to two vacant elderships,

"Mr. Lindsay," said he, "as you know there has been a long vacancy in Avay kirk, in the course of which two elders have died. Patrick Morris looked after Kaverkie and James Thomson the East Quarter. Their work is at present shared by the other elders but it would be more satisfactory if two honest men were now chosen. Will you consider this, Sir?"

"The appointment of an elder," I replied, "is a matter that cannot be undertaken without due consideration. I am not willing to proceed in the matter as yet, for as you all understand I know nothing about the place or the people.

When I judge the time is ripe I shall make intimation to you and examine the proposals set forward."

This they agreed to without further ado.

"Now, Mr. Smith," I proceeded, "I must enquire into the kirk records. What accounts have you of the session meetings and of the box and of disbursements?"

"Sir, I have never seen any records: indeed, if there were any at all before my time, they must be lost or eaten by the mice with which the kirk is plagued."

"But, surely Mr. Smith," I pressed him, "you have some papers anent the management of this kirk."

Thereupon he muttered something about a few years' accompts of expenses and disbursements.

"Show me," I urged him, "What is in the chest belonging to the session."

He then produced a few scattered and confused sheets, but, in regard they had little or nothing of discipline in them and hardly any sense could be picked out of the accompts the items being so badly set down, I did lay them aside.

"What of the registers of baptisms, marriages and deaths?" I continued in my examination.

Again he brought forth some sheets of small paper sewn together on which were roughly recorded baptisms and marriages, but nothing that I could see of burials.

"Do you not record the deaths in the parish and the burials in the kirkyaird?" I asked, somewhat impatiently.

"It was not the custom when I came here to keep a record of burials," he answered dourly.

"Sir," I retorted, "you know well that every session ought to record the affairs of the parish under its care. In the keeping of the kirk records you have shown negligence, but from henceforth I shall take care that you attend to these matters with more diligence."

Turning to the session I asked if they were willing that proper books, well bound, be got at the expense of the church for registering the meetings of the session and for making entries relating to the accompts of this they gave their assent. I then said that I, myself, would write the records of the meetings of the session, and that the others would be the task of Mr. Smith, whom I again exhorted to keep henceforth an exact account.

"Now, Mr. Duncansone, please to give an account of the state of the box," I went on, addressing Alexander Duncansone, the boxmaster, a middle-aged weaver, very forth-right in his manner, who dwelt in the Green of Avay.

"Mr. Lindsay, wae's me tae tell ye, there's little at a' in the kirk's box. The parish is but sma' an' there's only ane heritor o' ony consideration, whilk is Sir Charles. Sae its nae wunner that the collections are puir. At this verra meenit we hae but sax punds Scots

13

an' ten pennies. The box has to pey the fees o' the session clerk an' the schulemaister an' the bellman, forbye the dues tae the synod an' presbytery. Then, Sir, there are aye charitable bodies gaun aboot that we maun be helpin' like that puir wuman last week frae Kelso that had her hoose brunt in the great fire."

With a sigh Duncansone added, "Forbye, Mr. Lindsay, a deal o' bad copper aye finds its wey intae the collection."

Accepting this explanation of the low state of the box as reasonable I passed on to examining the utensils of the kirk for the administering of the sacraments and the decent burial of the dead. Here indeed the poverty of the parish was made plain to me.

"Where is the baptismal laver and the tallow cloth?" I asked.

"The kirk of Avay has never had a basin nor a cloth," spoke up the schoolmaster. "The minister himself has been wont to furnish these items.".

"What then," I continued with heavy heart for the poverty of Christ's kirk, "of the plates, cups, and tablecloths for the solemnising of the Lord's Supper?"

"These, Mr. Lindsay" explained James Dawson, a dyster of substance and senior elder who had reached his allotted span, "are ordinarily got from the Laird's house. The kirk has, indeed, a communion table, supporters, and forms but I fear they need repair."

Passing from thence to the burial of the dead I enquired, "Does the kirk have a handbell or mortcloth?" And again the answer was in the negative. These items were borrowed from other places.

My next business was to enquire into the conduct of the schoolmaster and accordingly I asked him to step outside while I examined the elders on this head.

"Now," I went on, "you must tell me if Mr. Smith is diligent in educating the young ones committed to his care. Does he instruct them carefully in the scriptures? Does he conscientiously give attendance to both kirk and school? On your consciences I charge you to give honest answers."

John Rennie, a cordiner, whose skin was as brown as the leather he worked with, spoke first.

"Weel, Sir, I can testify that Mr. Smith is an eident maister. The bairns are aye keepit in order an' ken the catechism brawly. They can a' write a guid hand, dae a coont, an' read frae baith the auld and new testaments." With this statement the elders were all in agreement, which gave me much pleasure that in this poor parish the lamp of learning was being kept burning.

James Rob, ploughman at the Bole, stood up."Before ye ca' back the maister I think we sud say tae ye, Mr. Lindsay, that the folk o' Avay are maistly puir cottars whereby they canna keep their bairns at the schule the hail year through. Ye maun ken, Sir, that in spring an' summer the bairns has tae leave aff their buiks tae help in the herdin'an' in fact in a' thing dealin' wi' the husbandry o' the place.

But when the hairst is in an' the herdin' ower we tak tent tae send the bairns tae Mr. Smith."

This I readily understood having been reared myself in a country place. Howbeit I took the opportunity, when Mr. Smith rejoined the meeting, to exhort him to use his utmost endeavours to give the young ones some insight into the knowledge of God and the principles of religion.

"You will remember, Mr. Smith, to pray morning and evening at the coming and at the going away of your scholars. You must also be sure to teach short forms of grace and of prayer that they may use by themselves. See to it also that each scholar attends the kirk punctually. Be as careful of the poor scholars for whom the session will pay you as you are of those whose parents pay for them. Punish all swearing," I entreated him, "with the utmost severity for it is, in truth, a sin that stinks in the nostrils of all good Christians."

"That I will, Mr. Lindsay," promised the schoolmaster.

Looking straight across at the bellman and kirk officer I went on,"Robert Stalker, see to it that the communion furniture is repaired straightwith and have every breach in the dyke of the kirkyaird repaired, for I will suffer no beast to roam therein and graze. You must answer to all these matters on your peril," I concluded with the utmost sternness, as I thought it best to make it known I was not to be trifled with.

This first meeting with the session I closed with prayer, calling upon the elders to thank God for His goodness in providing them a ministry after the long vacancy caused by the religious struggles of the times and the late Mr. Forbes' ill health.

As I walked back to the manse by the path leading through the kirkyaird the Sabbath calm came flooding over my spirit and I reflected that in truth my lines had fallen in pleasant places, though my heritage was not as goodly as I had expected. In time, however, I promised myself all things would be redd.

May 29th was the anniversary of His Majesty, King Charles II's birth and restoration and therefore I preached to my people on this solemnity, impressing upon them the goodness of God in restoring to Scotland the House of Stewart.

And it was at this time by the singular working of Divine Providence that I was brought into the presence of James, Duke of York, brother to King Charles. The Earl of Argyll had a grand town house in Stirling (which is about seven miles distant from Avay) close to the castel - called Argyll's Ludging. It was here that the Duke of York paid him a visit in the year of my coming to Avay - 1681.

From the Laird of Avay himself I heard of the impression made by the Duke of York who had been given the freedom of Stirling.

"Ah, Mr. Lindsay, what charm His Highness has, and his delightful lady and their daughter, the Princess Anne. I declare their aimiability has won all hearts yonder in Stirling. My Lady was quite taken with a novelty the Duchess has brought from England. 'Tis a new brewed drink called tea."

"Indeed, Sir Charles. How is this tea drink brewed?"

"To be sure I did not learn much of its making but it is a foreign leaf, very dry, and I believe the ladies place it in boiling water, drinking the infusion thereof."

"I think, Sir Charles, I prefer my own kind of brewing for, as the miller is always declaring, there's nought like "gude ale tae keep the hert aboon." I hear, Sir, that the Duke is much interested in the game of tennis."

"That he is. I had the honour of playing with him last week in the castel gardens. One of his gentlemen told me that His Highness, when in Edinburgh, played also at the Golf on the links at Leith."

"It is unfortunate that Stirling cannot vie with Leith in providing golf links, Sir Charles."

"Ah, Mr. Lindsay, but Avay offers the Duke a better sport than golf and His Highness has graciously accepted my invitation."

"Avay, Sir! Comes the Duke of York hither?"

I was astounded and Sir Charles, observing my surprise, laughed, "Surely you have not forgotten our Craigleith falcons, Mr. Lindsay. The Duke comes here next Wednesday to hunt."

"Avay is indeed honoured, Sir Charles."

"Aye, Sir, and Avay House shall not be found wanting in rendering all service to the Royal Duke. But Mr. Lindsay, before I go, here is a tale that you will enjoy."

"Of the Duke, my Lord?"

"Of the Duke of York and of the Earl of Argyll. 'Twill amuse you to hear of how that zealous Presbyterian Argyll was put out of countenance. His Highness was in a humour and addressed Argyll thus:

"My Lord, if you will do me one thing you may be the greatest man in Scotland."

Argyll, Mr. Lindsay, looks startled and asks dryly,

"What may that be Your Highness?"

The Duke replied: "If you do this I shall be singularly obliged"

Argyll, becoming a trifle impatient, repeats:

"What is it that you deSire me to do, Sir?"

There is a moment's silence and the Duke declares softly:

"Exchange the worst of religions for the best."

Sir Charles laughed heartily."I tell you, Mr. Lindsay, Argyll and his friends looked sour, but those of us who support the present church government smiled, for we knew it was a well-aimed hit at the Presbyterian opposition to the King and his brother."

The following Wednesday, at about three in the afternoon I was busy transcribing what existed of the old records and setting in order the new, when a great tirling at the manse door, such as might wake the very dead in the kirk-yaird, sent Mrs. Spowart, my housekeeper, a kindly widow of upwards of fifty years, running from her kitchen crying aloud:

"The Lord hae mercy on us! What gars ye tirl sae, whae'er ye be?"

As I laid down my quill I heard the voice of Charles Morris, the Laird's falconer, shout in agitation

"Haste ye! haste ye! Mrs. Spowart. Whaur's the meenister? The Duke o' York hae stumbilt on the hill an' twistit his leg. Sir Charles is helpin' him doon tae the manse."

As an afterthought Morris went on:

"He thinks it's ower far tae tak him tae the big Hoose."

By this time I was at the door. Morris, white-faced and trembling, called out:

"Mr. Lindsay. The Duke o' York's hurt -- "

"Yes, yes, Morris: that I have gathered. Tell Sir Charles I shall have everything ready. Mrs. Spowart, get kettles of boiling water ready and strips of linen."

When Sir Charles and his men arrived with the injured Duke I was prepared with the linen cloths and Mrs. Spowart had my biggest basin full of hot water. His Highness hobbled into my great chair

"Sir Charles," I ventured, "if I may help I shall be glad. In the course of my studies I learned a little of medicine."

The Duke signed assent and I came forward. I soon discovered that the trouble was a wrench of the ankle bone.

When I had bathed the injured part and bound it in linen strips, I looked up and saw for the first time full in the face, my unexpected visitor and patient –His Royal Highness, James, Duke of York.

The face into which I gazed was oval shaped, the chin resolute, the lips prominent though not over full, the long nose thin and finely proportioned, and the eyebrows bold. But it was his dark eyes, glowing with depth of feeling, that drew me to him. His voice, when he spoke, was exceeding pleasant.

"I am indebted to you, Sir. Your touch is more healing than that of my own physician. May I rest here until Sir Charles' coach comes? He assures me it will not be long.

"Indeed, Your Highness," broke in the Laird, "it should be here at once. I sent a man off for it the moment I discovered your hurt."

"Sir, I should be honoured," I replied with a deep bow. "I am a poor country minister but what I have is yours to command."

"Ah, Sir Charles, there is an expression of loyalty that many in Scotland would do well to copy. Tell me, Mr. Lindsay, is your church here a building set up after the Reformation or is it the old kirk in which the Mass was once celebrated?"

"Some rebuilding has taken place, Your Highness. Alexander Bruce, of the Bruce of Culross family, restored the west wall and had a tablet set in with his arms, but the floor and the crypt below belong to earlier times."

"So there is a crypt. What is proposed to be done with it?"

Sir Charles spoke. "It is my intention to use it, as a burial vault for my family."

"A worthy use, Sir Charles, but may it be long yet ere you have need for the Erskine Vault. Hark! Do I hear the sound of wheels?"

"Yes, Your Grace. The coach is here to take you back to Avay House."

The Duke of York rose and leant upon Sir Charles' arm. With a smile he turned to me:

"Come, Mr. Lindsay. A good physician attends upon his patient. Help me to the coach." '

With the aid of myself and the Laird, James Stewart got himself into the Erskine coach. The driver was climbing up into his seat when the Duke leant forward to me at the window. -

"Continue to serve the House of Stewart, as you have done this day, Mr. Lindsay, with affection and loyalty."

And before I could reply a word he leant back and the driver, a sign from Sir Charles, whipped on the horses.

The coach lumbered off down the kirk brae between the long line of trees, bordering either side of the road to the House of Avay. As it disappeared from view and the dust settled on the highway I felt, for the first time in my life, the stirring of a deep personal loyalty to the Stewarts, which, when the time was ripe, set me in a way of thinking, that at length brought me to this city where in the sunset of my days I pen my story.

I write not for vain self-glory, nor to explain why I have followed the House of Stewart, for that like the love of a man for a maid defies cold reasoning. It is a thing of the heart. I write simply that those who come after me may catch a glimpse of the romance of destiny that has been my life.

As the summer advanced and the labour was over I informed the Session of my intention to examine the people. James Dawson, the dyster, now well advanced in years and a man of quiet zeal for the kirk, spoke to me anent the sacrament of the Lord's Supper.

"Sir," he said, and I can catch again in memory the sincerity of his voice, "for several years bypast, by reason of the long vacancy and the late minister's lingering sickness before his death, we of this parish have not had the benefit of communion beneath our ain kirk roof. Many deSire such an occasion earnestly, even as the hart that panteth after the water brook. Will it be possible this summer?"

"Brethren," I replied, "much as I deSire myself to partake of the sacrament in this kirk, yet I cannot adventure on so solemn an action before I have examined the people twice or thrice. It is my earnest hope that by next Spring all will be in good temper to proceed to the tables."

Old James lifted himself painfully from the elders' seat for an ague racked his limbs:

"God's will be done, Mr. Lindsay. My years have been many and fruitful in this place. May I be spared to be at the Lord's Supper next year."

My heart was full at this expression of devotion and I am glad to record that when the time came the worthy old dyster was at the first table I served.

After my diets of examination when I reported to the Session anent the parishioners, I rejoiced that I was able to say I had found most families well versed in the Scriptures and knowledgeable in the ways of God.

And so the months slipped by as I went about my ministry throughout the parish and the common folks laboured at their day's darg.

In August Sir Charles Erskine went to Edinburgh to walk (along with the Lyon King of Arms) in the funeral procession of John, Duke of Rothes, Lord High Chancellor of Scotland, which melancholy ceremony was afterwards engraved by Alexander Kincaid, wherein you may see Sir Charles any time you chance upon the artist's plates.

At the end of the year there was much excitement in the country. Argyll, having been arrested for treason and incarcerated in the Castel of Edinburgh, managed to escape and went into hiding.

Of these matters I knew little personally, hearing only the general reports.

Four years later, of a summer's night, I was to be told from the lips of Argyll's own friends, the story of that daring escape.I

GRAVEL ON THE WINDOW PANE.

Charles II died on Friday, February 6th, 1685, but it was some days before the news came to Avay from the Castel of Stirling.

The following Sunday I preached from The Second Book of Samuel, otherwise called The Second Book of Kings:

"Know ye not that there is a prince and a great man fallen this day in Israel."

And there was scarce a dry eye in the whole congregation, for Charles Stewart had sought to govern his people well and all were sensible of it. Afterwards the Laird graciously commented on the powerfulness of my preaching.

My cousin Davie, with whom I had watched the Covenanting prisoners in Edinburgh in our student days, now a convinced Presbyterian and tutor to the son of a gentleman of the same persuasion, wrote to me in the month of April, describing a great equestrian statue of our late King that the Provost and council of Edinburgh had set up in Parliament Close.

Loving Cousin,

I trust you are in good health as I am. I write to tell you that I hope to be in your part of the kingdom at the end of this month so you may expect to see me. It will please you to hear that the town council of Edinburgh have set up a monument of Charles II on horseback in Parliament Close, where it was proposed some years ago to place a stone image of Oliver Cromwell, which figure now lies on Leith sands where it was landed the very time news was brought of Cromwell's death. The Baillies of the town, the hypocrites, did leave off their project to honour Cromwell and set about getting in its stead a statue of the restored Stewart and now, at long last is hither. The common folks were much amazed at it, crying out it was like unto the image of Nebuchadnezzar.

I have had some business across the sea from which I hear that the keepers of Israel slumber not nor sleep and I think it best to let you know this.

When I come I shall bring you the copy of Bishop Burnet's History you deSired me to obtain for you and which I got at little expense it being second-hand.

D Lindsay.

At Colinton, near Edinburgh.

April l685.

It was addressed on the back:

For the Rev. William Lindsay, the Manse of Avay, to the care of the postmaster at Stirling.

I was glad to hear of the fine leaden monument set up exactly two months after the death of the king though made uneasy by remark about the keepers of Israel, whose meaning I took to mean that Argyll and his party were conspiring in Holland against King James.

Davie, in his own way, was kind for he sought to warn me that a successful Presbyterian rising would mean trouble for Episcopalians like myself. For myself I was not alarmed: for the kirk I was deeply troubled.

That was April. May brought with it the old May-Day customs, which though frowned on by the kirk as relics of heathendon and Popery, were still engaged in by the country folks. Early on May-Day morning I saw a flock of young women setting off for the upper slopes of the hills to bathe their faces in the dew. I spoke to Mrs. Spowart anent this folly but she defended her sex valiantly.

"Awa' wi' ye, Mr. Lindsay: it's a grand fur the lassies tae weet themsels wi' the hay dew. I did it myself forty year syne an' bonnie red cheeks I had."

"But, Mrs. Spowart," I remonstrated, "it is a heathenish practice from the times when our ancestors worshipped the sun and the seasons."

"Nae doot ye're tellin' the truth Sir, for I'm nae scholar tae gainsay ye nor are the lassies on the braes yonder. They dinna think on heathen times when they gang tae he hill. Their thochts are on the wabster lads an' the daffin' when they win back the toun."

As Mrs. Spowart turned from me to what she was cooking she added, "Youth maun has its fling".

I could see it would be a long time before the old customs died out: folks, like Mrs. Spowart, would cling to their wonted way, the kirk approving or not. And I knew Mrs. Spowart represented the mind of every cotter in Avay.

Up there at the shepherd's cottage beyond the Nebit, John Wilson and his sons would be busy, too, this first of May. They would cut a trench in the heather, kindle a fire, and make a caudle of eggs, butter, oatmeal, and milk. Part would be poured forth on the hillside as a libation and then John, Robert, William, and Andrew, would take a cake of oatmeal having marked on it nine points. Solemnly each of the nine sections be broken off and cast into the fire and as the shepherds did this, they would name the enemies of their flocks — the eagle, the fox, the stranger dog - thus hoping to keep danger from their sheep.

Mrs. Spowart was stirring her kail when I announced my intention of going to see any if any persons were engaging in May-Day visitations to St. Serf's well. Spurtle in hand, my housekeeper asked:

"For why can the puir bodies no tak' the waters o' the well freely as aince wis the wey? It's fine an' caller though a wee taste bitter tae the tongue. I mind my grandSire tellin' me hoo mony, an ane wi a blue face. cam tae St. Serf's an' gaed awe' nane the waur o' their veesit."

"The Presbytery and the Privy Council have forbidden it, Mrs. Spowart, because such visits often lead to unruly scenes. You must remember the commotion at the well of Strathill a few years ago,"

It wis a' a misunderstandin', Mr Lindsay - jist a mountain oot o' a molehill, as ye micht say. Strathill, like St. Fillan's, is guid for them no quite richt in their senses...weel, a puir man an' wife frae Comrie brocht their only bairn, a laddie, ill o' a brain fever tae Strathill. Eh, Sir, it wis like the story o' oor Lord lang syne. The dementit laddie, efter bein' dippit in the well, ran wild intae a nearby fairmyaird, sendin' a' the swine i' the place fleein' liked crazed beasts intae the stank behint the hoose whaur a' were drooned."

"How do you know this?" I asked for I had not heard this way of the incident before.

"I wisny there, but my nevoy was a pleugh laddie on the verra fairm whaur the swine gaed daft an' he tellt me it wi' his ain lips."

"Ah, Well, Mrs. Spowart, whatever happened at Strathill, I wish no unseemly gatherings here," I replied, grasping my stick end making ready to set off.

When I reached the well there was no one there save John Muirs, a dull-witted servant lad employed by John Monteath of Westquarter and of the Highland country by birth. Some time previously the Session had rebuked this lad for hunting sheep with dogs on the Sabbath day from the top of the hills to the stubble grounds used for pasturage.

I felt sorry for the lad for he had little English, his own tongue being the Gaelic, and he was not accustomed to our Lowland Sabbath discipline.

"What seek ye here, John?" I inquired, in a kindly tone, to set him at his ease.

"White stones, Sir," he replied haltingly.

"White stones? What mean you?"

"In the glens white stones are lucky," and with that he ran off. I did not understand him then, but I now know that in Highland parts, where John was born, round white stones have a magical association as tokens of good fortune.

Nobody else being in sight I turned my steps up the glebe brae to the manse." I was near to the east stile of the kirk when I heard a great clatter of hoofs. Before I could turn a voice cried:

"Mr. Lindsay."

It was the Laird, Sir Charles Erskine. I could see he was perturbed and I at once thought something was amiss with my lady or the bairns.

"Is aught wrong with Master Henry, Sir?" I asked anxiously, for the lad was but three years old and in the throes of a bout of chincough.

"Nay, thank God. All is well at the House of Avay, but not in Scotland, alas! A messenger has come this hour post haste from Stirling Castel with tidings that Argyll and his party have set sail from Amsterdam and are to land in the North. I must away to see what is needful for defending the fortress of Stirling and closing the way to any rebel force advancing on Edinburgh."

"The Lord protect us all, Sir Charles. Blood will certainly flow ere long if Argyll's plans succeed. Our Episcopal ways are in jeopardy, I fear."

"You speak rightly, Mr. Lindsay. Yet a greater fear assails my heart. A Presbyterian victory may well mean the end of James Stewart."

"The king, Sir!" I exclaimed aghast.

"Mark my words, for I have seen the beginning and the continuance of this struggle betwixt the kirk and the restored Stewarts. James will not yield and what will not yield needs break when the force opposing it is stronger.

Pray God that those of us who love the House of Stewart may be given strength enough to scotch this snake Argyll. But I must not tarry longer. I look to you to do everything necessary in Avay for the King's cause in my absence. Urge all who are able to bear arms to join the royal host at Stirling."

With these words he spurred on his horse and was quickly lost to sight.

I returned to the manse with my mind in much turmoil. Though I had lived in troublous times I had never been touched personally by the strife. I had first seen the light of day in the year of the Restoration, 1660, and I had been but a bairn at my father's school at Dairsie when the men of the south and west marched to Rullion Green. My father had remained loyal to the Episcopal church as had done his father before him. Cousin Davie's father had wavered a bit and, as you will have realised, Cousin Davie deserted to the Presbyterian party.

When Drumclog and Bothwell Brig were fought I was studying at Sanct Androis University and it was all finished with before I was licensed to preach. Here in this quiet parish I had gone about for four years undisturbed, but now the drums of war were echoing at my ain hearth stone.

Would the peaceful slopes of the Ochils resound to the tramping of soldiers and the grass be dyed red with the blood of the slain? Or more dreadful thought still — would I myself, a minister of the gospel, lay aside the garments of peace and gird my loins with the accoutrements of war to defend my Kirk and my King?

For, when Sir Charles bade me defend the King's cause I saw again the dark eyes of James Stewart, Duke of York, now King James VII, and I heard again his voice:

"Continue to serve the House of Stewart as you have done this day, Mr. Lindsay, with affection and loyalty."

That was 1681. This was 1685 and the throne to which James had succeeded on the death of his brother Charles was in great danger

As it so happened this threat to the Stewart House was averted more quickly than at first thought possible. Yet I knew on that fateful day when Sir Charles brought the news of Argyll's attack that a time would come, be it soon or late, when I would go forth among strange men to serve the Stewarts.

It was with a heavy heart that I took my candle upstairs to my bed chamber that night and my sleep was troubled. In the weeks that followed rumours of all sorts flew about the countryside - Argyll was in Islay; Argyll was in Kintyre; Argyll had gone through Glendaruel; Argyll was approaching Stirling Castel. This last report caused the authorities to send more troops to Stirling of which many were sent along the Hillfoots to quarter. In my Session records I noted that one troop of horse was stationed in the parish of Avay. Furthermore all the fencible men were called into Stirling to attend the King's Host so that only old men, women and bairns were to be seen about the cottages.

Then came the news of Monmouth's landing in England, so that King James' authority was defied in both kingdoms. The Session began to be anxious about the administering of the sacrament that year. William Smith, the schoolmaster and session-clerk, spoke for them all:

"We were wondering, Mr. Lindsay, if you were intending to celebrate the sacrament this summer. Since you have not gone further with the diets of examination the people are asking at us what is to be done."

"Brethren," I answered, "as you are all aware, the troubles of our nation are great this summer and the disorder of the state is palpable. The recent invasion of the Duke of Monmouth has worsened matters so I must let fall my resolution of going further with the diets and of administering the Lord's Supper. In the meantime let us pray for a speedy ending to this disturbance and confusion to the King's enemies."

"Aye, indeed, Sir," spoke up Alexander Duncansone the boxmaster, "for e'en noo we are bein' asked tae help them wha has sufferit at the hands o' Argyll's wild men frae the mountains. There is ootside a puir object frae Bute whas hoose was brunt doon an' his cattle herrit. What am I tae gie him frae the box? The cratur's 'hopin' tae win tae Leith whaur he has friens."

I looked at the accompt book.

"You may give him twelve shillings Scots and recommend him to the charity of the next parish on his journey"

A week after this or thereabouts we heard that Argyll was captured and on his way to Edinburgh. It was the 19th of June and when the news came to Stirling the soldiers at the castel did fire their cannons which resounded a great distance around.

By the end of the month Argyll was executed and on August 13th a fast of thankfulness was observed in Avay kirk for God's goodness in delivering the kingdom from war.

Two days later, about ten in the morning, I was walking out the highroad along the Hillfoots towards Kaverkie, when I met the Laird returning from Stirling. Though Sir Charles was not a tall man he carried himself so well on horseback that his figure was arresting, seeming greater than it was in truth. His natural red colouring shaded over with the brown of the summer's sun, which emphasised the long, clean cut lines of his visage and gave him an air of authority and resolution. In body as in face the Laird had that sparseness characteristic of the Avay Erskines.

When he saw me he reined in his horse and smiled for Sir Charles was ever a genial man.

"Good-morning, Sir. I trust I find you well after these trying times bypast," I cried.

"Well, Mr. Lindsay, but wearied: wearied in body and soul. Howbeit the danger has been averted for which we must all be thankful. Yet much remains to be done. There are still a number of rebels at large that we would do well to bring in."

"I thought, Sir, the leaders had all been accounted for."

"Cochran has been seized and also Ayloff and Rumbold, but Hume of Polwarth has managed to Holland. Yet it is not the leaders alone we seek but the lesser gentry whose machinations are no less troublesome and inimical to a settled government."

"Is it true then that a company of foot has been ordered to Stirling Castel for that very purpose?"

"True, indeed. Erskine of Cardross is still busy in Stirlingshire among the Presbyterian faction and Thomas Forrester in Menteith. Strange, Mr. Lindsay, but Forrester once served in Avay Kirk." _

"Forrester who left in '74?"

"The same man. The Privy Council had a deal of trouble with Forrester and his conventicles so that like the other Presbyterian malcontents he went to Holland returning this summer with Argyll.

By the way one of your name is wanted too - a David Lindsay of Colinton near Edinburgh who is believed to be an associate of Forrester. No relation I hope !"

Sir Charles laughed as he spoke for he jested but I felt as if stabbed to the heart for this was news of Cousin Davie that I had not heard.

31

Taking my confusion for embarrassment at such a possibility Sir Charles leant forwards :

"Take me not so seriously, Mr. Lindsay. I jest. King James has no more loyal Lindsay in all Scotland than yourself as I know well, whatever rascally fellow this namesake may be!"

"You are kind, Sir," I stammered forth. "Pray bear my greetings to my Lady Avay."

"That I will," he cried, setting off at a gallop.

Though the morning was dry, rain came driving along the hillside from Stirling way by early afternoon and then as evening fell, a chill mist began to drift down on the hills.

Mrs. Spowart was from home, visiting for a day or two a sick sister in Tulliallan, so I lit a fire in the south laigh room I used as my study and tried to rid my mind of the disturbing news of Cousin Davie.

The hill mist brought the darkness down quicker than usual so that it seemed more like an evening in autumn than in summer. A weariness coming over me I was nodding in my great chair when the clock struck ten.

Scarcely had the last stroke ceased echoing when I heard a pattering on the window pane. Lammas rains I thought and drew myself even closer to the fire's warmth. A few seconds later came another drumming on the window and this time I jumped from my chair, for I knew it was gravel from the path cast against the glazing.

Its meaning was clear. Someone was seeking admission but not openly. I drew the bar on the front door, looking out cautiously into the grey dark. All was silent save for the rain falling steadily.

I was about to turn indoors when from the depths of the evergreen bush at the door a voice whispered:

"Tis I, Cousin Davie."

For a moment I was petrified. Then I managed to say :

"Davie! What brinqs you here?

"Hush! Are you alone?"

"Yes. Mrs. Spowart has gone —-."

But my explanations were cut short. Davie glided from the shadow of the bush to my side, and pushing me into my own house, closed the door behind us. Once inside the study he said quickly and sharply. As a man uncertain of his security:

"Fasten the window shutters, Will."

When I had done so and lit a candle he breathed more freely.

" I am not troubled for myself, Cousin Will, but I would not harm you. All I want is refuge for the night for myself and my friends We shall be off by first light and none needs know you have sheltered insurgents"

This last he said with a wry smile.

"Your friends? Where are they?"

"At present, Will,they are making free with the hay in your barn, where we have tied our horses.

We dare not put up at the common inns but are counting on our friends. They await my signal to come in."

"But who are you with?"

"Erskine of Cardross; Thomas Forrester who preached here before you, Will; John Ure, a Stirling man friendly to the Covenant who acts as my servant; John Drysdaill, a Dollar man, Erskine's servant. I can tell you, cousin we are all hungry men having eaten little since daylight."

My mind was in a whirl. Here was I, an Episcopalian minister and a loyal subject of King James, being asked to shelter Presbyterian rebels and foes of the House of Stewart.

But there was little time to think it all out and since blood is aye thicker than water I said to Cousin Davie that he had better bring the others into the manse.

Thus I came to hear much about the man Argyll from his own followers.

My unexpected guests soon finished the great meat pasty which the thoughtful Mrs Spowart had left to serve me the three or four days she was away. They washed it down with my own brewing of ale and drew their chairs round the fire.

Then and only then was a word spoken of the times and the situation in which they were placed. Mr Forrester looked round the room.

" It was back in 1674 that I said farewell to this house Mr Lindsay. Many a pleasant hour I spent in this very room"

"The fortunes of war, Sir" I replied

"As you remark, the fortunes of war and my dislike of prelacy. The air of Holland was less choking than the air of Scotland "

"You have not been back in Scotland since then ?"

"Only once did I come, staying from spring 1681 to spring 1682 "

Mr Erskine of Cardross broke in :

"That was when you came to see Argyll, was it not ?"

"Richt you are, Mr Erskine. I came to sound Argyll anent his feelings to the Scotch Presbyterians in Holland "

"I was at the College in Edinburgh then" observed Erskine.

"And I had completed my studies,"added Cousin Davie. "As for William, here, he was settling into his kirk."

"Did you see the Riding of the Parliament in 1681?" Erskine asked Forrester.

"Of a surety I did. I was lodging in the White Horse Close near to the Palace of Holyrood House. The Riding was a procession of great splendour, with Argyll carrying the royal crown."

As Forrester mentioned the name of Argyll a melancholy settled on the fugitives. Cousin Davie voiced their thoughts when he broke the silence:

"And to think now that four years later, he has been executed, in that selfsame street, by the common hangman, before the rabble,and his head affixed to a spike on the west end of the Tolbooth for his enemies to jeer at."

"Friends," said Mr. Forrester, "We must not forget we are under Mr. Lindsay's roof. He has taken us in this night in Christian charity. Those in authority whom we rail against are of his party : we would be better to talk of other things."

"Nay, Sir," I hastened to say, "I am in troth mightily interested in the Earl of Argyll: though I like not his principles I am not so blinded by partisanship that I cannot recognise nobility of spirit and I believe he died a noble death. I shall hear gladly what you have to tell."

"You are tolerant, Mr. Lindsay, a virtue sadly lacking in these times," Forrester hastened to say. "I can tell you something of Argyll's story and the others have their share too in it."

"Recount your part, Mr. Forrester, and we shall all gladly help," was Erskine's comment.

"I think, John, the fire needs another log," I said to Mr. Erskine's man, who was nearest the fuel.

When John Drysdaill had built up the fire, Mr. Forrester fell to his tale. The flames, leaping up the wide chimney place, sent shadows flickering on the rough cast walls of the room and across the faces of the listeners. Forrester settled his slightly corpulent figure deep into my great chair, laying his plump fingers along the arms. Then he began to talk and his powers of oratory became plain:

Vivid episode followed upon vivid episode. As I sat, spellbound with the drama of the narrative, the manse of Avay receded into the past, into month of December 1681 when the Earl of Argyll was taken a captive to the Castel of Edinburgh.

And I became as were a spectator, seeing, in a glass, mighty events pass before my amazed eyes.

PART TWO

A Tale Told By The Fire 1681 - 85.

Prelude to a Drama

It was winter 1681. A biting wind from the sea blew in over Arthur's Seat and whistled round St. Anthony's chapel. There was a smirr of rain in the wind that added to the unpleasantness of the night.

The Palace of Holyrood House was shrouded in darkness, save for the window of an upper chamber occupied by His Grace the Duke of York. Presently a servant came in.

"The Earl of Argyll deSires to speak with Your Royal Highness."

"Bring him here and see to it that we are not disturbed."

So Argyll is back in Edinburgh thought James. There is certain to be trouble now, for Argyll will not take the Test easily. What a commotion he had made all the time the Test Act had been discussed in parliament, objecting at this, objecting at that.

The Duke of York pursed his lips. Maybe it would be best to send Argyll to join Lord Belhaven in the castle.

James' eyes narrowed - no, not yet for Argyll. The fellow might hang himself if given enough rope and left alone.

There was this Commission of Enquiry into Argyll's heritable offices and rights. It promised to have interesting results pondered James. Yes, it would be well to wait and watch - aye and to strike when the chance came. The Duke of York smiled, the grimly satisfied smile of a man who foresees the downfall of his foe.

The rising wind flung the rain harder against the window and sent the draught swirling about the feet of His Royal Highness.

"This Scotch climate," muttered James ill-pleased and kicked the great log on the hearth.

"The Earl of Argyll, your Highness "

James looked up. Before him stood the small stockily built man who, in his own part of the Highlands, was a power greater even than that of the king. There was an air of determination and vigour about his person that compensated for his lack of stature. The keen eyes spoke of one who would not easily brook opposition. The lips were purposeful.

Though he had travelled far and the night was wild his general appearance was neat, betokening a man of methodical habits. James Stewart knew well that here was one not to be treated lightly.

 "Pray be seated, Sir," and the Duke indicated a chair beside the buffetstool. "To what do I owe the honour of this visit? I thought you tarried still in the wilds benorth the Clyde."

"Your Highness, I have returned as I said I would, bringing with me the writs and charters confirming my hereditary rights. But before I proceed further in that matter I would know the truth of rumours brought to me on my way hither. It is reported that I have been dismissed from the Court of Session of which I have been an Extraordinary Lord since 1674. Is that so, Sir?"

"It is".

The abruptness of the reply took Argyll by surprise. James observed with satisfaction that trick of manner which indicated that the Earl was disconcerted - Argyll's trick of keeping his thumb folded in his fingers.

"What, pray, is likely to befall me next?"

"What expect you?" James' voice was cold, haughty, with a tincture of a sneer in it. Argyll's proud spirit blazed with resentment. Rising from his chair and bearing himself with all the dignity of the noble line he represented, the Earl faced the Duke and spoke, slowly, deliberately, with aloofness.

"Your Highness, I did not seek the office of Extraordinary Lord. That office, I know full well, is at the disposal of His Majesty. No doubt a better man than I will be found to fill it. But if this action be to express a frown it is the first I have had from His Majesty_these thirty years."

Argyll paused but James said nothing, continuing all the while to look the fire. The Earl went on:

"I know I have enemies. Yet they shall never make me alter my duty and resolution to serve His Majesty. I have served His Majesty in arms and in his judicatures, when I knew I had enemies on my right and on my left, and I will do so again. If, however, any person have power to render His Majesty or Your Highness jealous of me, it will make my service the more useless to both and the less comfortable to myself."

James toyed with the seal ring on his finger. The situation was becoming ticklish. Argyll spoke loyally, yet it was clear that beneath the apparently calm exterior the Earl was seething with wrath. It would, perhaps, be well to rouse the man no further - as yet. The Duke of York cleared his throat.

"I have told you all I know on this matter."

"Then may I ask if is true that I am to receive a summons to attend a meeting of the Council tomorrow to take the Test Oath?"

James cursed inwardly. What else did Argyll know? How did he know? The fellow must have informers in the Council, at the Palace – these Highlanders hung together like lice on a beggar's rags.

"You have heard correctly."

 Argyll burst forth in wrath:

"Many weeks yet remain in which the Test may be taken. 'Tis only October. I have till January. Wherefore am I forced to swear straightwith?"

"It has been decided that you are to subscribe to the Act to-morrow."

Nothing but the curtest of replies reflected Argyll and never an explanation. A plot is afoot to trap me into supplying my enemies with the excuse for getting rid of me. He glanced at James Stewart, who continued to sit, inscrutable, indifferent. At last, as if the Earl's gimlet gaze had penetrated, the Duke of York shifted in his seat and said:

"On second thoughts you may leave off taking the oath till the next meeting of the Council on November 3rd."

No rapiers edge was sharper than the Earl's tone when he replied:

"Your Highness is kind. What I have seen of the fate of those who have taken the Test inclines me not to follow in their steps. In truth, it is they who have not sworn loyalty that seem most in favour."

The Duke of York laughed for he sensed that the Presbyterian Argyll was hitting at the Episcopal clergy who were still in office despite their not having taken the oath. That sardonic laugh stung Argyll into plainer speaking:

"I am surprised that Your Highness is so insistent on honouring this Test Oath for, of a truth, it contains much you must find not to your liking."

The thrust found its mark. James, the Papist, knew Argyll spoke truly. He lost his temper and snapped:

"My lord, the hour is late. I am about to retire "

"Sir," protested Argyll, "you have not as much as glanced at the documents I have inventoried anent my rights."

James stared coldly at Argyll, yawned affectedly and rang a bell.

"It seems Argyll's hearing is lacking. I remarked the hour is late."'

A serving-man appeared. The Earl of Argyll took his dismissal with a deep bow. The rain was falling heavily as he passed through the palace gates and turned up the steep slope of the south back Canongate.

A gust of wind caught his cloak, causing it to swirl about his shoulders. The Earl did not feel the inclemency of the night for he was preoccupied with thoughts of his interview with the Duke of York. He scented danger and his mind was full of gloomy forebodings. As he turned his footsteps into the courtyard of the Mint where he lodged he shivered from head to toe. It was as if someone walked over his grave.

The bright, cold light of a winter's morning shone over the castle of Edinhurgh and crept into the dark recesses of the wynds that led off from the High Street. An ill-fed tyke of a dog was nosing about in the gutter offal. At the common well in the Lawnmarket the servant lasses were busy drawing water.

Further at the Luckenbooths, Maclean, the silversmith, was fashioning the heart-shaped love tokens that gallants delighted to buy for their ladies. The craftsman, a slight built little man with fair hair and skilful hands, gave a final polish to the trinket lying on the bench before him and then paused to consider whether he would make the next a single heart or two entwined and surmounted by a crown. He was still considering when a clamour in the street outside distracted his thoughts.

"Jock, lad," he cried to his apprentice, "what gars the bodies shout?" .

"I'll rin oot an' see, Maister Maclean" replied Jock, ever eager for a chance to mingle in the bustling life outside on the causeway.

The silversmith was annealing his metal for entwined hearts when the lad returned breathless.

"It's the Earl of Argyll. He's been brocht tae the Parliament Ha' frae the castle in the Governor's coach."

"Gude sakes, leddie. I clean forgot. Argyll's trial begins the day. I doot he'll gang the same gait as his faither, the Great Marquess "

"Dae ye mind o the Great Marquess bein' beheaded" ?

"Fine that, Jock, the 27th of May, 1661. A great crood there wis tae. . He deed as he had lived, wi' nae fear o' man in his hert."

"Whit make ye think the Earl's gaun ti kiss the Maiden tae" ?

"Eh, lad, ye sudna jest aboot daith. The Maiden's a sair instrument fur them whae hae tae kneel doon afore the executioner. Argyll has ower mony enemies a' waitin' like hoodie craws tae pick at his banes. Forbye he didna tak the Test Oath o' loyalty as the ithers did an' the Duke o' York's

bonnie an' angry wi' him."

"Dae ye ken whit Argyll said at the Test, Maister Maclean?'

"Brawly. A'body that loes the Covenant kens that - fur the word sune got roond an' a printer set it a' oot on a sheet. I got ane mysel'."

"Read it oot, Sir. I wad like fine tae hear whit the Earl said tae the Cooncil"

"Here ye are. Read it yersel' Jock fur ah maun hasten wi' this luckenbooth. It's wantit the morn's nicht. Och, ye micht read the sheet alood fur I wud like tae hear it a' again."

Jock took the broadside and began to read aloud with painful hesitancy for schooling had been but scanty.

"I have considered the Test, and I am very deSirous to give obedience as far as I can. I am confident the the Parliament never intended to impose contradictory oaths. Therefore I think no man can explain it but himself. Accordingly, I take it, as far as is consistent with itself and the Protestant religion."

Jock looked puzzled:

"I dinna richtly understan', Maister Maclean, whit Argyll wis meanin' in a' that clamjamfry o' big words."

"Weel, lad, he wis jist sayin' he'd dae as he's aye dune an' that's act accordin' tae his conscience. But we maun spen' nae mair time on politics. Time's siller - dinna forget that, Jock. Gae awa' doon tae Maister Bryson, the lapidary, an' ask him tae gie me a sicht o' a wheen pebbles. An' dinna stan' listenin' tae lasses' clavers. Haste ye back."

Whistling a stave or two of a merry refrain Jock set off for Master Bryson's shop in the Canongate without as much as glancing across at the Parliament Hall where the fortunes of the Earl of Argyll were hanging in the balance. The trial had begun at ten o'clock with the reading of the indictment. Argvll was new defending himself. He spoke at length end with emotion but he felt the dice was weighted against him. The Justice-General - the Earl of Queensberry – and Lords Nairn, Collington, Forrest, Newton end Kirkhouse sat with faces that might have been hewn out of Rubislaw granite, so implacable and unbending they appeared.

Argvll handed over to the court letters he had ~received in the past from King Charles himself and other personages of importance, all testifying to his integrity and to his devotion to the crown.

When he finished speaking and sat down his face was haggard and strained and his small figure seemed even smaller with weariness.

Then followed the long drawn-out discussions of the court : the tedious arguments shout the relevancy of the libel. Acting for the defence Sir George Lockhart spoke for three hours. Thereafter followed the Lord Advocate for the prosecution.

Now Lord Nairn , one of the judges and well advanced in years, began to nod his head: the endless talk had a soporific effect on his senile mind. His thoughts began to wander. He tried to recall how he had listened to countless cases in this very hall, but his eyes kept closing and the memories were not clear. Then he gave up his efforts to recollect past trials and asked himself what was the use of listening to this one. It would be more comfortable in his own warm chamber where Betsy, his maid-servant, would have a crackling fire on the hearth, before which he could doze in peace.

So Lord Nairn tottered to his feet and shuffled from the trial room and went home.

The case dragged on. It was nine in the evening before the public hearing ended. The judges remained behind to make their decision. The hours crept by. Midnight rang out from the steeple of St. Giles. Still the judges disputed. Lords Collington and Kirkhouse were aqainst the relevancy of the libel: Lords Newton and Forrester were in favour.

Justice-General Queensberry was hoist on his own petard. His casting vote would end the deadlock but Queensberry, himself, had made an explanation on taking the oath and felt his judgement could not be impartial and therefore was reluctant to signify his opinion.

His colleagues yawned, speculated upon what he would do and secretly relished his dilemma. But Queensberry was not to be cornered. There was no way of escape - recall old Nairn.

A messenger went to fetch Nairn as the night watchmen called out, "one of the clock and all's well."

Not all is well mused Queensberry till Nairn is here. When the old man joined his fellow judges he blinked around them like an owl confused with a bright light and in a quivering voice asked why he had been called from his slumbers.

Queensberry, ignoring the complaint, commanded the clerk:

"Read over the reasonings of the case to Lord Nairn."

But Lord Nairn was old, very old. His mind kept straying. He wanted back to his bed. Queensberry was a fool he mumbled to himself as the clerk intoned the day's business. This was a conspiracy to deprive him of sleep but they would not succeed in their wicked plot.

He would sleep - and he did - before the very eyes of his learned friends.

"Wake the old dotard: 'tis time to vote."

Lord Nairn voted, fell asleep again and was not disturbed any more for this time the business of the court was over. Argyll's death sentence had been settled by Nairn's vote for the interlocutor as good as decided the case.

The second part of the trial took place the following afternoon. This was to decide whether the prisoner had indeed commited the actions set forth in the charge or not. The Marquess of Montrose presided and among the fifteen jurymen was Claverhouse.

No one was surprised when the verdict was returned - Guilty. All realised it was only a matter of time now till the death warrant came from London. That the sands of time were running out none knew better than Archibald Campbell, 9th Earl of Argyll. Shut up in the chilly, State Prison of the grey fortress on the rock overlooking the crowded lands of the city, the doomed man inevitably recalled that his father had been hastened to his death before the warrant arrived and was not unmindful that history has a way of repeating itself.

The key grated in the lock of his cell and he heard a voice growl:

"Nae mair than five meenutes, mind."

Into the bare chamber stepped Duncan Campbell, the faithful playmate of his childhood, with whom he had spent his foster years in Perthshire and who afterwards became his devoted personal servant.

"Sir, I am bringing you evil news. The Duke of York is saying that if the messenger from Whitehall be delayed he will, as Royal Commissioner, be pronouncing the sentence of death himself."

"Duncan, I still trust my King. He cannot fail to see the injustice of this trial."

"That maybe as you are thinking, McCallum More, but I am not trusting to it. The second sight came to me last night. I was seeing the man Charles Stewart speaking with an English Lord and I was hearing the Englishmen say with a sneer-

'I know nothing of Scotch law, but this I know, that we should not hang a dog here on the grounds on which my Lord Argyll has been sentenced.'

And it came to me that Charles Stewart was not wanting to lift his quill so that when at length he was doing so he was writing not with ink but with blood.

"There is danger, my lord. You must be leaving here."

"Escape?"

"That is so. Let James Stewart find the nest empty and the eagle beyond his reach.

"But the King, Duncan. He will not desert me. Tell my friends I wait till I hear what His Majesty pronounces on this matter."

"Sir, the King will be influenced by his brother. There is no time to lose. Let me arrange at once a plan of escape"

"No, Duncan. I must await a surer sign before I take such a step. If I break out from this castle I burn my boats and Scotland is home no more to me.

"Go now, in peace. Your friend, the guard, will let you see me a little time to-morrow."

"Your will be done," answered Duncan with a sigh.

Argyll was left alone with his thoughts.

ESCAPE FROM THE CASTLE OF EDINBURGH

The sentry at the castle entrance was bored. Nothing but talk, talk, talk of Argyll and order upon order to survey carefully all persons leaving the fortress. The Governor was surely a fool to imagine Argyll could escape. Strong John McEwan who guarded the State prison chamber would see to it that flight was impossible - a terrible fellow was Strong John for he had frightened even the Highland Host on their way through Crieff to quell the Covenanters of the West.

Aye, reflected the sentry, maybe it was as well not to be a great man. Poor folks had less chance of falling into royal disfavour. Another four hours on duty! Ach, it made a man ill to think of it and the sentry spat his disgust into the castle moat. Then, of a sudden the soldier stiffened. who was this toiling up the steep brae from the town? As the figure came nearer the sentry recognised the dress of a clergyman but the face was not that of any of the city preachers. Nor was the voice:

"I have permission to see the Earl of Argyll."

The accents were those of a Borderer. The soldier scrutinised the pass for the bearer's name - "John Scott, minister at Hawick."

"Ye're a lang wey frae hame, Mr. Scott."

"I happen to be visiting in Edinburgh and the Earl is an old friend."

"Richt forrit, Sir. Yir pass is a' in order. It's no verra cheery veesitin' a man that hasna lang fur this warld."

"Mayhap I can bring him some measure of comfort," replied the Rev. Scott as he passed beneath the entrance gateway.

48

Argyll was sitting on a low stool, his head between his hands, when his visitor entered.

"My lord — "

The Earl looked up.

"Scott, my trusted friend!" he exclaimed, rising to clasp the clergyman by the hand. "What brings you here, far from your pleasant valley?"

"Sir, I come to advise you to escape. You must act at once, to-night."

Argvll shook his head.

"You,too! All my friends seen possessed with the idea of flight, even my daughter, who has gone so far as outline a strategy she fancies will succeed."

"And an excellent plot it is: tis the lady's plan I come to beg you to follow out.

"Nay, Sir, I will not be won over. I await news from London."

"No news is needed, Sir. Troops, both horse and foot, have been brought into the city. The palace grounds swarm with them. Moreover, the baillies have gotten word to prepare rooms for you in the common Tolbooth."

At this last remark Argyll started in surprise:

"Rooms for me in the common jail? That can mean only one thing, Mr. Scott."

"It is even so, Sir."

Argyll gave utterance to his thoughts:

"Such arrangements are only made when an execution is to take place."

"Therefore, Sir, you must hearken to Lady Lindsay for whom I act."

"She has chosen an able advocate to plead her case."

"All is ready, my lord. We adhere to our original scheme for your leaving the castle and have perfected the plans for action afterwards which I shall now make known to you.

You are to quit the city by the Bristo Port. Horses await you there from dusk till an hour after ten o'clock. Remember the castle gates close at ten. Try to effect your escape two or three hours earlier.

From Edinburgh ride with your servant to Lauder, where fresh horses have been arranged . From Lauder make for Torwoodlee: there Pringle will have a guide and horses to get you into Northumberland. Once over the Cheviots you will be ably helped to London."

"Mr. Scott, I yet doubt whether to proceed with this business or not."

"I beg you, Sir. Your life is in extreme peril. It is to-night or never."

"You are kind, like Sophie, If I decide to make a bid for freedom this day I shall inform her, ere another hour has gone, by the mouth of Duncan Campbell whom I exoect here shortly "

"My Lord, consider this well. Not your own safety depends on this escape. The kirk and the Covenant in Scotland need a strong leader. If you die the blood of the church is spilt. If you win free, the kirk has a leader, who lives to fight another day with the forces of prelacy. Oh my Lord, think of the kirk and escape out of this fowler's net "

"I have told you, I expect Duncan soon, when he comes he will bring news of how the wind blows in London. Till then I promise nothing. Go to my friends and bid them remember me in their prayers. Do you tarry long in the city ?"

"Nay Sir, I travel back to Hawick tomorrow "

"My good wishes to you and your journey home. Whatever I resolve to do by the end of this day ret assured I will not forget my duty to the church "

"My Lord, the blessing of Almighty God be with you, farewell "

It was late afternoon when Duncan Campbell brought the expected intelligence.

"Sir, Ninian has arrived but half an hour since. The brave fellow has ridden hard to bring the Kings finding on your trial. The Royal Messenger, whom the Duke of York awaits, will not be reaching Edinburgh until tomorrow, for which we may thank God most truly. It gives us a brief space in which to act."

" To act ? What is the verdict ?"

"His Majesty has ordered the death sentence to be passed on you but the execution of it to be delayed during his Royal pleasure "

Argyll was stunned.

"Charles Stewart, I do not deserve this" he at length mumbled brokenly. " I have laboured faithfully in your service, I supported you in the days of Monck and the Commonwealth, when others bowed to the English intruders"

Duncan broke in on his master's reflections.

" Moreover Sir, the Castle guards have been doubled, the Governor has ordered a stricter watch and all leaving the Castle must now disclose their features to the scrutiny of the soldiers. Indeed as I was coming hither a low fellow was looking boldly into a lady's face and asking with a leer

 "Are ye the Earl O' Argyll, my dearie?"

For a moment or two the Earl paced his chamber floor before speaking.

"The decision is made Duncan. I try to escape tonight. Go at once to the Lady Sophia Lindsay. Tell her I am ready to follow out her plan. Bid her come at once with the livery page to carry her train and the other servant to bear the lantern. Horses are to be ready beyond the Bristo Port. Await me there and if all goes well, you and I shall be this night out of Edinburgh and riding south to safety. Are the instructions clear?"

"They are, my lord. I will be leaving now for time is pressing. Till we meet, McCallum More."

With a bow Duncan was gone. _

Argyll walked up and down his prison chamber. Outside he could hear the guard stamping his feet in the stone flagged passage. The candle on the oaken table beneath the tiny window flickered as the wind, swirling round the ancient battlements, crept in at the nooks and crannies of Argyll's room.

He crossed to the window. _Outside was the blanket of the night for the moon was in her third quarter and would not rise till near eleven. A flake of snow was blown against the pane and then another and another. Argyll began to wonder if Duncan had failed to deliver the message to Sophia.

Could the guards have guessed what was afoot and prohibited access to him? The Earl felt his mouth parched and, as he poured a drink of water from the flagon on the table, his hand trembled. .

Sophia loved him. She could not fail him now. Fail him? No, fail Scotland, for his old friend had spoken justly: the Kirk and the country needed a champion.

He must get away.

The fingers of his right hand kept opening and closing over his thumb in his agitation.

Somewhere in the castle a clock began to strike - one, two, three, four, five, six, seven. The last stroke died away and Argyll was still alone. Outside the snow had ceased to blow against the window, while inside the tallow of the candle ran drunkenly over the candlestick.

Feet were approaching. Argyll stopped his pacing to listen. Voices sounded afar off and gradually came nearer, nearer. The door creaked on its hinges. The doomed man turned slowly, fearfully, lest his hopes be dashed to the ground. He sensed someone in the room and looked to the door.

"Father. "

God be thanked: it was his child.Sophia. The words stuck in his throat. The guard was speaking to the lady, behind whom stood two servants:

"I'll be back in half an hour, mistress."

In an instant she was in his arms and he was saying repeatedly, confusedly:

"Sophia; my dear Sophia."

Then she took command of the situation as she loosened herself from his embrace. ~

"Quick, my lord. You must change clothes with my page."

Argyll looked at the page, a tall, awkward, country lad, wearing a golden wig and his head wrapped in cloths so that he appeared as if he had been worsted lately in some common brawl. Fortunately the Earl was not a big man and the exchange was done swiftly and easily. In low, hurried tones Lady Sophia spoke to her page:

"Now, Francis, when we leave, you are to lie down on the couch and feign sleep. If the guard comes in, keep your face well-hidden and speak softly. If you are bade rise, stand in the shadows. You must keep from them as long as possible the fact that you are not my father. Do you understand?"

"Aye, my lady." _

The Earl addressed his substitute.

"You do well, lad. To-night, doubtless, you feel you serve me and indeed you do, but of a truth you serve a greater one than I, for in helping me to escape you further the work of Christ's persecuted kirk in this land."

Eagerly the lad replied:

"My lord, my faither was a puir, honest cottar that fecht at Bothwell Brig. He ne'er cam' back: he fell defendin' wi' his life's blude the banner 0' the Covenant. Prood it is I am tae dae this nicht's wark."

"Pray God that we all meet again in happier times," observed Argyll and then fell to discussing family matters with Lady Lindsay.

Soon the guard could be heard returning, coughing and cursing the elements. Lady Sophia went over to the page taking her father's place. When the soldier opened the door of the prison chamber he saw a heart broken woman, sobbing and clinging to the man who, with bent head, was trying to comfort her. Tears streamed down her lovely face and her noisy weeping drowned the man's words.

The guard coughed and cleared his throat.

"Ye've haen yir time, mistress."

The lady sighed deeply:

"Farewell, father, farewell. If not on earth, we meet in Heaven."

A gawky page lifted his mistress's train. The -servant-man, who had all the while kept watch at the door, held high his lantern. The prisoner in the room uttered a stifled groan and flung himself on his bed. The jailer turned the key in the lock. With an anguished cry of "Father," Lady Sophia buried her face in her hands and stumbled along the ill-lit passage-way.

At the first sentry the little party was challenged:

"Wha gangs there?"

"The Lady Sophia Lindsay and her servants," answered the man with the lantern. The sentry turned his light full upon the tear-stained face, letting it rest there a little space. Next he swung its beams on to the serving-man.

"Wha be this?" the soldier demanded roughly.' _

"My man-servant, James Campbell," replied the lady.

The guard's lantern was pushed closer to the servant's face. After a searching scrutiny he turned his attention to the page

"An' wha, in God's name, be this a' tied up like a clootie dumplin'?" he demanded, peering into the Earl's face.

James Campbell knew this was where he must act with boldness. He brought his lantern close up beside the sentry's, saying with irony in his voice:

"Hae a guid look, my mannie. Dee ye no see it's the Earl O' Argyll?"

Campbell's scornful laughter went echoing round the turrets and battlements. The sentry was enraged:

"Ye think ye're gey smart, ye muckle Hielan' gomeril, but keep a ceevil tongue in yir heid or I'll spit ye on my sword like a salmon on a leister. Gang on, my ledy, an' learn yir servant better mainners."

At last they came to the castle entrance. The great gate was opened and the lower guard drawn out double to make a lane for them to pass. Lady Sophia led the way. Then the officer of the guard stepped forward, grasping the page by the arm as he followed his mistress.

"What pretty lad serves my lady?" the soldier enquired mockingly.

"Would you not learn to be a man with His Majesty's soldiery and fire a train of powder rather than carry a train of velvet?"

Before Argyll could answer the Lady Sophia turned quickly, deliberately twitching her mantle out of his grasp.

"Careless loon," she cried in exasperation. "Can you not keep my mantle off this muddy ground?"

And feigning anger she slapped the soiled, wet train across Argyll's face. The captain laughed:

"That will teach him to attend to his business."

"Ah, Sir, you see how a lady is plagued with a country bumpkin of a lad. This fellow is more suited to the byre. Have you picked it up again, dolt?"

The Earl succeeded in looking the embodiment of clumsiness. James Campbell came nearer, swinging his lantern:

"What the deil ails ye at the laddie? Gin he's a wee bit tongue-tackit he's nane the waur o' that. Hae ye catched up my lady's goon, noo?"

"Aye," mumbled Argyll.

The officer was good-humoured:

"Nought ails me, but something ails your mistress's lad for, having dropped her mantle, he wonders why she scolds. Pass on, friend, before he does more to annoy the lady."

Behind them clanged the great gate and they were swallowed up in the darkness of the night. Below, cheek by jowl, lay the wynds and tenements of the town, where twinkling lights spoke of life and warmth and security. Not a word passed the lips of the three who picked their way across the rough ground to the waiting coach. In jumped Lady Sophia hastily. Argyll and James Campbell sprang up behind. The driver cracked his whip. Down the castle slope the coach rumbled until at the foot of the Castle Hill it stopped in the shadow of the Weigh House. The two men slipped down and came to the door. Lady Sophia spoke softly:

"'Tis here we must part, my lord. James will accompany you to the Bristo Port." Her voice faltered: "God speed you."

Campbell signed to the coachman and then turned to Argyll:

"This wey, Sir. Haud close tae me."

They turned into the Bow. A tavern door opened, casting a broad beam of bright light on to the snow-covered causeway. Out staggered a drunken roister, singing uproariously, "The Jolly Beggar"

"And we'll gang nae mair a rovin'

Let the moon shine o'er sae bright."

Campbell smiled:

"It's a gude thing fur oor rovin', Sir, that there's nae mane - fur the present onywey."

"Aye, Jamie. I'll get a good start under the cover of this darkness."

No more was said as the two men crossed the Grassmarket towards the Candlemaker Row. The streets were ankle deep in mud and slush. Argyll's thin shoes were sodden and at each step he took there was a sound of squelching.

"Ye're feet are gey weet, I'm thinkin," whispered Jamie,"but the man that waits ye ootside the gate has dry class fur ye."

"My friends have indeed been kind but I gladly suffer the discomfort of the body, which brings freedom to the spirit."

At the Bristo Port the waiter was in talkative mood.

"An' whaur are you twa birkies gaun the nicht?" he enquired.

Campbell, taking the Earl's arm and giving it a warning squeeze, replied:

"Gaun? I'm gaun hame wi' this drunken blellum that canna haud a wheen drams."

Argyll, seizing the cue, clung to his friend and belched.

"Has ye far tae gang?"asked the gateman, lifting his lantern to inspect the travellers more closely.

"Tae Liberton. It'll be a sair trauchle or we win the tap o' the kirk brae."

The watch laughed.

"I doot ye'll stick at the Dams fur yir frien's fair miraculous wi' the drink.' Gaun on, Sirs, an' joy be wi' ye."

"Little joy there'll be whaun his gude wife sees him," commented Jamie.

"God, aye," replied the gateman in a feeling tone that spoke of personal knowledge of such things,

"Weemin are aye awfu' ill at a man haein' a dram wi' his cronies."

"Aye," agreed Campbell, "weemin are kittle cattle."

Then heaving Argyll up on his arm he exclaimed crossly,

"Deil tak ye,man Geordie. Staun' on yir ain legs."

The Earl swayed and sagged and, rising again, stumbled. Jamie sighed:

"It'll be the mornin' or we see Liberton kirk tower,Geordie, gin ye gaun this gait."

They staggered forward. The gatekeeper went back to his fire. A little distance ahead was a clump of trees in the shadow of which a man stood with two horses ready for the road.

James Campbell was on the look-out. When he saw the figure with the horses he broke into whistling: "*I'll gang nae mair tae yon toun.*"

The man in the shadows replied with the opening bars of: "*The Lowlands of Holland.*"

Jamie spoke quietly:

"Duncan."

"Right you are. Duncan Campbell it is."

"Duncan, my trusted friend," exclaimed Argyll joyfully.

"Happy I am, Sir, to be seeing yourself. Quickly,change your stockings and shoes and let us away."

"Not here, Duncan. We must put a greater distance betwixt ourselves and the city."

Turning to his daughter's serving-man he said:

"Farewell, James. Words of thanks are bare recompense for what you have done to-night but when fortune brings me back to my own I shall not forget you. Hasten to your mistress with the news that all has gone well."

"God speed you, my lord."

Argyll and Duncan mounted and were away, swallowed up in the darkness that also lent cover to James Campbell as he set off to enter the town, not by the Bristo, but by the West Port..

Craigmillar Castle was in sight when Argyll decided to slacken speed.

"Pause here, Duncan, in the shadow of the bushes. I shall change into my riding boots now."

He drew off his thin, sodden shoes, exchanging them rapidly for the dry ones Duncan produced from his saddlebag. Then Argyll remounted. A snowflake floated down on to his hand. Let the snow fall he thought: it will cover our tracks.

"Let us on." »

Both riders spurred their horses. The night wind sang a song of victory for the Earl of Argyll who had escaped from the castle of Edinburgh; and so it was that Argyll made his way to London where he sheltered till in September 1682 when he went to Holland.

The great log that had filled the manse grate burnt through at last and fell with a crash on the hearth stone. The spell of the speaker was broken. The Rev. William Lindsay came back from the past that his visitor had recreated for him. Mr Forrester spoke;

"It was there in Holland that I made my acquaintance with Argyll and from.there I sailed with him on this ill-starred venture some eight weeks ago."

"Aye," observed Erskine of Cardross, spreading out his hands before the fire, "the hopes of Presbyterian Scotland are bound up with him, and now it seems all over."

"Despair not," cried Cousin Davie, " we live to fight another day for the Covenant."

"Tell me, gentlemen," the Rev. William Lindsay broke in, "what has taken place these past weeks. News here has been but scanty. Stirling Castel has been strongly garrisoned and troops have been quartered along the Hillfoots, but of what has happened elsewhere I know nought."

Mr. Forrester turned to Mr. Erskine:

"I have played the prologue in this tale. Will you take up our story and tell Mr. Lindsay of our coming to these shores."

"Gladly," replied Erskine of Cardross and leant back in his chair. His brown eyes shone brightly, vivifying his pale, tired countenance. Despite the privations of the past weeks that had obviously emaciated his body for his clothes hung loosely about him, his voice when he spoke, was firm and determined.

"My family have suffered much these last ten years, Mr. Lindsay, in the cause of the Covenant. My brother, Lord Cardross, as you no doubt know was driven last year to seek freedom of worship in America. In his last letter he told of how he and his friends are even now building a town in Portroyal which they intend to call Stuarts Town."

Did you not think of joining him?" asked the minister of Avay

"Indeed I did but it was decided I should stay in Scotland to perfect my law studies. Howbeit the continued persecution of my family - my mother you will remember was fined 4000 merks for not attending the curate's services - forced me to go to London whence I passed over to Holland in

March of this year."

"You would meet many of your countrymen there."

Mr. Forrester laughed softly:

"'Twas there he met in with me."

"And with that meeting my tale properly begins," said Erskine, motioning to Drysdaill, his servant, to add some peats to the logs on the fire.

INTERLUDE IN THE LOW COUNTRIES

In the cobbled streets of Rotterdam Dutch housewives went about their purchases and Dutch merchants strove to sell their wares. The air was filled with shrill voices, speaking in a tongue with which John Erskine of Cardross, but lately come from Scotland, was not altogether at ease.

He was a fresh featured, somewhat plump lad of medium height, whose chestnut wig falling in ringlets over his shoulders, made him look older than his actual twenty three years. His full red lips were slightly parted and his hazel eyes were bright with interest as he gazed about him with the curiosity of a stranger drinking in an unfamiliar sight; for his eye had that moment caught an artist sketching the interior of a courtyard, where a servant maid was bringing forth a flagon of wine to two elderly gentlemen. -

Erskine smiled. Who at home would ever think of putting on canvas an Edinburgh Wynd with a lass bringing fresh vegetables from the Landmarket, or picturing even The Sandhaven at Culross with a boat coming in from Preston Island? And here his long nose wrinkled as if he were snuffing the well-known breezes of the Forth.

Queer notions these Dutchmen had: aye and a queerer language. It was a blessing thought Erskine that he was lodged with deuce Robert Gibb, sometime merchant in Stirling,for there, at least, he could hear a kent tongue spoken.

Erskine turned into the alley leading to the Scots kirk and scanned eagerly the signs that swing to and fro above the shop doors. Gibb had said to look for a lion armed – the Bruce emblem. He advanced slowly. Aye, yonder it was: the coffee house of James Bruce, the trysting place of all exiled Scots in Rotterdam.

The young man hurried, pushed open the door and paused a moment. Then he stepped forward into a low-raftered room, the floor freshly sanded. Tobacco haze blinded his vision. A hum of voices filled his ears. In a trice he was back in Scotland for the accents rising on all sides were those of home. A lump came into his throat and through the mist that filled his eyes he saw a man approach, who grasped him heartily by the hand , '

"Erskine, my lad, thrice welcome. What news from home? Come join me and my friend, Mr. Forrester, who has suffered much for the faith."

As in dream Erskine heard himself saying:

"Dr. Blackadder, you are indeed kind to an exile."

"No exiles, here, Mr. Erskine: James Bruce's coffee house is Caledonia in Holland," replied Blackadder, leading the way to a table in a far corner of the room. As he passed among the men filling the room he caught the sing-song tones of the west country and the broad, vigorous accents of Buchan.

A thick-set, scholarly looking man in his thirties rose to greet him with a smile.

"Welcome to our little community, Mr. Erskine. We had news of your being on the way. My name is Forrester."

Erskine bowed:

"I am glad to make your acquaintance, Sir. I believe we both have interests in the same parts of Scotland."

"Menteith for me, Mr. Erskine."

"Boquhan and Cardross for me."

"Pray be seated, gentlemen," said Dr. Blackadder.

Soon all three were deep in an exchange of news. When young John Erskine returned to his lodgings that day he no longer felt a stranger in a strange land for he knew that in Thomas Forrester he had found a friend.

A month later Erskine was in Leyden whither Forrester had recommended him to go to finish his legal studies. Under the tutorship of Professor Matthias he had started to study the Institutes, in company with Charles Ker, my Lord Lothian's son. But Erskine's law studies were destined to be of short duration.

The April day had been remarkably fine, with a warm gentle air, and, as in the evening he sat at his chamber window overlooking the market square of Leyden, John Erskine found it difficult to keep his mind on his writing up of the Professor's notes. Instead his thoughts kept straying to Cardross and the hawthorns in blossom and the pretty islets of Inchmahome.

Suddenly his memories were broken in on by an impetuous knocking at his study door. Startled into wakefulness he called out abruptly,

"Who knocks?"

"'Tis I, John. Let me in Erskine."

The importunate visitor was John Forrest, a fellow Scot, studying medicine. Erskine rose and unbarred his door.

"What brings you in such haste and with such clatter?"

"Great tidings. I have heard Argyll intends to return to Scotland soon, in a week or two, and even now is gathering men and munitions. What think you? Are you for joining him?"

Forrest was breathless, his eyes shining with excitement. Erskine, taken aback, demanded:

"How came you by this news?"

"From the lips of my Lord Stair. I was in his company but an hour ago when he made the news known."

"What intend you?"

"I am for Scotland and the Covenant. I depart to-morrow for Amsterdam where my lord Argyll is at present. I shall offer him my services." '

Erskine's reply came stiftly, decisively:

"Agreed, my friend. I shall arrange to-night to have my books stored and will travel with you to Amsterdam. When leave you in the morning?"

"Seven sharp. Meet me at my lodgings if your intention holds. Farewell for the present. Like you I must put my affairs in order ere I sleep this night."

The morning sun was glinting on the fields where the peasants were toiling as the two young Scotsmen made their way on foot towards Amsterdam. It was late evening when they caught their first glimpse of the city. Low dark clouds hung over the red tiled roofs and the air was laden with moisture. But it was even worse next day, April 23rd, 1685.

Sea fog came rolling in from the Vlie , the passage from the Zuyder Zee into the North Sea. John Erskine, as he directed his footsteps to my lord Argyll's lodging , felt it chill him to the bone. Amsterdam a grey city by a grey sea: it reminded him of Sanct Andrews and the haar that came creeping in by the castle and over the ruined pile of the cathedral. He could scarce see the knocker and, when the servant opened the door, the fog went swirling past him into the house.

"Mr Erskine of Cardross to see Mr Carr."

He was careful to use the name under which Argyll was then passing. When he was brought into Argyll's presence he found himself in a large panelled room where a fire glowing on the hearth kept the mist at bay. The Earl rose to receive his visitor.

"Mr. Erskine, it is a pleasure to meet you."

"My Lord, I am honoured."

"Allow me to present my trusted friend, Sir Patrick Hume of Polwarth."

The man, who had been standing at the window turned.

"Your brother, Lord Cardross, was known to me, Mr. Erskine." '

"I have heard him speak of you, Sir."

Argyll motioned the young man to a seat by the fire.

"My friends tell me you are deSirous of joining our attempt to free Scotland from Prelacy." _

"It is indeed my dearest hope, Sir."

Argyll gave his visitor a searching look:

"Do you think I have much chance of success?"

"My lord, how can you doubt it? I hear you are well provided with arms. Moreover, what of the astrologer Holwell's prophecy? I have seen the picture in his Catastrophe Mundi of - as he describes it himself - "a little Highlandman, as the habit sheweth, brandishing his sword over a field of dead bodies." Surely it is a foresight of your victory."

Hume spoke: "You will have doubtless heard of strange happenings in Glasgow, Christmas last?"

"To be sure," replied Erskine. "I was taking some classes at the college of Glasgow then. Several of my friends declared that a shower of bluebonnets appeared in the air and vanished as they reached the ground. All thought it presaged a rising in Scotland."

Argyll turned his keen gaze full on his visitor.

"These things may be so, but you understand, Mr. Erskine, that if you throw in your lot with me and our attempt fails, you lose all. Your family has suffered much already. Consider well before you agree to join me."

His voice sounded gravely as he spoke.

"Perhaps, my lord," broke in Hume, "it would be well if I acquainted Mr. Erskine with the decision made by our Common Council some days ago."

"By all means. Then the lad will know to what he commits himself."

Sir Patrick searched among the documents on the table.

"Ah, here it is." I

He cleared his throat and began reading:

"Last Friday, Sir John Cochran presiding, the Council governing this expedition agreed to declare and undertake a war against the Duke of York,for restoring the true religion and the rights and liberties of three kingdoms; to add to the Council when a landing was made in Scotland any suitable persons; to elect the Earl of Argyll as general; to draw up a declaration of war."

Hume laid down the document saying, "These are our resolutions, Mr. Erskine." '

"In addition," said Argyll, "I may add that our plans are made with my lord Monmouth, who is to attack in England. To make the union between our forces clear two of the English party, Rumbold and Ayloff, accompany us to Scotland, while our own Fletcher of Saltoun goes with Monmouth."

Erskine rose to his feet.

"My lord, I have long thought of what I should do when an hour, such as this, came. No man who thinks rightly could refuse to venture all he has in this world for the interest of Christ against so many enemies. The liberties of the nation, the property of the subject and the lives of all our honest countrymen and friends are inseparably joined with this project. 'Tis my belief that standing or falling of the Protestant interest in Europe depends in a great measure upon the event of this undertaking in Britain."

"Well spoken, Mr. Erskine," cried Sir Patrick with fervour.

"Pray God our countrymen feel as you do when we land,"was Argyll's solemn comment.

"My worthy friend, Mr. Veitch, is at present in the Borders seeking to stir up adherents to our cause and Pringle of Torwoodlee is active in Moray. Among my strongest supporters here I number my secretary, William Spence, who bears about on his body the marks of the Edinburgh torturers. Then there are William Blackadder whose field preachings are known throughout all Scotland; Sir John Cochran, ever ready to carry out my commands; John Balfour of Kinloch and George Fleming both of whom sent the traitor Sharp to his death on Magus Muir."

Argyll paused and then added quickly, "And, of course, my friend here, Sir Patrick. You have heard of his concealment in Polwarth vault by his dear daughter Grizel."

"I am honoured, Sir, to be in such a noble company of witnesses," said Erskine. ,

"Now to the immediate business!" went on Argyll briskly. "Provide yourself without delay with the necessary equipment for such an undertaking. See to it that you get a good buff coat and a serviceable cuirass. A musket will be required and I would advise pistols also. Five days from now join the "Anna". James Wishart is her captain."

The Earl seated himself at his table and wrote. When he had finished he sealed the document with the great gold ring he wore and handed it to Erskine.

"There is your pass to the ship and with it your commission in my forces. Ensign Erskine, you take the sword in a just cause. God defend the right."

Hume and Erskine murmured, "Amen," simultaneously and the newly-appointed ensign departed. As he passed out into the street the fog closed around him. It clung to his cloak and gathered in beads of moisture on the cloth's rough surface. Fog on an April day....nature was perverse. Did it signify ought?

Erskine shivered and quickened his pace. The sooner he was at sea bound for Scotland the better thought the young Scot

RETURN TO SCOTLAND

About seven on the night of Saturday, May 2nd, 1685, despite a contrary wind, three ships - the_David the Anna and the Sophia, - left Holland, Argyll, with almost 3000 followers, had at last sailed for Scotland. Then, even before they had cleared the banks on that part of the coast, the wind, veered.

Erskine, as he stood on the deck watching the distance between the ship and the friendly shores of Holland grow greater, noted this change of wind with satisfaction. His thoughts turned to home. He could see Cardross House, a narrow, tall, plain harled building with its ancient tower reaching yet higher. The birds would be nesting now above the stables. Would his mother he busy with her sewing? The light faded and Erskine went below.

Elsewhere on that great ocean another ship was speeding, not to Scotland, but to England, to tell James VII and II that Argyll and the covenanting exiles in Holland were bound for Scotland. And when he heard the tidings His Sacred Majesty smiled a little, but after a serious fashion, and sent immediate word to his Privy Council in Edinburgh to summon to the defence of their country all heritors, who with the standing army and the militia would provide a force of some 60,000 men. One third of this army was to guard the Borders at Selkirk; one third to dominate the Highlands at Stirling; one third to control the west at Glasgow.

By the time Argyll's company sighted the Moray Firth the Privy Council had obeyed the King's orders.

The steep cliffs of the Aberdeenshire coast glistened in the morning sun as the Sophia and the David drew alongside the Anna. Argyll called a council of war with Sir John Cochran and Sir Parick Hume.

"The approach to the west can be made by two routes. This and he pointed to the map, "is our present position. From here we can proceed along the north coast to the west either by the passage betwixt Orkney and Shetland or by passing through the narrow strait of Pentland. For mine own part I favour the passage to the north of Orkney."

So they agreed to take the route by the islands that led them to their first disaster. That very afternoon, the wind suddenly and unexpectedly dropping, a light mist began to settle on the sea face. The whole of the next day fog persisted till towards evening it thinned a little and they found they were in Scapa Flow and anchors were dropped in Swanbister Bay.

Aboard the Anna there was much activity. Mr Spence, my lord's secretary, had expressed willingness to go ashore in search of pilots to bring them to safer waters. Spence was an Orcadian with an uncle in Kirkwall. In addition to getting pilots they were to do their best to gain recruits. But the Bishop of Orkney was a zealous supporter of the king. Hardly had Spence and his companions entered Kirkwall when they were arrested by the Bishop's orders on the charge of being servants to a known rebel.

When the news of what had befallen Mr Spence's party reached the vessels sheltering in Swanbister Bay, Argyll at once sent out a raiding party to secure hostages so that he could treat with the Bishop in an exchange of prisoners.

Some hours later the long boat returned with hostages that included James Stewart, Laird of Graemsay, his son and five other country gentlemen. Argyll was delighted:

"Now , my lord Bishop, you must release our friends. "

A message was then sent to say that the exchange of hostages was to be effected by noon the next day. But noon came and the Bishop remained silent. Argyll was forced to continue on his way, having lost the first round to the King and his supporters.

As the David drew away from the mainland of Orkney Erskine spoke to Sir Patrick Hume.

"Do you believe in the power to see into the future?"

His companion smiled:

"Saul visited the witch of Endor."

"I am thinking, not of a witch, but of a Dutch wizard."

"What is on your mind?"

"There was a man in Amsterdam who foretold that a little Highlander would take prisoner a man called James Stewart, of the blood royal. 'Twas said my lord was much taken with this prophecy."

"I have heard some such rumours, Mr. Erskine, but my lord spoke not of it to me."

The younger man looked the older man very straight in the face.

"The prophecy has been fulfilled, Sir Patrick, but I fear it bodes us little good."

"Fulfilled?"

Erskine raised his hand in the direction of the Anna.

"Yonder, on my lord's ship, is James Stewart, Laird of Graemsay."

Sir Patrick Hume stared at Erskine: "of the blood royal. I had not thought of it. Graemsay is descended from the Earl of Orkney."

"Aye, indeed, he that was a natural son to James V."

"You are a shrewd young man, Mr. Erskine. I like it not either. We have not come hither to catch such a petty fellow. Pray God better fortune come to us soon."

But Sir Patrick's prayers were in vain. Ill fortune dogged their voyage down the west coast of Scotland.

First they were becalmed in the Minch. Then strong contrary winds blew up so that they could only enter the Sound of Mull by tacking. Glad they were to shelter for a night in the shadow of the gently sloping hills forming Tobermory Bay, where years before Argyll's father had sought to raise the treasures of a sunken galleon, grim relic of the Great Armada. The following day the little squadron moved on till the bleak, rugged mountains of Jura and the rocky shores of Islay came in sight. Here

Argyll was confident he would raise six hundred men. Marked indeed was his chagrin when the scouts returned with the intelligence that Atholl and his men had gotten there before them and forced the people to declare allegiance to the government.

The leaders of the expedition were summoned. Argyll spoke abruptly,

"To-night, gentlemen, under cover of dark we land our men on this island. Atholl lies at Killarow. We must destroy them."

But again ill luck befell the covenanting army. The enemy, getting wind of what was intended, moved swiftly and silently to Kintyre. And thither also Argyll directed his party. Then for once Nature was kind and calm seas were flowing when Argyll's ships rounded the Mull of Kintyre and passing the steep headlands of Kilkerran, where the rock falls sheer into the water, came to Campbeltown on the twentieth day of May.

The air was pleasant and here and there along the bay fishermen were busy with their nets. Argyll's men arrayed in helmets and breast armour and armed with shining weapons presented a stirring spectacle as they came ashore.

In the twinkling of an eye the nets were abandoned and the cottages of the village left empty and unattended. Every man, woman, and child was flocking to the great Celtic cross with its richly sculptured foliage and massive disc-head of more than three feet in diameter, that stood in the main street. The air became noisy with the excited talk of the folk and the clatter of the soldiery.

Suddenly a trumpet sounded high and clear and silence fell upon the throng. When the last notes had died away Sir John Cochran read their declaration of war against King James VII, the Roman Catholic prince of the kingdom.

A large number of the onlookers were Lowland Covenanters so that when he was finished loud shouts of acclamation rent the air. But that was all Argyll got there for men were loath to leave their homes and throw in their lot with so small a force.

From Tarbet the Earl crossed to Bute, bringing his vessels to rest beneath the great black hills confining Rothesay Bay, and here it was that the relations betwixt Argyll and his Council of War came almost to breaking point. He was for making the Highlands the arena of his activities: the others were for the Lowlands. Thus it came about that he remained in the Highlands while two of his ships sailed to Greenock. A small party entered Greenock but were unable to raise recruits. When they rejoined Argyll at Castle Toward their booty was forty bolls of meal, some small boats, and thirty volunteers, so that the expedition into the Lowlands was without glory.

The Council again convened. Calmly and emphatically Argyll examined their position.

"The English warships are closing in om us. Retreat to an impregnable situation is imperative. Beyond the Kyles of Bute on a barren , rocky islet up Loch Ridden stands the castle of Eilan Dearg. No warship would dare the narrow passages leading to this fortress, nor can cannon be trained upon it from the land. "

"What of Monmouth ?" asked Sir Patrick Hume.

"There is as yet no intelligence of his having landed in England," replied Argyll, "and we do not strike in the Lowlands till Monmouth sets foot on English soil."

There was nothing more to say so Argyll's covenanting army sailed to Eilean Dearg. But in a day or two Erskine and Forrester, chafing at this enforced inaction, begged to leave and go into their own country - Stirlingshire, Cardross, Menteith - where their influence might bring out men to support the cause.

A week later John Erskine of Cardross stood in the shadow of the barn door at Cauldhame farm some three miles west of Kippen kirk , looking across the valley to the hills of the north. All seemed peaceful, yet somewhere in the valley the enemy were lurking. How long, O Lord, how long ? thought Erskine. Assuredly he and Forrester had been fortunate in finding this hiding place with their serving man Drysdaill's friend Andrew Clark, the farmer of Cauldhame. Forrester appeared round the corner of the byre.

"Any sign of Clark upon the road ? Yonder, Erskine. Is it not a horseman?"

Erskine strained his eyes in the fading light:

"It looks like Clark but we had better retire. We cannot take risks."

Quietly they closed the barn door and swung themselves up into the stuffy loft where they hid by day and from whence they went by night to seek support for their cause.

Time passed slowly till they heard the clatter of horse hooves in the yard and the bluff tones of their host walling to his wife. Presently the barn door creaked on its hinges:

"Come doon, Sirs. I hae news for you."

In the farm kitchen a peat fire burned low and from the pot swinging on the swee came the pleasant odour of meat cooking.

"Weel," said farmer Clark when they were all seated and enjoying a pipe, "the hale o' Stirlin's gaed wild. Yester e'en a messenger cam tae the castle wi' the news that Argyll some days syne had crossed the Leven an' pitched his camp at Killearn an' that the King's men frae Glesca had cam up tae Killearn tae fecht. But Argyll, the cunnin' tod, leavin' his camp fires burnin', slippit awa' in the mirk an' won ower the Clyde tho' there were as mony guairds there as there's puddocks in Flanders Moss."

"God be praised" burst out Forrester.

"There's mair tae come, Mr. Forrester. I wis'standin' talkin' tae a Marshall O' Westquarter in Avay about the price o' barley, jist ootside Jamie Norie's gran' new hoose whaun wha gangs fleein' past, as tho' a warlock wis hingin' tae his tail, but the curate o' the Port o' Menteith. Later I heard he had ridden tae tell his brither curates that Argyll wis too near fur their weal."

Erskine was overjoyed:

"At last, my lord has left the west and north. Was there word of Monmouth?" _

"Naethin o' that, Sir. The only ither thing I has tae tell ye is that Geordie Gourlay in the change-hoose declares that the Laird here is aboot tae send oot the fiery cross tae raise the country folk agin Argyll an' that he has gotten an order tae tak the men folks intae Stirlin' tae arm them fur the King's service."

"Then 'tis clear," observed Erskine. "I shall risk going to Cardross to-night."

"And I will to Menteith,"exclaimed Forrester.

But Erskine was not long at Cardross House when ill news came of the Covenanting army. English warships had got to Eilean Dearg and Argyll had been forced overland to Striven and then to Killearn where the enemy came so close to them that they left with their camp fires still burning. About a mile from.Renfrew a party of soldiers captured Argyll as he tried to cross the Cart waters.

Fearing the enemy would turn their attention to Cardross now that Argyll was taken Erskine decided to return to Kippen where in July news came of Monmouth's defeat in England.

At the cross of Kippen the baron officer read a proclamation concerning the king's victory over the rebels and announcing that a company of foot was about to come into these parts to search out John Erskine of Cardross and Thomas Forrester of Menteith.

The moon was well up that night when Erskine left Clark's barn and set out across the fields in the direction of Gribloch where Forrester was in concealment. A gentle tirl at the pin of Gribloch smiddy door repeated thrice was the sign that gave Erskine admission to his friend Forrester.

The two men talked far into the morning.

"Come to me the day after tomorrow at Clark's barn, an hour after sunset," said Erskine. "We shall make our way as best we can eastwards to Culross where I know my kin there will get us off to Holland."

"Will you take another of our suffering countrymen and his servant with us ?" asked Forrester. " 'Tis Master David Lindsay, dominie to a young gentleman near Edinburgh, who these last few years has kept my lord well supplied with news of affairs in this country."

Erskine pondered and then replied:

"Be it so. And now I must away for light will soon be breaking over the hills."

It was August 13th 1685 when the fugitives rode out of Kippen. The two serving men were to go openly with the ponies to Stirling since it was unlikely that attention would be paid to country fellows and from there to the hill road below Logie kirk where they would await their masters. The others were to travel on foot to the crossing of the Teith and then by Bridge of Allan to the Abbey Craig.

By mid-day Erskine, Forrester, and David Lindsay had reached the thickly timbered slope of the Abbey Craig in safety. After some searching they came upon a natural cleft in the rock, screened over with a tangle of bushes. There they lay till night fell and they were free to descend to the farm of Craigmill at the foot of the craig where Erskine knew horses could be got.

Dickson, the farmer, was overjoyed to see Erskine.

"Horses, Mr Erskine. Ay, Sir, ye can hae them.wi' pleesure."

"Thanks, my friend. We will be off at once for I hope to be in Culross to-morrow. My brother's man will bring back your horses."

"As ye will, Sir. God speed ye."

At Logie Kirk the horsemen joined the servants already at the trysting place. Blair was as silent as the grave when the little cavalcade jogged through it. Menstrie burn was running full as they plunged across it and in a cottar house a rush light flickered feebly. The dampness of the day had now turned to rain and mist was creeping down from the hills so that it was more like a night in late autumn than one in August.

Forrester broke the silence:

"We are now in the parish of Avay where once I was the minister."

"Why, Sir," cried Lindsay, "even now it is my cousin who occupies your place there."

"Your cousin?" exclaimed Erskine.

"He is an Episcopalian."

"Would he give us shelter, think you ? This is a stormy night to travel in if we may avoid it."

Davie Lindsay, somewhat taken aback at the suggestion, pondered a moment or two.

"I believe he would. Will was ever a kindly lad."

So it came about thus that five Presbyterians and one Episcopalian sat down together in the manse of Avay and lived again the stirring tale of Argyll. The clock on the wall struck one. The Rev. William Lindsay rose from his chair:

"Gentlemen, your tale has been a lively one. Pray God that some day in this land of ours folks of your persuasion and folks of my persuasion may dwell together in peace."

"Amen," echoed Mr. Forrester.

"Only a few hours remain till daybreak," continued the minister. "Let us take what rest we can till then."

"We leave at first light, Will," cried Cousin Davie.

"Fear not, I shall waken you betimes."

The Wood Hill looked dark and gloomy as the cold, pale grey of dawn came creeping up over the summit. Slowly the darkness began to thin. At the manse of Avay five men led their beasts from the minister's stable to the high road leading eastwards. A sixth man watched them in silence. One of the horses snickered and reared up, joyous to smell the fresh morning air. The farewells had already been made.

"This way," said Erskine to his companions, pointing to the avenue of trees where the road from the kirk hugged the bottom of the hill.

Cousin Davie Lindsay and Erskine went off at a canter. Drysdaill and Ure followed after them. But Thomas Forrester, half turning in the saddle, looked back to the manse that once had been his home and to the young man at the gate. He called out softly:

"Mr. Lindsay, I was a stranger and ye took me in."

Then, with a swift turn of the body, he was away. Now the light-of morning filled the whole valley.

Another day had begun for William Lindsay, minister of the parish of Avay, in the shire of Stirling, in the year of grace 1685

PART THREE.

The Rev. William Lindsay Continues His Narrative 1686-1747.

'TWEEN GLOAMIN' AN' THE MIRK.

I have ever found that the minister in me will out; so that when I look back over the years that followed upon that August night when Cousin Davie with his rebel companions sought sanctuary beneath my roof at Avay I find my recollections framing themselves in the words of the scriptures. For indeed these were years when life followed its wonted cycle of "seedtime and harvest, and cold and heat, and summer and winter and day and night."

Sir Charles Erskine busied himself with the affairs of the shire and the business of the baron court; the villagers did their daily tasks and were neither better nor worse in their lives than before; as for myself I pursued my calling with diligence and prayed earnestly for the King each Sunday and heard after a time that Cousin Davie and his friends had gotten safely to Holland. All this while I enjoyed good health but in the Spring of 1688 Divine Providence thought fit to lay me low of a sickness of the bowels.

Mr. Francis Mitchell, chirurgeon in Alloa , tried me with various physick, but to no avail. Then, in despair, he decided to try Nature's cure and sent me to Aberfoyle for a course of goats milk. In all I spent six weeks in the wild Highlands, coming back to Avay with the flux stopped.

The day after my return Sir Charles came to the manse. There was a twinkle in his eye when he spoke.

"So you have journeyed into the Highlands, Mr Lindsay, and lived to tell the tale! By my troth! a veritable miracle. Howbeit I am here on serious business. I was talking to Mitchell when you were in Aberfoyle and he told me that the damp of this decaying manse will kill you. You must apply to the Bishop anent repairs and I shall support you."

Upon application to the Bishop of Dunkeld an order for visitation was at once issued. In due time two workmen of repute, Tobias Bachop in Alloa, mason, and James Howstoune, wright , in the same place, were brought to take a full inspection of the manse, both high and low, and also the office houses. When the workmen had made their calculations it was found that immediate repair was necessary. I was given power to proceed with the work to a sum not exceeding one thousand pounds Scots. Now all this was greatly pleasing to me for a personal reason anent which I have as yet said nothing, being somewhat backward in relating things intimate. But I can put off no longer and trust I shall not be over embarrassed in setting down the flowering of love in my heart: nor too blinded with tears (aye, old even as I am now) when I come in due order to tell of domestic bliss cut short by what I now believe was the inscrutable wisdom of God, though at the time 'twas as the waters of Merah - bitter almost beyond endurance.

John Burns at the Knapp was a substantial farmer and man of zeal for the kirk. Like myself he came of a family that had remained loyal to Episcopalian ways in good times and in bad times, so that I always had pleasure in stepping into his kitchen of an evening to spend an hour in conversation. He was a burly, well set-up man just turned fifty, whose ruddy countenance and roughened hands bespoke his life of hard toil on the land. His hair, black as the coals that came from the pit at the Coblecrook, curled naturally across his almost square-shaped head. Mrs. Burns, rosy-cheeked, homely in her manner and quick in her movements, reminded me of my own mother, who had died the year I left college. Their only child, Jean was some seven years my junior. When I first came to Avay she was to me a child of thirteen, busied with her mother in the manifold activities of a farmer's household — milking the kye, churning the butter, spinning the wool from the Knapp sheep, baking a bannock on the Culross girdle.

But as the years went by I found my chief interest at the Knapp turning from John and his comfortable spouse to Jean. From a child she blossomed into a lovely lass. The miniature that lies on my desk, before me as I write, does her scant justice. Her hair was a living auburn that in summer took to itself all the warmth and vitality of the sun and in winter brightened the grey skies. The artist's colours are dead, dead as she is to the world, but not to my heart. Her eyes were blue as the harebells on the Ochils and her lips red as the berries that each autumn hang on the rowan tree at the door of the manse . Her head reached but to my shoulder and when she smiled my spirit within me quickened towards her.

It was the year after Argyll's rising failed, when Jean had passed her eighteenth birthday, that I began to realise her beauty and to find happiness in her presence.For a year I said nought but pondered it much in my heart. Then in the autumn of 1687 I spoke to John Burns, asking his consent to court his daughter. The good man was overjoyed and Mrs. Burns, too, gave me her blessing, whereof I was heartily glad. But greater still was my bliss when I found that Jean herself was not ill-disposed to my attentions. So it was that the decision to set the manse in order after my return from Aberfoyle, gave me especial joy, for now it would be fit for me to bring to it a bride.

The workmen were busy all summer rebuilding the eastern end and the northern wall. Floors were pavemented afresh and new rooms made in the upper storey divided with partitions. The old worm-eaten timbers in the south room were taken down and fresh ones set up. While all this was being done, the farm folks were toiling in the fields leading in the harvest. At the Howe Croft above the kirk the reapers advanced, bent low, sickle in hand. Behind them came men and women tying the corn into sheaves with wisps of straw and the bairns setting them on end to dry in stooks.

I could hear the women singing as they laboured one fine morning when Tobias Bachop came to tell me that the manse was well and truly repaired. Thus, when John Burns invited me, at the end of August, to share in the Harvest Home feasting at the Knapp, I made up my mind to ask Jean to share my manse and my life.

The great barn at the Knapp was filled with.happy, carefree villagers, when I entered it in company with Mrs. Burns. At one end a huge trestle table groaned with food and drink, to which all could help themselves freely. At the opposite end the fiddlers were obeying John's command:

"Rossit weel, yer fiddlesticks, lads."

Above them hung the last handful of corn, the "Maiden," tied with a bow of gay ribbon. The air was noisy with chatter and laughter. Then in genial tones John called for silence, which being got with some difficulty, he went on to announce:

"Tak' yir pairtners fur a reel."

The evening advanced, but the dancers tired not,though the sweat ran in rivulets down the faces of the fiddlers. I stepped outside for a breath of cool air. Over the hills the gloaming was beginning to creep. In the distance the Abbey Craig and Dumyatt were merging with the darkening sky.

Nearer at hand Craigleith's deep front loomed up black and frowning. '

As I stood there contemplating the wonder of the earth a light hand was laid on my arm. I looked down and by me was Jean, a dainty figure in a gown of blue satinet.

"Do you not enjoy our rough merry-making, Mr. Lindsay?" she enquired timidly.

"Nay," I replied, taking her by the hand. "I am right glad to see my people rejoicing in due season, but the air in the barn is hot and I came out here for a blow from the hills."

She smiled, adding sweetly:

"I would not have your evening spoilt, Sir."

My heart leapt up to hear her gentle concern for my happiness and I knew the time had come to unburden myself to her. '

Just beyond the Knapp the Carnaughton burn runs lightly from the Grey Mare's Tail downhill, through a planting of trees, to join the Devon at Cobblecrook.

"Will you step with me to the burnside, Jean?"

She murmured her assent and we crossed the stubble ground at the back of the house. I could feel the blood mounting to my face and I hoped that the gleaming grey hid my confusion from the girl at my side.

As we entered the shadow of the trees a rabbit scuttled off into a bush. Taking my loved one's hand I led the way down to the water's edge, where an ancient oak spread its roots among the rocks. Turning I held out my other hand to steady her as she descended the rough, sloping ground.As our hands met I drew her to me.

"Beloved," I whispered from lips that were now close to hers. I kissed her gently, folding her in my arms. In the fast fading light I could see her eyes were bright as stars and I knew my love was not unwelcome. I lifted a hand to caress her soft hair, murmuring over and over again:

"Heart of my own heart, I love you."

Then very simply she said, "And I love you, too, Sir."

"Not, Sir," I cried, lifting her face till our eyes met. "Call me Will, my Jean." '

'Twas then, for the first time in my twenty eight years, that I knew how thrilling a name could sound when spoken with.the heart's deepest affection:

"Will."

"Jean."

My lips, brushing her brow and cheeks, sought to convey the tenderness my tongue found difficult to express. After a while I did speak:

"Will you marry me, my dearest love, and grace my manse? I have not much of this world's gear but I pledge my solemn word to cherish and love you till death do us part -aye, and beyond the grave too."

Beyond the grave - for more than half a century now I have kept that pledge to the girl who, on the night it was given, raised her head from my bosom to reply:

"I seek not riches, Will.'Tis for yourself I love you: because you are a good and a kind man I come to you freely

So it came about that we plighted our troth across running water as is the custom of lovers in country parts. And as she clung to me in her innocency of heart I prayed God I shoukd never fail her trust in me, so that when she whispered to me some moments later:

"Kiss me again, Will," I stemmed, with a struggle, the strong tide of passion that was walling up in my being and embraced her gently and tenderly.

When we returned to the Knapp, night had fallen, between the gloaming and the mirk I had woo'd and won a bonnie lassie.

The next day I laid down my marriage pawns with the session clerk - two lex dollars - as an earnest of my intentions. At the Knapp Jean and her mother began to prepare against our wedding day for I was of a mind to proceed with the business straightway, Mrs. Spowart being now much hindered in the work of keeping the manse on account of her rheumatics of the body. Moreover I was disquieted with rumours of an intended invasion of the country by the King's son-in-law, the Protestant William of Orange. Indeed the farmers on the east coast were much inconvenienced that summer and autumn for the militia were called out which did take men away from the harvest.

On the Ochils and the Campsies beacons were got ready to warn the countryside if William landed. Also another company of soldiers were sent to the Castel of Stirling which became a veritable powder magazine.

Our nuptials were solemnised on October 23rd 1688, a Wednesday, in the kirk of Avay, Mr. George Turnbull of Alloa officiating and my lord, Sir Charles Erskine, with his wonted graciousness, condescended to be present thereat, which was not only a great honour but also mightily pleasing to me since I had neither kith nor kin of my own, Cousin Davie being in Holland with the exiled Presbyterians.

For the occasion Jean had gotten a grand silk gown, white and sprigged with wide lace ruffles at the sleeves which were short, reaching but to her elbows. Her slippers were scarlet and her only ornament the plain gold ring I lovingly gave her. She needed nought else being in herself a bonnie bride.

From the kirk the bridal party rode to the Knapp, where in the best room, to the front, looking across the valley to the King o' Muirs farmstead, Jean's numerous aunts had the feast prepared. But ere we sat down we watched a company of Jean's young friends setting out to win the marriage broose or dish of brose. For this they had to race on foot from Jean's home to mine. Three lasses and four of the farm lads set off at a word from John Burns.

Patterson, the smith, afterwards told me that a great congregation of the townsfolk had foregathered at the Bridge of Avay and at the manse yett to encourage the runners and to congratulate the winner.

"Guid sakes, Mr. Lindsay, I ne'er heard sic lauchin' in a' my days. Maist o' the folks frae the cottar hooses at the burnside were standin' at the brig, their een fair stickit on the Langbank. Then we got a gliff o' the youngsters rinnin' doon frae the Knapp tae the highroad. As they cam tae the Strathy Well Tam Young shouted:

'Rab Drysdale's leadin' the wey wi' that limmer Phemie Galloway no far ahint them.'

An' wha sud be standin' ahint Tam but Phemie's mither an' sister wi a wab they had been shrinkin' in the burn. Oot cries the mither:

'Oor Phemie's nae limer, Tam Young.'

Up flies the young ane: Gie the tyke a clout, mither.'

Wi' that she taks her wat wab and skelps it clean across puir Tam's chops. A'body lauched loud. Things micht hae gaun tae waur gin the rinners had no, at that verra meenit, passed the Butter Ha'.

The crood cheered, the deals o' the brig dirled aneath their fleein' feet, an' as my nevvy, wee Dauvit Tamson, skelpit up the brae richt on' the heels 0' Phemie Galleway I cudna help shoutin':

"Haud on, Dauvit; ye're daein' grand, man." Eh, Mr. Lindsay, I wis sae taen on tae see Dauvit daein' sae weel that I ran up the brae efter him an' wis jist in time tae.see Rab Drysdale win yir yett, first i' the broose.

I smiled at Patterson's account of this time honoured custom, remarking jocularly

"So the minister's broose will be long remembered in Avay, John?"

"Deed it will," he agreed as he bent forward over his forge.

Nor have I myself, ever forgotten that sumptuous bridal banquet provided by the good people of the Knapp.

Jean and I sat at the head of the table, or, to be exact, tables, for every inch of floor space in that big room was occupied by a board, groaning with a superabundance of food.

Burns was a happy man that day. The kitchen maids never ceased to serve the guests. When I had said grace my father-in-law called out in his accustomed hearty fashion:

"Noo, freends, rax oot fur yir horn spune an' try the gude-wife's lang kale: nane better in a' the countryside."

Mrs. Burns demurred at her husband's praise:

"Na, na, John."

"Aye, aye, wife," he declared, "an' sae is a' else that's tae come."

Next were the bannocks freshly made. With a twinkle in his eye, John became voluble in his praise of the bannocks. Turning to the guest on his left, a fellow farmer, he said:

"Hae a bite o' the bannocks, Drumwhalley. They're gey guid - the Knapp's ain barley meal, of coorse: it maks a' the difference."

Drumwhalley entered into the spirit of the jesting:

"Jist wait till I'm mairrit an' ye taist Drumwhalley meal."

This caused great merriment as Drumwhalley, now past sixty years of age, was well-known to have been courting a spinster at Caroline for the last twenty years and no nearer venturing upon matrimony than he had been the first summer he called upon her. '

The next dish was salt herring with a cog of ale. To my amusement one of Jean's uncles leant across the table to confide in me:

"This is byordinar guid ale, Sir, frae Kilbagie, grand fur sindin' doon the saut herrin'."

Very right he was too in his judgement on the drink.

"What's neist, mistress?" demanded John of his wife.

"Has ye nae een, man?" she countered in jest, pointing to a gigantic ashet on which were piled up what she described as caller nowt-feet.

Meanwhile plates with thick whangs of Knapp kebbuck were constantly being passed up and down the tables. Last, but not least, in our feast came the bride's pie of which everyone present had to partake, even though in so doing he choked, being already maw-crammed with food.

At length the wedding banquet came to an end and the company repaired to the great barn, the younger ones to dance and the older ones to share in the general rejoicing. Jean and I danced the first reel, for unlike the Presbyterian clergy, I was never against the pastime of dancing, which I considered an innocent and healthful pleasure, if carried out in seemly manner.

John Guild, the piper, blew till his cheeks were like to burst and the rafters of the barn like to crack. Along one side was a table dormant, heaped with bannocks and cheese and close beside it huge casks of ale and tappit hens with whisky in plenty.

The evening was far advanced when we came to the final dance, which in these country parts was styled "Bab at the Bowster." This began with one of the bachelors present taking a bowster, or cushion, in his hand and dancing round the room to the fiddler's music. When the fiddling ceased the dancer placed his cushion before a spinster who knelt thereupon and was kissed by the bachelor. This was repeated until all the unmarried members of the party had danced upon the floor. As was to be expected "Bab at the Bowster" caused much daffin' among the lads and lassies and much recalling on the part of the older folks of the days of long syne when they had engaged in the same sport, wherein some had even met their life's partner. '

But think not that the ceremonies were over, for we were still to enter our own house. Outside the Knapp, in the yard, the horses pawed the ground and whinnied as we prepared to leave for the manse. Great was the lighting of lanterns and tarred tows so that a traveller, passing along below on the king's highway to Stirling, and seeing the bobbing lights must have thought that many a Wil o the Wisp roamed the Ochil slopes that night.

When we alighted at the yett and approached the manse threshold I saw Mrs. Spowart waiting to receive us with something held aloft.
~

"What think you Mrs. Spowart has?" I whispered to Jean.

"Twill be the sieve of bread and cheese," she replied laughing. And so it was.

Then, as I lifted my bride over the stone of the doorway, her cousin Lizzie broke above her head the Infar-cake, a shortbread specially prepared for the occasion. At this the company about the door began to sing:

"Welcome to your ain fireside

Health and wealth attend the bride!

Wanters noo your true weird make,

Joes are spaed by the Infar-cake."

The guests came behind us into my study where Mrs. Spowart had a blazing fire of logs and peats roaring up the chimney. The broken pieces of the infar-cake were handed out to the company, who would hope to dream that night of their own true loves. Despite her aches and pains, Mrs. Spowart hobbled to the hearth. With the long broom, that I knew so well, in her hand she turned to Jean:

"Mistress Lindsay, welcome tae the manse: may the moose ne'er leave your meal-pock wi' a tear in its e'e. Soop the hearthstane an' sae be the lady O' yir ain hoose."

And so Jean swept my fireside for the first time and her entry into my home was completed with the gift of the firetongs. i

"A parting cup, my friends" I cried, serving them all with some of my own brewing upon the excellency of which I prided myself and not without reason. Soon the last of our bridal party was swallowed up in the dark of the brae road leading to the village and the clip-clop of horses hooves faded on the night air. Jean and I were leaning on the manse yett. She was looking westwards to the Knapp that no longer was her home and I wondered if perchance her joy was tinged with the sorrow of separation from familiar surroundings. I put my arm about her to comfort her. My mouth was upon her hair as I whispered:

"'Tis not far to the Knapp, Jean. You may visit your parents daily."

Her voice sounded choked with emotion:

"Oh, Will."'

So we stood at the yett, clinging together on that October evening, our bridal night, while above us the stars shone clearly. When I judged she was more composed I said softly: ,

"Shall we go in now, beloved?"

Jean turned and looked to the house. Then, of a sudden, in the tongue of the country folks she observed:

"The lum's reekin' brawly."

And in the same speech I replied:

"Lang may it reek for you, my dear, dear wife."

We went into the manse, closing the door tightly behind us.

CLAVERHOUSE IS DEAD.

That my uneasiness for the peace of the nation had not been a wild flight of the fancy was made clear but a week or two after my marriage. It was a dull November afternoon, about the third or fourth of the month (though I remember not exactly and my journal here is dated only by the month) when the Laird's falconer, Charles Morris, came hastening from off the hill, where he had been observing some hawks.

Sir Charles, as he afterwards told me, met Morris high above the farm toun of Burnside at the glen that later became famous for its silver. Morris, at first, could scarce speak for lack of breath and obvious agitation of mind.

"Sir Charles," he gasped, "the beacons ower by Tulliallan and Culross has been lichted. An' gin I'm no mistaken there's a faint lowe ayont the Forth in the Edinburgh airt."

As Morris spoke the blood drained from Sir Charles' face

"Are you certain, Morris?"

"Sir, there's nae doot aboot the lowes on the Fife coast."

Then, as if the same thought had entered into the minds of both men at the self-same moment, they turned with one accord westwards, where a bright tongue of flame was bursting upwards against the grey skyline. Morris could hear Sir Charles draw in his breath sharply as in horrified tones he exclaimed:

"Stirling Castel beacon! God help us all! William of Orange has landed. Bear the ill news to Mr Lindsay and ask him to bid John Guild, the piper, inform the people that I expect them to remain steadfast in loyalty to King James."

In the weeks that followed I learned in piecemeal fashion sometimes from Sir Charles and sometimes at Presbytery meetings in Stirling - what was taking place throughout both kingdoms.

On the 18th of December the great doors of the palace of Whitehall closed behind King James. The Dutchman established himself in St James's and our lawful king, with his infant son, went to France; heart broken he was that his two daughters Mary, the wife of the Dutchman, and Anne - had deserted him,seeking instead their own interests.

Winter passed and the spring of 1689 came, yet there was no settled government in the country. Whatever William of Orange might be in England he was not king in Scotland. If there was any authority at all it was that of the Presbyterians who wherever they could manage it set themselves up in power.

Throughout the spring rumour smouldered beneath the heather on the Ochils that John Graham of Claverhouse, Viscount Dundee, would restore King James. For Dundee and his men made a dramatic departure from Edinburgh, passing like a whirlwind to the north. On the 11th of April William of Orange and his wife, Mary, were proclaimed rulers of the Scottish kingdom at Edinburgh. And Dundee had proclaimed for the House of Stewart. He had gone into the Highlands to raise the clans.

It was the beginning of a great struggle that still goes on, though now, in 1747as I write I wonder if it has ended.

Soon it was reported that Mackay and the Scots Brigade were pursuing Claverhouse, but the master of Dudhope knew the land and played with his foe as a cat with a mouse.

Late one night, about the third week in July, Sir Charles sent for me. When I entered the great parlour the candlelight fell upon, not only the Laird, but also his two older sons. James, the heir, who had just turned twenty, was a dour, thick—set lad with a weather beaten countenance, whose mind ran ever on military sports. John, in

94

contrast, was a lad of finer mould. Despite his youth - he was but sixteen he was already tall and well-proportioned. He was kindly and his interests lay in the management of the estate. The lad smiled to me as his father spoke:

"Mr Lindsay, grave news has reached me. My lord Dundee has been successful in raising the Highlanders but Murray of Atholl remains obstinate. Howbeit Murray's factor has seized Blair Castel for the King and Dundee."

"Blair Castel", I exclaimed. "It is the gateway from the Lowlands to the Highlands."

"Aye, indeed. Now the King's forces have it they must keep it, for upon possession of it hinges any possibility of restoring King James."

"What of Mackay, Sir Charles ?"

"It is my news of Mackay that forces me to act to-night. He is on his way north to Blair."

Sir Charles looked across at me where I sat opposite

him by the fireside.

"Mr Lindsay, James Stewart and James Graham need the help of every loyal Scot. My son and heir, James, rides with me tonight to join Dundee. John remains to attend to the estate. Will you draw a sword in the King's cause ?"

I felt the blood rushing through my veins. In the pale light of the room I saw , not the eyes of Sir Charlws but those of James Stewart, who had won my heart that summer day in 1681 when I had bathed his bruised ankle in the manse of Avay. Then I saw the eyes of my dear wife, eyes I might never behold again if I went forth into battle. It is ever a struggle to choose betwixt duty and ties of personal affection, but I thank God that there was given me that night the strength to follow the hard path of duty.

"When do you leave ,Sir Charles?"

"Expect me at the manse within the hour. If we ride hard we should get beyond Perth to Blair well in advance of the Dutchman's soldiers. We will bring a horse for you."

When I got back to the manse Jean was waiting for me anxiously. Briefly I told her of my decision to throw in my lot with the King's men. There was little time for endearments but I took Jean by the hand as I quickly advised her how to act in my absence. Too soon the clattering of hooves were heard on the road outside.

"Come not with me to the yett, Jean. Rest by the fire and let me bear away with me the picture of the firelight on your bright hair."

"My dearest life, wherever you go, carry me with you in the secret places of the heart," she murmured.

A moment longer we clung to one another and then drew apart. I crossed to the door. My heart was full as I said:

"Forget not, beloved, that deathless and happy are the united in spirit."

I passed out into the night to join the Laird. We did not travel by Dunblane for while I had been setting affairs in order at the manse another messenger had arrived at Avay House to say that Mackay was expected now along the highroad to Crieff by Dunblane. We therefore, turned east to Dollar.

Soon we passed through the Yetts O' Muckart and came near to the shores of Loch Leven where, at an earlier time, another stirring scene in the history of the Royal House of Stewart had been played. In Glen Farg the croft steadings were all without a peep of light. When we entered Perth a sleepy-eyed, tousle-headed lad was carrying water across the yard at the Inn of the Annunciation. Sir Charles hailed him.

"Is the landlord stirring , yet, lad ?!

"Aye, Sir."

"Go tell him that three gentlemen are here that would breakfast without delay."

Mine host appeared almost at once.

"This wey, gentlemen. Hughie, gie the horses some aits an' water an' dinna stand gowkin'."

The innkeeper was talkative and we learned that Mackay was expected that very day. A hot July sun beat down on us unsparingly that morning as we advanced to Dunkeld. It must have been the 26th of July for the battle (which I know was fought on the 27th) took place the next day. When the grim.walls of Blair Castel came in view we stopped at a small changehouse. There we discovered that Murray, having abandoned Blair, was somewhere about the Pass of Killiecrankie awaiting Mackay. But what heartened us was the report that Claverhouse was coming with all speed over the Pass of Druimuchdair and by the Garry river to Blair itself.

At last, when the heat of the day was over, we saw Claverhouse ride into Blair. His face was lined with fatigue but his eyes were animated. His lips were thin and set in a firm line, the mouth of a man who knew that much was at stake. The hands that held the reins, were long and purposeful. At his side hung his sword, devoid of ornament, the weapon of a practical man. He bade Sir Charles be present at the council next morning.

Next day we learned that we were to attack towards evening. Mackay was in the Pass. Our position was to be on the hillside by the burn with Claverhouse himself. For two long, weary hours we waited on the slopes above Killiecrankie till the evening sun sank behind Tulach hill.

Then our leader signalled to Clan Maclean who, without need of any second bidding, sounded the onset. The Macleans with the Macdonalds were on the right and Locheil with his Camerons in the centre. We were on the left with Dundee's own horse and the Macdonalds of Sleat and the Stewarts. I, who had never engaged in any battle save the battles of schoolboys, watched as if rooted to the ground. Slowly, at first, the clansmen want down the hillside, flinging aside their bright checked plaids and holding their muskets in readiness. Then they swept forward like some wild, unchecked mountain torrent.

All this time Mackay's men were firing but the Highlanders refused to answer till they met almost face to face. At that moment every musket was fired, and then out flashed the swords, and the men from the glens drove the foe into the frothing waters below.

When darkness hid the enemy and the noise of fleeing men died away I came upon James by a great rock beneath which the Garry boiled. He told me of an incredible feat of daring. An English soldier, pursued by a fierce Highlander, had, with a mighty leap, cleared the chasm and fallen safe on the far side.

Finding no trace of Sir Charles about the burn of Clune we betook ourselves to the clachan of Blair where we feel in with the Laird, his face grief-stricken.

"My lord, what ails you ?"

"Claverhouse is dead"

Dundee had fallen, shot in the side. Sir Charles had seen the gallant soldier die. His last words were:

"How goes the day?"

"Well for the king, but not for your lordship."

"It is less matter for me, if the day goes well for the King."

A deep breath and life was extinct.

As Sir Charles recounted this to me the tears ran down his cheeks and I was not without being affected myself. The defeat of the enemy was complete. Mackay rode into Stirling with less than seven hundred men and without powder or weapons, for these he had perforce left behind him, scattered about the bracken on the braes of Killiecrankie or lying deep in the amber-coloured pools of the river where the speckled hill trout sport. Later that day when we had rested our battle-wearied limbs Sir Charles took me aside.

"Mr. Lindsay, the death of Claverhouse has much upset the King's business in these parts. There is none to command as he did." '

"Aye, my lord, this victory is become as ashes in our mouths," I observed sadly.

"We must think of the future. It is better to save ourselves against another day, than to deliver ourselves now an easy prey to the foe. I advise we return to Avay, there to await the issue of events.

"Your counsel is wise and just, Sir Charles.' We have played our part like men for the King and the Kirk and have nought wherewith to reproach ourselves. Better, as you say, to keep alive the flame of loyalty to the House of Stewart by conserving it now against a happier time."

We returned by the way we had come. Wherever we stopped the country folks were speaking of the death of Claverhouse and when I gathered Jean to my heart late on the night of our second day's journey from Blair her first words were :

"Alas! Will, to think that Claverhouse is dead."

Claverhouse is dead - Claverhouse is dead " - like the o'ercome of a song it kept repeating itself in my brain till I thought I must go mad and shout from the hilltops: " Fools, 'tis not Claverhouse that is dead! It is Scotland and the Stewarts and the Episcopal kirk that are dying, dying,dying."

For Scotland and the Stewarts I had for the time being done what I could. For the kirk I would continue the fight. So the next year, 1690

, when, by Act of Parliament, I, being an Episcopalian , should have left Avay , I refused and remained there (the Presbyterians called it "intruded") till 1696 when,for personal reasons as well as by force of increased government oppression , I quitted my charge.

To the explanation of all these things I shall come in due course , if Providence sees fit to spare me till the writing of this tale is done.

THE OCHIL EYE.

Throughout the winter of 1689 and the spring of 1690 the Laird and I watched events in the Highlands with anxious eyes. In a desultory fashion the resistance to King William was carried on by General Cannon and those of the Highlanders, who had not returned to their glens. But in May 1690 we knew that even this last shadow of opposition was vanquished when news came to us of the defeat at Cromdale.

Sir Charles had been in low spirits ever since our return from Killiecrankie and now he appeared cast into the very pit of dejection. At that time he was wont to send for me with much frequency and I would betake myself to Avay House to spend there an hour or two in political conversation or, when talking seemed to cloud my lord's brow over much, we would turn to the game of backgammon.

It was on one such occasion that Sir Charles broke off our conversation on matters of state, speaking instead of his family and in such melancholy accents that I was greatly put.about. ,

"Mr. Lindsay, I am disquieted about James. He is ever asking that I procure for him a commission in some Scots regiment serving William of Orange."

"The lad is indeed a soldier, Sir Charles. That I saw with my own eyes at the Garry last summer."

"Aye, indeed, but he is one who fights for fighting's sake. I would my sons supported the House of Stewart as I do."

"Has Master James no wish to join the exiled Court ?"

"Alas, no. He declares the Dutchman is here to stay and states roundly that we who acknowledge him.not are fools."

"Be not despondent , my lord. God willing it will be many years ere James is called to be the master of Avay House, by which time he may have seen the folly of Dutch William on the throne."

The Laird sighed and then spoke of his other boy.

"Robert is a good lad. He progresses in his studies and shows much interest in the body and its diseases. If all goes well I shall send him.to Edinburgh in another year or two to learn the art of medicine there."

But the Laird was destined not to see his son a physician. Divine Providence that appoints our coming hither and our going hence took Sir Charles Erskine from our midst in the month of June 1690, exactly two weeks to the day from the time of the conversation I have recorded and in the forty seventh year of his life.

James became second baronet of Avay and strait joined King William's army. In vain did his mother plead that his father would rest uneasy in the vault beneath Avay kirk and that the estate needed him.

"John can look after the estate. He knows more of it than I do, mother."

"But James, you cannot go just now," protested the Lady Avay. "The notar is come for your father's affairs must be set in order." .

James was adamant:

"John can do as well as I could."

So John and I and the notar made up the inventar of goods,debts, gear and sums of money, which pertained to the deceased Sir Charles Erskine of Avay, knight, so that it might be given up to the Commissariat at Stirling by his lady Dame Christian Dundas.

Time has long since wiped from my memory the exact details of Sir Charles's estate but I do mind well the work we had to get everything recorded. In the stable there were work horses (some I think old) and there were mares, as well as a stand saddle horse and two little pomme horses. In one byre were kyne and a few oxen and in another byre were some stots and one bull.

Then we had to estimate the bolls of meal in the girnell of Avay.

When we came into the house we went from.room to room , setting down the utencill and domicill oak chests and buffet stools and a fine cabinet of the mother of pearl that had belonged to Sir Charles's father.

My lady, with the tears in her eyes, helped us to set down the details of the clothing of the deceased – from the best pair of breeches and sewn waistcoats and fine black cloak that the Laird had kept for his visits to Edinburgh to the old apparel and well-worn shoes in which he loved to be at ease when living at Avay and the familiar broad hat with plume that many a time had lain on the table in my study, when its owner had stepped in to speak with me.

All this I found very affecting as doubtless also did John though he kept a stiff upper lip. We were not required to make an inventar of the jewels as Sir Charles had done this himself but three months before along with the drawing up of a list of legacies he wished to be observed in the event of his death. Poor Sir Charles, he must have felt within himself some premonition that he had not long for this world. My own opinion is that the fall of the House of Stewart quite broke his spirit but the doctors declared he died of an internal sickness.

The debts resting to the dead were few and easily made up - some cottars who had been given loans for Sir Charles was ever ready to help his people, and a neighbour Laird who had got a hundred pounds Scots. As for the debts resting by the dead these were simply the wages of the servants and the expenses of the doctor and chirurgeon who had attended Sir Charles when he took to his bed.

About three months after the making of this inventor my lady sent for me. John was with her in that spacious west room in which I had been wont to visit Sir Charles. When I was seated my lady began in gracious tones:

"Mr. Lindsay, Sir Charles had ever a great respect for you. He spoke to me often of your good influence in the parish. He was very sensible, as I also am, that under your care the kirk in Avay had prospered and that under your guidance the cottars have improved considerably in their ways.

From the people themselves we have heard of your kindly ministrations to them in illness and in health, in fair weather and in foul. Though the parish is scattered you have never hesitated to go to the people, not only in time of day, but also in the night time if need arose."

At such praise I was, as you will understand, much abashed and tried to protest, but my lady went on:

"Moreover, Sir Charles had deep satisfaction in the knowledge of your loyalty to the House of Stewart."

As Lady Avay spoke, she lifted from the table beside her a small box, which she held out to me.

This, Mr. Lindsay, is a legacy left to you by Sir Charles - a token of his gratitude for the services you have already rendered to our family and to King James - a token of his faith that if ever Erskine or Stewart need you in the future, you will answer their call."

I rose from my chair in agitation and scarce could speak, for conflicting emotions of affection, gratitude, and grief, struggled together in my bosom.

"My lady, how can I express my feelings?"

"Do not try, Mr. Lindsay, but open the box and see what my dear,departed lord wanted you to have."

I did so. And I looked for the first time upon the ring that ever since has been worn on the little finger of my right hand. I laid my pen aside for a moment even now to gaze upon it. I was thirty years of age when I placed this ring on my finger and now I have attained four score and seven years.

Fifty seven years of constant use have not dimmed its beauty nor diminished my affection for the Houses of Erskine and Stewart.

The stone is one of our Hillfoots agates, oval in shape and ringed as agates sometimes are, the outer elipse being white with a ring of dark brown next and the centre a paler shade of brown, so that the whole gives the appearance of a human eye, whence its local appellation of The Ochil Eye.

It is mounted in silver, the metal having been hammered over the edge of the stone. The band of the ring is broad with curiously inter-twined knots of a design common to the Celts resting betwixt the setting and the band on either side.

Around the setting, or bezel as I believe the jewellers term it, are engraved these words:

"Vous y regnez seul."

"You reign there alone" I muttered, puzzled.

In the space betwixt the first and last words is carved the emblem of a heart. My lady spoke:

"The motto, Mr. Lindsay, has long been in use in our family. It can be understood as an expression of loyalty to an individual or to a cause. I think you will understand why Sir Charles bequeathed this to you as a keepsake."

"Lady Avay, I understand perfectly."

John, who had all this while been a silent spectator, now broke in. '

"Mr. Lindsay, I want you to know that I share not James's sentiments. I believe as my father did in our rightful kings and in the Episcopal kirk."

My lady smiled:

"There, you have won another Erskine. Now take a glass of wine with us before you leave."

John brought forward the wine bottle and glasses. A carafe of water stood on the table.

"Mother, Mr. Lindsay, I give you a toast."

As he spoke, young John Erskine passed his glass over the carafe: .

"To the King - over the water."

Thus was the first Jacobite toast given in the House of Avay. The following spring there was a great coming and going betwixt the Knapp and the manse. Then the last week of March Mrs Burns came to stay, bringing with her the huge cheese that was to celebrate the birth of our child.

Well I recall how I felt that third day of April, late in the evening when the wail of a new-born infant filled the house.When the knock came to the study door it was Mrs Spowart, our faithful old servant, who brought the child in swaddling bands.

"Mr Lindsay, it's a man bairn. Naethin' cud be luckier

I was dumbfoundered.

"What sall ye name the lad ?" she asked kindly.

My eye fell on the ring I wore.

"I think I shall call him Charles."

And.Charles it was. When the news was conveyed to Avay House my lady graciously sent down some wine for Jean and John Erskine offered to be godfather to my child, which I accepted with joy.

Three days later Charles Burns Lindsay was baptized in Avay kirk and the entry made in the register. Jeans mother,with a grandmother's pride, carried the infant from the manse to the kirk. The first person we met, to whom we offerd the bairn's piece, was John Marshall in the Strude, who accepted the customary piece right gladly.

As time went on the Presbyterian Assembly became more and more insistent that Episcopalian clergy should be evicted from their charges but I in Avay, enjoyed a peculiar protection. The young Laird,being an ardent King William's man, the Presbytery wished not to offend him by asking him.to remove me. He suffered me to remain because his mother and his brother , John, valued my friendship.

The last time I saw Sir James was about the end of June 1692. Having got word that his regiment, the Scots Brigade, was to depart for the Low Countries, he came home to Avay for a day or two to see his mother.

The following summer a messenger from the postmaster at Stirling came to Avay House, with the news that Sir James and Captain Murray, brother to the Laird of Polmais, had been killed in Flanders some weeks previously.

These sad tidings were conveyed in a letter from a fellow officer who wrote to Lady Avay of her son's end . Part of the letter I noted at the time for though I regretted his fighting for Dutch William, yet I was glad he made a brave end.

" I regret, Madam, to tell you of your son's death in action on the 19th July last at Landen in Brabant. We engaged there in a most desperate battle. Vast armies were employed and though we were defeated, all fought bravely, not least your son. Our brigade was

forced from their ground by the Swiss who attacked with bayonets. Sir James endeavoured valiantly to stem their onslaught, the last sight I had being his sword upraised to meet a band of Swiss who were bearing down upon us.

Your son died as I think he would himself have chosen to meet death, that is, in the heat of battle. To know that may in some measure lighten your grief. I know not if you are acquaint with Flanders, Madam, but I can tell you that here in summer the fields are all bright with scarlet poppies, so that you may think of his lying at rest beneath a pleasant soil, not much different from the lands of which

he was the Laird."

So John, the Jacobite, became the third baronet in Avay.

NO SECOND SPRING.

Our next bairn was born in the September of 1693 when the dark purple-red elder berries were hanging in heavy clusters on the trees in the glen. We called her Mary after her maternal grandmother.

As the months and years glided by and Mary came to celebrating her third birthday, young Charles took increasing pleasure in his playmate and many a day the noisy laughter of happy children kept me from the sermon I would be busy composing. The bairns followed me, wheresoever I went, ever chatting according to their childlike fashion.

Mary was still at that stage, when in the company of strange adults a child is struck dumb, though she would prattle to me without ceasing if I did walk her about the glebe or take her to the cottar houses in the Green of Avay. But her brother Charles was ever ready to speak. One day he would be wanting me to catch a rabbit that he might hold it in his arms and stroke its fur; another day he would be asking to be lifted up to see into the nest of the thrush that built beneath the thatch of the byre.

He was also greatly devoted to Widow Spowart, sitting for hours on end, wide-eyed at the kitchen ingle, drinking in her unending treasury of country lore and legend. Every bogle in Stirlingshire it seemed was known to our aged servant.

Witchcraft , indeed, was a matter of much discussion among my parishioners, who believed implicitly in the existence of the weird sisterhood and were far from pleased when I suggested that the so-called witches might be none other than senile old women more deserving pity than persecution. I rejoice that in my time at Avay there was none accused of witchcraft.

Since I have the bairns in mind it is not unfitting that I should mention what was done in Avay at this time anent the schooling of the children of the parish.

From the time of my coming Mr William Smith had laboured industriously in the teaching of reading and writing and the repeating of the catechism, with the singing of psalms, and in all I was well pleased with his work.

Mr Smith had been wont to keep his school in the church but by reason of the scholars using the elders' seats and the stools belonging to some of the indwellers, and the bigger boys being not overcareful so that the seats suffered skaith, the Session decided to pay Mr Smith forty pounds Scots wherewith to furnish a schoolhouse. Moreover Mr Smith got 13/4 Scots for every poor scholar learning Latin and 6/8 Scots for those learning English .

Several poor bairns were provided with Bibles and the best at the catechism got eight pence from the box to encourage them. All this writing of scholars and learning has brought it to my mind that I have not, as yet, spoken of Master Robert Erskine, whom Sir Charles had hoped to encourage in the study of medicine.

My lady, knowing of her husband's intentions for Robert sent him, the year before my Mary was born, to Edinburgh to a Mr. Hugh Paterson, surgeon-apothecary, who received the young gentleman into his house to teach him his art.

Robert Erskine had been four years with the Edinburgh chirurgeon when he came to see me in the late summer of 1696, being on a visit to his family at Avay House.

For a while we spoke of Robert's apprenticeship:

"Only another year, Mr. Lindsay, and I shall have finished my training," said Robert, not a little excited.

"You have found Mr. Paterson a good master?" ,

"That I have. He has told me most freely much of his knowledge of pharmacie and already I have, in his company, waited upon several of his patients."

"Ah, but you must not tell me too much about that, must you?" I jested.

"Even so. In my indentures I bound myself not to reveal my master's secrets and not to disclose the secret diseases of his patients." ~

"And right glad I am to see you observe your oath, Master Robert, and that you waste not your time in Edinburgh."

Robert laughed heartily.

"Waste my time! You know not Mr Paterson. He is for ever lecturing his apprentices about idleness and drunkenness, forbidding us to frequent alehouses and taverns and reminding us we agreed in our indentures to be sober and lawabiding."

Robert flung himself, laughing, into a chair.

"What is the news of the parish? Are there any sick?"

"The old folks have their customary rheumatics," I replied, "and yesterday Henderson's youngest child was complaining of a sore throat."

"A sore throat. I trust 'tis not a spreading fever."

"I think not. The bairn has had a bout of the chincough and this may be some after stage."

"I like not that, Mr Lindsay. I think I shall step down to Henderson's cot."

Robert Erskine had not gone an hour when he came back, perturbation showing in his face.

"I am almost certain that Henderson's child has a fever. You must warn the village folk."

The young apothecary was right. Within a few days Henderson's child was dead and the disease was sweeping through the village, so that I was night and day at the bedsides of dying bairns and comforting heart-broken parents.

As soon as I had become sure that the epidemic was increasing I had bade Jean keep the children from me, thinking that thus all would be well at the manse. All this took place about the time the country folks term "the hint o' the hairst", though that year the grain was not cut from the fields for it had been blighted by easterly haars.

The trees on the manse brae were beginning to change colour, but the inclement weather had robbed them of much of their customary brightness of hue. On the hedges the hips were scarce turning from their summer green so that one day, espying a solitary scarlet spray as I came up the brae from the bridge, I pulled it, thinking the berries would pleasure Charles who was ever fond of Nature's gaily coloured plants.

I was swinging the branch in my hand as I came within sight of the manse. Inwardly I was cast down for I had seen much suffering of body and spirit in the days bypast by reason of the fever plague.

Outwardly I tried to assume an appearance of calm and trust. As I raised my eyes towards my home I saw Jean at the gate, looking for my coming. A sudden stound passed through my heart for I knew her presence there could only mean something of ill omen.

She came to meet me, half running.

"Oh, Will, the bairn is taken with a fever."

I ran, almost stumbling in my anxiety, into the house and upstairs to the little room where my daughter lay. One glance was enough.

"I'll get John Guild to ride at once to Alloa for the doctor," I said to Jean. "Meantime, my dear, get a good fire going in the grate. There is nought like heat for such cases. Give the child more bedclothes."

When I returned Jean and Mrs Spowart had heaped more blankets on the bed and a fine fire was blazing up. I closed the window tightly.

The poor bairn tossed and moaned and great beads of sweat hung on her flushed countenance. Jean was almost beside herself with anxiety.

"Will, do you not think this heat is too great for the child ?"

"Nay, my love, it is the treatment for a fever for the more the patient sweats the more the fever will come forth from the body."

We sat down together at our child's bedside, taking it in turns to give her sips of water.

"Will, pray for our bairn."

And I whose daily habit it was to pray found the words, for the first time, stick in my throat. As I leant across the bed to hold the little fever-torn body in my arms, I felt my own tears drop on my wrists. In utter anguish of soul I could only call aloud time and again:

"O, God, save our bairn."

Mr.Broun was not able to come till noon the following day, there being much sickness in the countryside. He had scarce entered the chamber when the Angel of Death spread his wings over our innocent child and I entered in upon the most harrowing and dreadful experience of my life.

Three days later Charles took to his bed and died almost as swiftly as Mary had done. Twice within a fortnight I was called upon to follow the little coffins of my own children to the kirkyaird.

Heavy of spirit myself I had perforce to stem the flood of grief welling up in my heart for their distracted mother needed all the comfort and solace my love could give her. The villagers were kind beyond telling to us in our sorrow. Charles Morris, the falconer, brought a pigeon to tempt Jean to eat and Andrew Smout, the tavern keeper , sent up some fine French brandy for the same purpose. Not a day passed but some kindly woman body came to the door to enquire after my wife's health.

By the end of the month of September the fever was on the wane in the parish and I was beginning to think that the hand of Providence was to chastise us no more at that season for our manifold shortcomings.

Howbeit I was to come close yet again to the borderland of that valley of the shadow in which I know even now I daily tread. Then I shrank from it, for it was to take from me the creature I loved most on earth: now I welcome its easeful shades for it brings me ever nearer to the glorious reunion I have deSired for nigh on fifty years.

The first Sunday of October 1696 was bright with autumn sunshine. A goodly congregation had gathered in the Kirk that forenoon including many from neighbouring villages. When I got into the manse after the Session meeting Mrs Spowart was awaiting me anxiously.

"Eh, Sir, but the mistress is nae better - deed she's waur. I dinna ken , but, oh, I dinna like the look o' her."

I waited to hear no more, hastening to our bed chamber upstairs. The fever flush had heightened since morning and I knew I must send John Guild in haste to Stirling for the best doctor there.

When he came he advised bleeding, which he performed with four leeches behind the ears. This he followed up with some cooling physio compounded of hillfoot herbs. All that day I sat by the bedside, leaving it not to eat, so that Mrs. Spowart brought me some of her nourishing chicken broth but I had little heart to sup.

Through the long hours of the night, along with Jean's father, I watched my beloved struggle in her delirium and cry aloud. When the first grey streaks of dawn came stealing into the room the fever seemed to abate and she fell into an insensibility. Monday dragged out its wearisome length and night followed day. Jean's mother kept vigil with me in the sick room by day and her father shared the long watches of the night. The fever returned again with renewed intensity over Tuesday night and long valiantly did its victim struggle for breath.

By Wednesday evening my wife was without strength to combat the plague any more, fatigue and raging thirst and loss of blood had entirely weakened her body. The knock in my room downstairs struck seven, each stroke echoing in the bed chamber upstairs. Jean lay propped up on three bolsters; her face, having lost its hectic flush, was now as white as the linen sheet spread across her breast; and from her lips had fled the scarlet hue of youth and beauty. Only her hair retained its vigour as it lay spread out on the bolster, glinting like burnished copper in the light of the candles.

I knew she was going from me and nought I could do might stay her. I could only sit , holding her hand, clinging desperately to mortality ere it slipped from my grasp, hoping against hope that even on the brink of the grave she might be restored to me.

The knock struck eight. Slowly, with effort, the eyelids opened . The mouth began to work. Her father and mother drew close to the bed head. I rose and leaned over my dying wife , clasping still her hand. At last the words came , though scarcely audible.

"Our prayer, Will."

She wanted me to repeat the prayer we had said together each night since our marriage , the very last thing before sleep came upon us. I slipped my arms about her as was our wont -

"Father in Heaven , keep us true to Thee, and to one another."

I looked down into her eyes. She smiled gently, sighed but once and was no more.

The weeping of a mother mourning her child filled the chamber as John Burns led me downstairs.

A sharp October wind was blowing off the Nebit when we laid my Jean beneath the mools in Avay kirkyaird. As in a dream I heard myself repeat the familiar words of the burial service.

"I am the resurrection and the life ---- --"

But there was no reality in it. I went on intoning and then my voice ceased. Some person standing by placed a cord in my hand. My wife - nay, my life itself - was going down into the earth to remain there till the day of judgment. I knew the faces about me were those of friends yet I could distinguish none.

The yellowing leaves from the kirkyaird trees came dancing about my feet and some went fluttering down into the open grave to lie on her coffin. I remember thinking how Jean would like that for she was a true child of the Hillfoots to whose heart Nature in all her seasonal changes was dear.

And where she rested was a spot of her own choosing for when the bairns died she asked me to lay them at the east end of the kirkyaird. There, she said, the eye may best look down on the road leading from the valley to the east stile of the kirk that, on Sundays, is thronged with folk from.Kerseypow or Shevihall or the Howtoune of Sauchie.

There the eye may best look up to the Ochils that to an Avay man or woman are the breath of life itself. Years cannot dull the eye of recollection and I see it all before me plainly this very moment. I have left instructions that when I am gone my heart is to be taken back to Scotland and buried there in Avay with the dust of my beloved wife and bairns and mingle too with the yellow autumn leaves.

116

I went back to my empty manse and to Mrs. Spowart but not for long. Early in November the Presbytery of Stirling again deSired I should demit my kirk, being of the Episcopal persuasion. This time I raised no objection but went straightwith to Avay House to consult with the Laird. Sir John was most understanding.

"If it is your deSire to go, Mr. Lindsay, I shall not press you to stay; but you serve the kirk in Avay well and I would have no presbytery hound you from it."

"Sir John, as you doubtless comprehend I have little heart to remain beneath the manse roof. Every corner is full of sad memories."

"Yes, indeed, I know how you feel. But, tell me, what shall you do when you go? Life is not easy for an Episcopalian clergyman in these times."

"Perhaps, Sir John, I shall get a post as a tutor, or I may try my fortune abroad."

The Laird thought a while.

"My brother, Henry, wishes to advance his studies,but my mother deSires him to stay at home. The lad is ,as you know, in his fourteenth year. Come to Avay House as Henry's tutor and help me with the estate. What say you ?"

" I accept gladly."

For my valedictory sermon I preached on the text:

"Here we have no abiding city."

Finally I commended my successor to the congregation. Then,having pronounced the benediction , I stepped down from the pulpit and stood at the west door where I took each of my people by the hand. The last bread I broke in the manse of Avay was my breakfast the following morning. Then I walked through the chambers that had brought me so much joy and so much sorrow.

117

When I had gone over all the house I took up my cloak and hat and, slipping my old and treasured Horace beneath my oxter, passed over the threshold , drawing the door behind me.

Thence I went into the kirkyaird where the cut sods were still noticeable. Another life was beginning for me.

The winter wind blew through the thick Avay-woven grey cloth of my cloak and I clasped my hands together for warmth. The ring on my finger turned about , for grief had emaciated my body,

I drew my hand out of the folds of my cloak. The Ochil Eye, with its inscription of loyalty, gleamed bright in the hard winter light. I thought of Sir Charles, lying not far from my Jean, in the Erskine vault; I thought of James Stewart, King of Scots, exiled in France; I thought of the love I would never again know on earth.

"Jean, Jean," I called out to the silent grave, "no other woman can ever take your place in my heart. O, my beloved, vous y regnez seul."

THE ILL YEARS

The years that followed my leaving the kirk of Avay —the years that brought the century to a close - were ill years for Scotland. Season upon season frost and rain and haars blasted the crops while famine stalked the land and beggary increased beyond belief. So great was the poverty that the Presbyterian kirk was obliged to license beggars with parchment badges, commanding that no charity be given within the bounds of the parish save to those so authorised.

In the northern parts of the country there were vast tracts bereft of human and animal population.

Roof thatches fell in on cold chimney places , and land that once had felt the plough and waved with fair crops was quickly covered over with heather and bracken so that it became as if the hand of man had never been upon it.

Over at Tulliallan so great was the poverty and so numerous the burials that the kirk session could no longer supply coffins to the poor, it being arranged that the bottom of the public kist be on hinges to allow the bodies to be dropped more expeditiously into shallow graves.

During these ill years Sir John was much exercised on the subject of agricultural methods and would often lament the backwardness of the farmers. But my farming friends had other ideas.

"Dae awe' wi'the rigs ?" cried Burns , "An' close the grund aboot wi' hedges ? Hoo ere we tae pasture the cattle an' hoo wull we get eneuch caller air tee winnow the hairst ?"

"Aye," joined in Drumwhalley, " does the Laird think the puir herds can fill their bellies wi' hedges ? Ye ken as weel' as me the snaws that cover these hills free December tae March. Nae beast cud be left oot here a' winter. "

"Only a coof widna bield the silly craturs,"declared Burns.

"Forby," went on Drumwhalley, " the Laird'; got a bee in his bonnet about sheep, He wis tryin' tae tell me I sudna tak the lambs free their mithers in May , but he didna say hoo I wis tae get milk fur the hoose. Gin I wis see daft as believe him. It's grand fur the laird: he's ne'er short o'siller or gudes. The kain hens that gang tee Avay Hoose are byordnar."

The mention of hens brought a fresh outburst from Burns.

"Aye, an' the kain eggs . No content wi' the size o' the eggs as Nature ordained, the Laird maun be passin' them through three rings, and countin' twal tae the dizzen fur the first size, fifteen tae the second, then auchteen tae the third,"

"My friends," I protested , "these are but the customs of our country. From time immemorial the subject has rendered service to his lord."

But the farmers would have none of my chiding and continued in their old ways.

In December my lady received a letter from Robert who was in Paris whither he had gone two years before to further his study of surgery and to engage in botany. This epistle caused much rejoicing for in it Robert informed my lady that he was shortly to be recognised as Doctor of Medicine and hoped to be admitted a Fellow of the Royal Society.

The close of the year was indeed a solemn occasion For being the end of the century it bore with it more of a sense of finality than others had. As I sat in my chamber in Avay House that Hogmanay of 1699 and watched the flickering flames in the grate, my mind wandered over past years.

It wanted but fifteen minutes to midnight. I slipped from the house and made my way behind the stables to a point of vantage on the hillside. As I stood looking towards the village the first snow fluttered down on my woollen cloak.

Down there in the kirkyard I thought, these flakes will be falling on my loved ones, making beautiful my desolation.

And I had a strange feeling as if I was passing from the death of the heart to the resurrection of the spirit. The old century was going, going, going.

Then it was gone.

The first of January, 1700, had arrived. Far away from Avay, in the palace of St. Germain-en-Laye Scotland's exiled king raised his glass to the future and to his son - James Francis Edward Stewart.

THINGS O' THE STATE

The new century brought my pupil , Henry Erskine, to his eighteenth birthday and to the decision to seek his fortune abroad. A Glasgow merchant with interests in the Jamaican molasses trade and known to Doctor Robert needed a young Scotsman to train in the trade. So Henry left Avay on the morning of September 1st, 1701, never to return, but of that tragedy I shall write hereafter.

A week or two after Henry's departure word came to Sir John that the King, James Stewart I mean, had died at St.Germain.

"Sad tidings, my lord, "I said."I had hoped to see our king restored for I do believe he intended well for his people. Nor can I ever forget his gracious bearing the time your father brought him here when he stumbled on the hill."

Sir John smiled. "He won you that day."

Involuntarily I voiced aloud my thoughts:

"I wonder if the Prince will ever see our shores."

"What think you of a Stewart restoration?"

"Sir, Scotland has little reason to relish Dutch William and the English. Glencoe and Darien are not easily forgot. If rumour is, for once, not a lying jade, we may expect some action from the Duke of Hamilton."

"The moment Hamilton awaits," observed Sir John, "is the hour of King William's death."

That moment came in the spring of the next year when an English mole cast up a hillock where King William was riding: his horse stumbled and the Orangeman had a fatal fall. The day the intelligence of this reached our part of the kingdom I chanced to be in Stirling.

Stepping aside to the Rampant Lion hostelry for some refreshment I found myself in the company of the Lairds of Touch, Kippendavie, and Keir. These gentlemen invited me to a private room to share their claret. As we raised our glasses Touch, a staunch Jacobite, spoke:

"To the little gentleman in the brown waistcoat."

I believe that would be the first time that grown men had solemnly drunk a toast to a mole.

Sir John, as Member of Parliament for Burntisland, was present in 1703 at the opening of the parliament in Edinburgh. National feeling ran high for it was feared that Queen Anne's English advisers would force a union of parliaments. Little did I think that I was witnessing the last Scottish parliament and seeing also the last carrying of the ancient symbols of Scottish independence – the Honours Three - now shut up in the Castel lest they fan into flame some yet smouldering ashes of patriotism.

Tears blind my eyes as I write for but a year ago I thought to come again in my old age to that wind-swept city by the Forth and see these Honours grace Charles Edward Stewart, grandson of the Stewart that first engendered my loyalty. Alas! That dream is shattered. Howbeit I must keep to an orderly setting out of events and leap not back and fore.

In the early morning when we left the Erskine family house in Miln's Square beside the Kirk at the Tron and made our way to the Abbey of Holyrood House, a grey mist hung over the tall lands. The long cobbled street was unusually clean, the middens having been removed and the people forbidden to fling out rubbish and stale water that day. Absent too were the country carts that daily brought butter and eggs and vegetables, for the roadway was to be kept clear.

At Holyrood attendants were busy arranging their masters' apparel. Impatient horses whinnied. Then the heralds began to arrange the

123

cavalcade according to the etiquette of feudal times, the lowliest first and the greatest last. From a window in the palace a herald summoned each member by name, who then rode to the gateway where another made certain the correct order was observed. The sixty three members of the royal burghs rode first. Sir John representing Burntisland wore the customary black velvet and rode upon a grey pad.

Behind him came the nobility, the heredity members, and the Dukes, resplendent in costly robes. After them in a blaze of scarlet and gold came the pursuivants and the Lord Lyon. Then followed in velvet and ermine the nobles privileged to carry the golden crown that once the Bruce had worn , and the sceptre and the sword of state, gifts of the popes to our medieval monarchs ;and it was a thing to be noted that these men alone were bareheaded in all that great train.

Last and greatest was the Royal Commissioner with attendant gentlemen. While we were awaiting the signal to set off Sir John acquainted me with many of the dignitaries there present.

"Look, Mr. Lindsay, yonder is the Duke of Hamilton."

"The taller of the two, my lord?"

"No, the shorter, with the black, coarse complexion and haughty mien."

Hamilton, indeed, bore in his person a superiority of manner that testified to his royal ancestry and made me speculate if there might not be much truth in the report that he hoped to gain the throne for himself when Queen Anne was gone. My attention then fell upon a man of exceeding plain manner but handsome figure. He seemed to be on good terms with all about him so that I asked Sir John who this genial personage might be.

"The Earl of Seafield, Chancellor and ex-secretary of State."

"Seafield I exclaimed. "From all reports he is not to be relied upon."

"True, true. Did you hear Lockhart called him a blank sheet which the Court might fill up with what they pleased"?

"I did, my lord. Pray, who is yon tall, awkward figure with the choleric countenance, whose poor servant seems to be getting the worst of his master's tongue?"

Sir John laughed.

"Athole, Mr. Lindsay, well-known for his fiery temper."

Dropping his voice to a whisper my master went on,

"He is expected to join the Stewart cause openly one of these days."

Then in normal tones he said, "Close beside Athole is one you know well."

I raised myself forward on my toes to get a better view of the man of whom Sir John spoke. At that moment Athole moved aside so that I beheld clearly a striking figure, whose full curled wig, falling about his shoulders, added to his natural grace. The long shapely nose and finely curved lips of the Erskines, I recognised full well. Yet it was not the man's physical appearance that distinguished him: it was his air of charm and purposefulness - something of the country gentleman with something of the politician, something of the planner with something of the patriot.

"Why, 'tis your kinsman, the Earl of Mar."

Little did I realise that day how soon Mar would influence my master to side with the proposed Union of Parliaments, thus causing him to abstain for a while from active support of the Jacobite party.

All the while we were speaking I was aware of a man of about fifty years of age, very thin in the body, low in height and stern of face, who from a little distance behind, regarded us somewhat sourly. '

125

"Andrew Fletcher of Saltoun, member for Haddington,"replied Sir John to my enquiry. "He likes me not for I am sib to Mar. Fletcher will fight any attempt towards Union to the bitter end."

Further conversation was, at that moment, cut off for the heralds announced the procession was to set forth. As I turned to lead forward Sir John's horse I caught a glimpse of the Royal Commissioner, Queensberry, sparse, black visaged, with an air of gentility and very magnificent in his brilliant robes.

The morning haze had now lifted and a May day sun shone brightly so that the country folks from Duddingstoun and Portobello and Leith, who had gathered on the slopes of Arthur's Seat, had a fine view of our silks and ermine and velvets as we clattered over the courtyard at Holyrood and passed beneath the ringing arch of the Gatehouse Pend. Up the steep causeway of the Canongate we rode, passing Huntly House and Moray House, from the windows of which many a woman with painted face and tired head (like Jezebel in the Scriptures) did hang out. At the Netherbow Port the gates stood ready open, that we might pass without hindrance from the burgh of Canongate to the toun of Edinburgh.

The regular soldiers and the City Guard with their Lochaber axes lined the streets that the crowds of spectators might not push forward or throw squibs or other fireworks to fright the horses and interrupt the ceremony.

The people were strangely silent. I know not if this were so by reason of the solemnity of the cavalcade or by reason of the numerous pamphlets that had directed public attention to this Riding of the Parliament, declaring that since a Union was to be forced on us the Honours of Scotland would never again be carried through the capital but be put away to humiliate Scotland. This I could not believe possible. Yet subsequent events proved the pamphlet writers correct and myself wrong.

At the Kirk of St.Giles carpenters had set up long banks of timber for dismounting at the Lady Steps, beside the opening to Parliament Close. There I saw the Lord High Constable of Scotland, with his baton of office, and his guard behind him, make obeisance to the members, who then advanced to the Lord Marischal by whom they were conducted into Parliament Hall with its fine oaken roof.

Here I left my master, leading his horse (as did all the other attendants) to the Lawnmarket where the townspeople admired both beasts and trappings, for the animals of the great nobles wore rich footmantles ornamented with heavy silk fringe and gay with heraldic devices and magnificent in silver and gold braiding.

It was a stormy sitting of Parliament over the question of the succession to the throne: Sir John told me on his return to Avay in the autumn.

"Parliament has passed an Act of Security, Mr Lindsay, but Queensberry reuses to give it the royal assent".

"What, Sir, is the tenor of this act ?"

"In brief, we have set aside the English act that passes the crown, on the death of our present Queen Anne, to the Hanoverians."

"Who then is to reign?" I asked eagerly.

"The Royal power is to be invested in parliament till they select a successor of the Stewart line and of the Protestant religion. Moreover that person can only rule both kingdoms if we are granted equal trading rights with England."

I shook my head.

"This strife wears our country down. We should bring the Prince home now,"

"So," said the Laird, "think the Edinburgh Jacobites but for my part I think our country's pressing need is agricultural and commercial expansion. The Prince is too young and his mother an ardent Roman. Later perhaps - "

"Come he soon or come he late," I broke in , "I serve him as I served his father at Killiecrankie along with your father."

I held up my hand so that the candlelight fell bright on my Ochil Eye.

Vous y regnez seul.

"Aye, my lord, once a woman shared the love of my heart but now, on earth, all my devotion is for the house of Stewart . Their restoration alone can give fresh life to my suffering Episcopal kirk and bring prosperity to Scotland."

My master was serious.

"Many like you are for immediate action but I have had much intercourse with Mar these past months and he advises a more cautious policy for the present. Nothing is to be gained by dethroning Anne - remember she is a Stewart."

"A Stewart in name, but not in spirit,"I countered,sorry that Sir John was so swayed by Mar's opinions.

In the midst of the national unrest private grief came to my lady. From the time Henry left Avay till midsummer 1703 he wrote regularly to his mother and many a lively picture he drew of the black-skinned folk on the plantation. But when no more letters came Sir John wrote to Doctor Robert in London. By luck Robert was friendly with a military surgeon in the Indies to whom he applied for news of his brother. This good man replied but it was high summer 1704 ere the sad news reached us in Avay that Henry had been drowned.

Later that year Queen Anne agreed to the Scottish Act of Security but the following year the English retaliated with an Aliens Act, whereby we were not permitted to export to England our cattle, linen, or coals. Moreover this Aliens Act threatened to treat the Scots as aliens so that the temper of our people daily grew uglier.

Very near to breaking did matters come as the Queen became more persistent for a parliamentary union of the kingdoms.

Strange, nay almost miraculous, was the unification among Scotsmen, brought about by the very thought of such a possibility as the union. Then did the lion and the lamb couch together for Covenanter and Episcopalian, rich and poor, Highlander and Lowlander, were one in their abhorrence.

Nor did I fail to observe that when this business of the Union became more urgent and the spirit of nationalism more keen, my master, swayed by the Earl of Mar, began to say openly that if the Union meant stability and freedom to trade abroad, it should be entered into.

It was while agitated in the throes of the Union conflict that I met again John Erskine of Cardross, the Covenanter, who had sought refuge beneath my manse roof along with Cousin Davie, when Argyll's rising failed away back in 1685.

Though a distant kinsman of my master there was no coming and going betwixt the two households, their political opinions being divergent. Mr. Erskine had returned to Scotland in 1688 with William of Orange, buying later the estate of Tulliallan in the Kingdom of Fife from the Earl of Kincardine's creditors. He was also governor of Stirling Castel and member of parliament for the same town.

The Black Colonel, as he was known to the people on account of his appearance, took up his abode in a fine red-tiled house on the Sand Haven at Culross, styled the Colonel's Close. And from there he came but once to Avay - towards the end of July 1706 - borne on a good roan horse but more, indeed, on the wings of his wrath for he had just then heard that all the Articles of Union had been agreed to in London.

Sir John and I were busy on the estate accompts when the Colonel was ushered in to our presence. He waited not to introduce himself nor to exchange any of the usual ceremonies but, coming straight to the long table where bills and inventories lay scattered, rattled upon it with his fist, crying aloud:

"John Erskine, what say you to this black union?"

Sir John, with his wonted civility, at once rose.

"My dear kinsman, welcome to Avay House. Pray be seated. This gentleman here is my factor, Mr. William Lindsay, before whom you may speak freely."

At the sound of my name the Colonel turned abruptly in his seat to look bluntly into my face.

"Lindsay? An Episcopalian minister?" he barked at me.

"The same, Sir, and your servant."

Turning to Sir John our impetuous visitor went on to say:

"Mr. Lindsay and I have met. He once gave me the hospitality of his hearth. If he is your factor, John, you have an honest man. But I came here to know if you intend to fight the Union."

The Laird spoke quietly and deliberately.

" It is not without something to commend it , in as much as it gives our country trading privileges with England. It surprises me that you who are both Whig and Covenanter would wish to oppose this matter of united parliaments. "

A snort of indignation filled the room as the Colonel exploded:

"Your kinsman, Mar , has poisoned you with his English sympathies. I tell you this - both of you - that staunch Covenanter though I am , yet would I rather sign a league with the Jacobites on a drumhead than accept this wicked union."

" Aye , indeed ," I cried. " All true Scots must unite against this measure ."

" There , " declared Sir John , looking straight at Colonel Erskine , " you do not want the proposed union because you fear as a good Presbyterian churchman a return of Episcopacy: Mr. Lindsay, the Episcopalian, does not want it for he hopes for a return of the Stewarts, who champion Episcopacy. If you both get what you want - no Union – you will then turn and rend one another. And where, in that case, stands Scotland?

"Where, indeed?" retorted our visitor. "Where will Scotland be with a Union? Cromartie judged the situation well when he declared that this Union would be "as a blood puddin" to bind a cat - that is, till one or the other be hungry and then the puddin' flies.""

"Freedom of trade must be our first consideration,"replied my master. "If the Union gives us this (and I believe it will) you will live to bless its treators."

This last was more than the choleric Colonel could stomach.

"Treatorsl" he roared. "Nay, Sir, you mistake your word - traitors!" '

And with that final denunciation of the Union and the Commissioners he swept out of the room, sending the spaniel that lay at the door flying in trepidation beneath the table.

A minute later we heard his horse clatter off down the avenue. Sir John and I fell to our accompts again but my mind was much troubled, for I could see plainly that the Laird, despite his royalist leanings, was not at this point prepared to come out with the Jacobite party. Only time and bitter experience were to teach my master and Mar that this Union was an ill thing for Scotland and to bring them both in the year 1715 to support James Francis on the field of battle.

But I could see in that year of 1706 upon the horizon the gathering cloud of a Stewart rising. Then it was to me,as to Elijah of old, a little cloud like a man's hand. Yet I knew that soon the heavens would be black with clouds and wind and rain; the clouds of discontent that the Union must bring; the wind of adventure that would drive a young man to seek a crown; the rain of disorder that needs inevitably follow upon such circumstances.

Aye, indeed, a storm was brewing.

NEWS OF THE BLACKBIRD

Winter 1706 - 1707 saw the last stages of the parliamentary battle anent the Union. Sir John was much in Edinburgh where all the talk was of this lamentable affair, with many an ill word for Mar who had produced it. Everywhere there were soldiers for Queensberry, uncertain of the temper of the citizens, was attended throughout the proceedings by a guard of musketeers at whose head the angry populace hurled the cry, "No Union."

I was in the Cross Keys inn, near the cathedral of Edinburgh, when I first heard of Lord Belhaven's spirited opposition . The November haar had sent me in for a dram to which I had but started when a lawyer's clerk came in. At once he was surrounded by a group of anxious men keen to hear what Belhaven had said. Well can I imagine the noble lord flinging out his hands in appeal to his listeners:

"I think I see our ancient mother,Caledonia,like Caesar, sitting in the midst of our Senate , ruefully looking about her , covering herself with her royal garments , attending the fatal blow, and breathing out her last with et tu quoque mi fili ? .None can destroy Scotland, save Scotland's self , Hold your hand from the pen."

Yet the protests of the common people were as nought. In January the signatures were got and Queensberry was off to London post haste. The final step in this wicked business was the signing of the exemplification of the Act of Union on the 19th of March by Chancellor Seafield. Scarce was the ink dry when it was known that the traitor had dismissed the signing with the comment:

" There's ane end of ane auld sang."

On the 26th of March 1707 I went , a little after one in the afternoon , to see the Honours of Scotland carried into the castel. Nor was I alone for it seemed that the honest tradesmen and many other patriotic folks of the capital had gathered also that they might pay a last tribute of respect to these symbols of independence, now become what Lord Belhaven so justly foretold they would become - the *"Spolia opima"* of the English Hannibal.

As the officers of state passed up to the Castel a decent woman at my side burst forth.

"Wae's me that I sud hae leevd tae sic a day. The bonnie gowden croun wi' a' its braw stanes tae be seen nae mair!"

"Aye, in troth, mistress," spoke up a man, "a curse on England. 'Twas a bad day for Edinboro' when Jamie the Saxt rode oot o' its gates fur Lunnon."

"An' noo the Parliaments gaun tae," joined in a baxter, "there'll no be a banquet frae ae year's end tae anither. It's a toom pouch I'll be haein'."

"We'll a' be haein' that, baxter," broke in a swarthy fellow, who from the tools he carried was by trade a carpenter.

"Tak a guid look.at thae lands," and he pointed to the tall buildings of the Lawnmarket. "Mony a fine bit o' work I dae fur the gentry dwellin' yonder. Wait_a wee an' they'll a' be flittin' tae Lunnon. Syne it's English pouches that'll be rattlin' wi' Scotch bawbees."

Though my own heart echoed the gloomy forebodings of those worthy citizens as I rode back to Avay, a glimmering of hope kept me from utter despondency. My duties as factor to the Avay estate had acquainted me with several of the Stirlingshire Lairds who like myself favoured the Stewarts.

My inclinations being known I was not altogether surprised when word came to me about three months later that Keir deSired to see me at the changehouse of Archibald Ogilvy , hard by the bridge carrying the highway from Stirling to Crieff over the Allan Water.

By the time I had ridden along the Hillfoots, skirting the Kirk of Logie and coming down into Bridge of Allan, I was glad indeed to pass beneath the lintel of Ogilvy's inn and feel the cool air of the parlour where Keir, Kippendavie, Touch, and Garden were enjoying a pipe.

Keir was a jovial young man, much given as are all gentlemen to the bottle. His countenance was one that was not readily forgotten _ sparse but finely arched eyebrows, a shapely nose, laughing eyes. Yet there was more to Keir than his physical appearance: his ready tongue and pleasant voice gladly drew me into his company.

Kippendavie, of medium height and inclining to corpulence - he always had more waistcoat buttons left undone than the rest of us, was a genial man upwards of forty years of age. His complexion was florid. The Laird of Carden was stockily built with beetling eyebrows. Like Keir he counted it a proud boast to say he could drink any man under the table.

In contrast Touch was a tall, raw-boned fellow of thirty odd years , who contrary to fashion wore his own hair and drank sparingly.

When I had refreshed myself with a stoup of Ogilvy's ale Keir fell to business,

"Mr Lindsay, you know that one Colonel Hooke has been here enlisting support for the king across the water. We have pledged our support of James V111 and now I am to let Hooke know about other Stirlingshire gentlemen. What of our neighbour, your master , Sir John?"

"Sir John will not come out at present. Mar has led him to believing the Union will bring prosperity to all."

"Fools," exclaimed Kippendavie,"Do you not think he might he persuaded to give a general promise of support only to be put into action when the King sets foot in Scotland?"

I gave a wry smile,

"No, gentlemen, his mind is full of new schemes for trade and agriculture and he declares that peace is a first necessity."

Keir looked grim.

"Erskine and Mar will learn that this Union is but a stick to break their backs with. Let them be. What of you?"

Before I could answer Touch leant across the table,the sunlight through the inn window falling upon his high cheek bones, intensifying the earnestness of his face.

"Forget not that the Stewarts are friends of the Episcopal Kirk. Join us under Keir's leadership."

"Right gladly," I replied.

"Would to God all your fellow countrymen thought as you do," burst out the Laird of Keir. "When you are needed my messenger will come to you. What token shall I give him to accept as proof of your identity?"

I rested my hand on Ogilvy's broad oaken table so that the gaze of all present was drawn to my Ochil Eye.

"This eye-shaped agate and the inscription on the bezel thereof is proof enough of my loyalty."

"What says the lettering?" asked Garden.

Before I could reply Kippendavie who was seated next me read aloud:

""Vous y regnez seul" - and it is accompanied with the heart emblem. Troth, Mr. Lindsay, a very fitting ring for a Jacobite."

"Assuredly," declared Touch, "for sit who may on the throne in England the Stewart ever reigns in the Scottish heart."

"Truly spoken, my friend," observed Keir. "Now, Mr. Lindsay, that you may know my messenger is no Government spy seeking to entrap you, here is our password:

"The Blackbird is expected"

Hardly had Keir finished speaking when Carden, who whistled bonnier than any lintie on the Ochils, broke into that song which all Jacobites knew as a tribute to James Francis –

"Good luck to the Blackbird where ere he may be "

So I journeyed back to Avay to await there the spin of fortune's wheel.

That tumultuous year 1707 ended on a happy domestic note at the House of Avay, for Sir James entered into a contract of marriage with Mistress Catherine Sinclair, daughter of Henry, 8th Lord Sinclair.

In the spring of the following year three important events took place. Sir John brought his bride to Avay House, the dowager Lady Avay took up residence in Edinburgh, where her son Charles had been made Professor of Public Law, at the house in Miln's Square, and early in March a lad from the Mill of Keir came to me as I was watching the tenants at Braefoot turning over their land.

"Are ye Mr Lindsay, factor to the Laird of Avay ?"

"I am, what is your business lad ?"

"My master, the Laird of Keir has sent me. I am to see your ring Sir "

The Ochil Eye gleamed in the bright March morning light as I held forth my hand.

"And your message is ?"

The lad gave one look at my hand.

"The Blackbird is expected. You are to he at Ogilvy's changehouse before dusk,"

"Tell your master I shall not fail." with these words I returned hastily to Avay House where I requested Sir John to allow me to depart For some weeks, as I had pressing business to which I had even now been called."

My master gave me a long look. Then he replied:

"Mr Lindsay, I think I can guess your business. These are difficult times and each man must dree his ain weird,"

"My lord, you are most understanding."

Sir John thought a while before he added:

"I think this expedition is premature. If you find things go not as you expect return hither as silently as you go. None need be any the wiser for meantime I shall give it out that you are gone to a cousin in the north who is ill."

"Pray God I have more success than you think likely."

Sir John grasped me by the hand,

" I value you as a friend. God protect you."

When I came in by the Allan Water I could scarce distinguish in the rapidly waning light the white washed walls of Bridgend. As I rode into the cobbled yard a lad, whom I recognised as one of Touch's men, came forward to take my horse.

"Ye're tae gaun in tae the laigh parlour, Sir,"

The south door in the garden being open I passed into the house, treading the flagged passageway to the far room. A bright fire glowing in the chimney piece, sent my shadow dancinq on the white plastered wall. The candles burning steadily in their brass and wooden holders revealed my fellow Jacobites, booted and spurred,

"Lindsay," cried Keir, taking his hand from the pistol that lay before him on the table.

"Your servant, Sir, I come as arranged,"

"Come heat yourself at the fire. Ogilvy will in with supper and then to business."

When we had sampled the roast mutton cutlets , the dish of hens, and the raisins the landlord set . before us, Keir told us the intelligence we had got the night before.

"Gentlemen, the king is about to sail from Dunkirk with a French fleet. The hour has come for us to act."

"What is your plan?" enquired Kippendavie, giving voice to my own thoughts,

"Tomorrow morning I propose that Touch and Lindsay leave with me for Brig 0' Turk where I shall advise those well affected to the cause, that they hold themselves ready to join him. You, Carden and Kippendavie, will proceed to inform our friends about Dunblane, and then come to join us at Brig 0' Turk. From thence we shall pass in company toLoch Earn where it is arranged I am to meet in with one called Fleming. What we do thereafter depends on the instructions Fleming has to impart to us, friends we are on the eve of a great adventure. Let us call Ogilvy that we may drink to our Master' s health."

Which being done, the landlord placed before us pewter stoups of fine French wine with cream on the top and we raised them to James VIII of Scotland.

Very early next morning I was roused from my slumbers by the lusty crowing of a cock on the inn midden, Through the shutters of my chamber window the light of day was penetrating into the room. I was still in that state of half sensibility betwixt sleep and waking when there fell upon my ears the sound of running feet followed by a loud tirling at the pin. I heard the voice of the landlord and the agitated tones of the runner. Then Ogilvy came hurrying to the adjoining room where Keir and Kippendavie lay.

There was the sound of a chair overturned and voices were raised that bespoke hurried consultations. Next my door was flung open.

"Rise quickly, Mr. Lindsay. We must away."

It was Keir and with these words he was gone again.In shorter time than it now takes me to relate our little company was assembled in the laigh parlour. The runner in the dawn had been John Henderson, portioner in the Corntoun, a friend of Ogilvy's. He had gotten word from a chapman that had come out of Stirling at sunrise and had stopped for a sup of brose at Henderson's croft, that a company of soldiers, under one named Campbell, were coming that very morning to search Bridgend as a suspected Jacobite howff.

"We follow the plan I set out last night, gentlemen,"said Keir hurriedly. "The only change is that I shall stop at my own house for but time to arrange that my horses be taken away. I would not that my animals fall into the hands of this curst Campbell."

Just then Garden's serving man, who had gone with Kippendavie's man, to watch over the Carse of Stirling, from the high ground opposite to the changehouse, came crying that he had seen the glint of weapons from a line of soldiers marching across the Corntoun.

Without further ado we all, masters and servants,hastened into the yard of Bridgend, sprang to the saddle and with Archibald Ogilvy's - *"Good luck to the blackbird"* – ringing in our ears we pounded across the narrow, high arched bridge, spanning the Allan Water.

Sparks flew from the horses' hooves as we took the King's Highway to the North, bound post haste on the King's business.

HIGH TREASON

A little beyond Lecropt, at the House of Keir, we parted from Carden and Kippendavie. All that day we rode through the pleasant wooded valley of the Teith, stopping at both cottage and mansion where our friends were to tell that the King was coming to his own. By late afternoon the thatched roofs of Callendar came in sight. Soon we were splashing across the ford at Coilantogle and trotting along the shores of Loch Venachar.

At Brig o' Turk the change-keeper was from home when we tied up our beasts in the stable but his lady was not long in attending to us. We has just fallen to our food when the sound of horsemen approaching became plain and in a few minutes, Carden and Kippendavie entered, accompanied by a Mr Alexander Stewart of the Ardvorlich family; one Major Graham, a Perthshire Laird, and to the great pleasure of the Laird of Touch, his very own brother.

These gentlemen, having met in with our two friends, had decided to travel with us to Loch Earn, for they were also deSirous of speech with Mr Fleming. We were at our last dram before retiring when we heard the voice of one without enquiring if some gentlemen had lately come hither. On the instant our hands went to our swords or pistols as the case might be. Then there was a knocking at our door and at the same time the whistling of the song of the blackbird.

In a trice Keir sallied out:

"Enter, Sir, and say your business."

Into the pale light afforded by the cruizie came a gentleman of middle age as I guessed. He was of medium height, with a round face and sallow complexion.

"Newtoun" exclaimed Mr Stewart.

The stranger was Patrick Edmonston of Newtoun.

"Sir, you are very welcome,"said Keir, "but how did you know we were here?"

Newtoun smiled,

"I came early this morning to Stirling anent some private matters and there did hear that a certain Sergeant Campbell had returned in high temper from Bridge of Allan, having found that you gentlemen had flown from Bridgend. He had hoped to arrest you on suspicion of being in contact with our blackbird."

Touch cried out:

"Glad I am for once that a Campbell vulture has been deprived of its prey,"

Newtoun continued:

"Having also heard by other means that Fleming was in the Perthshire Highlands I decided you had likely gone to join him, I called on Ogilvy as I passed the Allan,"

"'Tis well you journeyed without delay, "observed Keir, "for we leave for Loch Earn to-morrow,"

We left Brig 0' Turk early next day going eastwards to the Pass of Leny. At Balquhidder we turned aside to acquaint some persons by the name of Macgregor of what they might shortly expect.

From there the road rose sharply across moorland, where in the greenness of the heather plants I was made aware of the coming of spring. Then we rounded a bend in the track and down below us lay the waters of Loch Earn.

And there at the changehouse at the head of the loch Mr Charles Fleming, brother to the Earl of Wigtoun, and special emissary from King James, but lately come to Scotland, awaited the Stirlingshire Lairds,

"Come, Mr Fleming," said Keir, "tell us of the King's preparations to come hither,"

"Aye, Sir,"joined in Ardvorlich, "we would know the true way of things for many conflicting reports are abroad."

"Gentlemen, it gives me pleasure to acquaint you with His Majesty's commission to me. I sailed from Dunkirk, coming to the Scottish coast at the Castel at Slaines. From Slaines I travelled to Lord Strathmore's in Angus,"

Keir leant forward;

"What are His Majesty's general orders?"

"The King is about to leave France but no one is to rise till sure news is received of his actual landing in Scotland, whenever this intelligence is got the King's supporters are to seize whatever is needful for the cause,"

"Stirlingshire is well prepared", broke in Keir. "Not a house I called at yestreen but had its hidden weapons,"

"The nobility," went on Fleming, " also wait in readiness - Nairn, Breadalbane, Drummond. The Highland chiefs have the clansmen in readiness,"

"How came you to send me word that I might expect you hereabouts?" enquired Keir.

"It came about thus, Sir. I journeyed from Castel Drummond to Lord Kilsyth's where I was told of you and your friends and that none knew better what support would come from the folks about the Ochils. But, by then having heard that His Majesty had landed , not in the south , but in the North, it became imperative for me to hasten to the Highlands. Wherefore I considered it might be possible for us to meet here,"

"The King landed,Sir?" said Touch, "and can you say where ?"

"No, Sir, I hope for more certain intelligence as we journey on."

"What way intend you to travel?" asked Ardvorlich.

"From here by Crieff to Perth where I feel more exact news may be got. Will you with me?"

With one accord we replied,"Aye, Sir,"

The journey from Loch Earn was without hazard and as we came near to Perth it was debated whether we should enter in company or if it would be morn judicious to separate, coming in twos or singly to some inconspicuous and prearranged place.

Being at this point in our journey within the parish of Methven I ventured to unburden my mind.

"My friends, the minister of this place is known to me, being of my own persuasion. I suggest we call upon him for be there any news of the King it is almost certain he will be informed."

"What is his name?" asked Mr. Fleming.

"Mr. Thomas Rhynd, chaplain to the Laird of Balgowan."

"I have heard of him," observed Kippendavie. "The Presbytery of Perth are at him, like hounds at a fox, for he is said to continue to use the Prayer Book in his services."

"He sounds a likely man to aid us," said Fleming."Let us on to his house."

When we arrived at the manse of Methven it was the lady of the house who welcomed us in, saying she expected her husband shortly from Perth whither he had gone that morning anent some charges being raised against him.

"If Mr. Rhynd is new come from Perth we shall have the latest intelligence of national affairs," I observed to my companions. '

And so it was, though the news in itself was disappointing for Mr. Rhynd declared there was yet no sign of the King's fleet about the Forth nor any information of him.

There was a rumour upon which we placed little reliance that James was at Blair Atholl where the clansmen were believed to be gathering.

We pressed on to Dunkeld, reaching the changehouse late on Saturday night. Mr Fleming having spent the greater part of Sunday trying to get word of the King's whereabouts from several Jacobites in places roundabout , and not being successful, a council was held,

"Gentlemen," said Mr Fleming ,"I regret to tell you that no certain news is to be got of the king. I begin to fear all has not gone to plan."

"What then is to be done?" asked Keir.

"I shall go east from here," answered Fleming,"retracing my way to Slaines, from where if the worst happens I can return to France, you, my friends, I advise to return to your homes till surer word is to hand of what is going on,"

And cast down though we all were at this melancholy ending to our riding forth we knew it was the wisest course. Next morning Mr Fleming and those travelling east left us, The Stirlingshire Lairds and myself waited another day, hoping against hope for the news we longed to hear. However, it came not, and the landlord beginning to be curious about our business, we left at first light on Tuesday morning, riding west into Strath Brand,down the Sma' Glen we hurried.

By noon we reached the Earn at Kinkell, where we got a much needed meal of roast mutton and the horses were rested, From there we journeyed in less hurried fashion towards Blackford. Here in the mid-afternoon I parted from my companions. Their way led by Greenloaning to Dunblane and Stirling.

My way was now to be on foot over the hills to Avay House, for we had agreed it would be best to separate about Strath Allan and each to get home as safely as possible.

"Are you sure of the way , Mr Lindsey,"asked Keir, "The Moss is treacherous going."

"Have no fear,Sir," I replied, "Many a time I have come to Blackford with a weaver from Avay, taking his web to the Crieff market,"

I turned swiftly from the highroad, making my way by a narrow path to the hills.I kept climbing and in time came to Glen Bee. Soon I crossed the water of Devon. Then at last I came upon a level stretch of moor with great patches of black earth that I knew to be peat hags. I was come to the Moss and near to home.

The light was beginning to fail so that speed in traversing this dangerous part was all I cared for.

Accordingly I decided it would be quickest and safest to wade the course of the burn which I did so, and by this means came safely to the head of Glen Winnel.

Before me were the familiar shapes of the Nebit and the Wood Hill. Striking off to the east I came down through the trees behind Avay House.

Dusk had now fallen. What with the lack of daylight and the weariness of my bones (for I had ridden hard since cock-crow and crossed the Ochils and soaked myself to the thighs in hill burns) I kept stumbling over tree roots and scratching my face and hands on the bushes.

I waited for a while at the rear of the house to make certain that all seemed normal. Then I slipped in by the postern gate and making my way to Sir John's chamber whistled softly a stave or two of the blackbird song.

In a minute the door was opened and my lord beheld me in amazement. I stepped inside.

"What news, Sir?" I cried, "for I have heard none this last week."

He laid his hand on my arm as if to support me.

"Your blackbird has flown."

Later that night when I had refreshed myself and supped, Sir John related what had taken place while I was in the Highlands.

"You had been gone only a day, Mr. Lindsay, when word was got at Stirling Castel that James Stewart had left Dunkirk and proposed to land in Fife- It was not, however, till about three days later that the French fleet entered the Forth. I rode over to Dysart to see my father-in-law there and to gather what information I could of the invading forces."

"Did you see the French ships?" I asked.

"Indeed I did, Sir, for in company with Lady Avay's father and brother I went to a point of vantage and from thence viewed the fleet at anchor off the May Isle."

"What was the feeling in Edinburgh, Sir?"

"Gentlemen of your way of thinking were indeed expressive of their sentiments, drinking to the King's health in the very streets and striking fear into the hearts of those who uphold the Government. Leven, the commander of the castel marched his men to Leith sands to do what he could should the invaders try to come ashore on the south. Then, yesterday, the English fleet under Byng came sailing up the Forth and routed the French ships."

"Did any suffer in the affair?"

"Only the Salisbury was taken. The French commander De Forbin was in luck for a strong breeze that got up helped his escape."

"What think you is intended now?"

"When I left Fife this morning 'twas said everywhere that James and the French were going north to the Cromarty Firth to land there but I think we will not succeed,"

"Why, my lord ?"

"Yesterday, the breeze at sea was strong: this morning heavy gales were blowing up in the Forth, If such winds continue De Forbin will hesitate to land."

Events turned out as Sir John had judged. When the French ships reached the Cromarty waters the tempestuous gales had veered north and gave no sign of abating. In addition several ships had become separated from the main body. James begged to be put ashore to continue the struggle by himself, believing his people would flock to him once he was on Scottish soil. De Forbin refused and headed off for France.

The Government lost no time in seizing known Jacobites: my master's kinsman, Mar, was very active in these afiairs, Belhaven was sent to Edinburgh and Fletcher of Saltoun flung into Stirling Castel.

Also seized were my friends the Stirlingshire Lairds.Strange to relate they were the only ones against whom the Government thought they had enough evidence for prosecution.

Though Queen Anne's warrant for the trial of my fellow Jacobites was given out at Windsor Castel in July 1708 it was not till November that matters were settled.

Nothing else was talked of in the taverns and coffee-houses of Edinburgh while the trial was going on. Especially interested were the legal men who felt the evidence of the witnesses to be inadmissible on the grounds that they were "socii criminis".

Accordingly not a sound was to be heard in the high Council-House at noon on November 23rd when the finding of the assize was made known - "NOT PROVEN".

Then the cheering rose in the High Street and floated down the wynds as the news of the verdict spread like wildfire. So ended what the Government called the "Trial of James Stirling of Keir and others for High Treason."

The day following the trial I rode out of Edinburgh with Keir, At Stirling bridge we parted.

I turned east to Avay and as I centered along the Hillfoots my companion's parting words kept sounding in my ears - " What has happened is but the beginning, not the end."

THE BRAES O' MAR.

In the years that followed our attempt of 1708 to set the Chevalier de St. George on the throne life along the Hillfoots kept an even tenor. At Avay House another generation of Erskines came to fill the rooms with the carefree laughter of childhood. Master Charles was born in May 1709. When the time came he followed his father in the estate as 4th baronet and, such is the strangeness of life, he died with great honour as a soldier, this very year of 1747 in which I have taken up my pen to write this tale. A few years later Henry, at present the 5th baronet in Avay, was born. Many a fine ploy they had with their sister Barbara (born after the Fifteen) and their numerous cousins, the Haldanes and the Sinclairs.

Lady Avay, that is Sir John's wife, grew to be a much respected figure in the parish, her care for the poor folks being as generous as had been his mother's ere she removed into Edinburgh. My lady's youth and gentle smile and kindly manner endeared her to the heart of every cottar. Indeed it was not long after her coming to the village that the weavers paid her a gracious compliment by callingthe patch of snow that every winter lingers high up on the hill behind the house 'Lady Avay's Web. '

Over the water James Francis, the Old Chevalier as he is now called, was then a young man , busy gaining martial honour , fighting with the French against Marlborough at Oudenarde and at Malplaquet, in Scotland discontent with the Union was plain. In the Parliament at London the English embers were exceeding foolish in their attitude to the Scots.

Duty on the exports of linen caused trouble. To tax linen was to cripple an important Scots manufacture but the English M.P'S ignored this , being more anxious to assist the Irish linen,

151

when challenged in parliament one upstart Southerner dared to say:

"Is not Scotland subject to the sovreignty of England? Is Ireland to be ruined to humour a few obstructive members from the North ?"

Then ,as Sir John told me, came a memorable moment. Lockhart jumped to his feet, calling out

"Scotland never was, an' never will be, subject to England."

All this led Jacobites like myself to hope that the Union would be severed and the King recalled. The Earl of Mar began to talk of giving over the Union and even Seafield, who had signed away his country's freedom, now thought otherwise and even tried to get a Bill to the House o' Lords to dissolve the Treaty of Union.

Events began to quicken their pace in the year 1713.

The long war on the Continent between France and England came to an end. The French king Louis, that the terms of the peace might be fulfilled , had to refuse shelter to the Stewart court in exile. Then Sir John brought news of Queen Anne's death and of the succession:

"Mr Lindsay, the German has gotten to the throne."

"George of Hanover ? I cried. "Who called the Privy Council to proclaim the Hanoverian king?"

"Argyll and Somerset."

"Argyll! The curse of Scotland is the Campbell clan. "

Throughout the next year nothing of moment happened but by early summer 1715 certain English gentry fled to France; the Earl of Mar came to Scotland ; and I, the Laird of Avay's factor, heard a summons that brooked no denial.

It came about thus. Sir John was in London in June 1715. We, at Avay House , were busy laying out the grounds for the Laird was anxious to emulate his kinsman, Mar, who had made the Alloa estate the talk of the whole shire. James Gibb, the architect, had altered Alloa House, while the policies had been laid out by the Frenchman, Le Notre.

I was overseeing the Avay gardeners one bright afternoon when my lady came to me.

"Are the men working diligently ?" she enquired.

"I have no complaint to make of them. The narrow walk has all the earth laid on it that it needs and the broad walk progresses satisfactorily. At present, my lady, we have seven carts and eighteen men at work."

"I am glad to hear that, Mr. Lindsay, for I observe that if you or I be not here, John Harley keeps not the men to their task."

At the mention of Harley's name I shook my head.

"John Harley's ideas of gardening are not Sir John's, my lady. He's a thrawn old fellow who regards the Laird's improvements as new-fangled nonsense."

My lady laughed.

"Then you must act the diplomat and hurry him on. There has arrived this very hour some neep seed that Sir John wishes us to try. Know you how or when to use it?" .

"I regret not. 'Tis a new thing of which I have no knowledge save that the English call it turnip."

"Trouble yourself not about it. I shall send word to brother-in-law Monzie for directions. He has tried it: in truth, I believe 'twas he who recommended it to your master

"Is there no word of Sir John's return, my lady?"

"Nothing at all. This long silence worries me greatly

Here lady Avay's voice sank and shook a little. "I trust he has suffered no upset on the road hither, for the last time he wrote of his coming north he mentioned he might travel with four horses wanting a postilion. I replied at once that in such an event he must take care to get a good coachman.

"Madam, I can hardly think he has left London yet. For had he done so he would have sent you some message to meet him at Edinburgh as is your wont."

"I know not what to think," answered my mistress sadly.

"Sir John cannot have forgotten that the sheep markets are near and yet he has not instructed either you or me what to buy."

"You speak truly, my lady. 'Tis an awkward situation. Only yesterday the man who sold us the stots last year was here enquiring if we wanted more beasts and I had to send him away till the master come home and direct me."

Oh, dear! exclaimed Lady Avay. There is also the buying of the cows for killing. If we leave off getting them now we'll pay dear for them at the end of the year."

"Be comforted, my lady; the black cattle I have sent to Perth fair will get a good price and Andrew Smout has taken the gelding for which I bade him fetch ten guineas at least." ,

"Andrew will make a good bargain, I have no doubt. Now, Mr. Lindsay, I leave Avay this day for Stirling to visit Lady Jean Erskine for a few days. Sandy Stewart attends me and in my absence I look to you to see that everything here goes forward."

"I shall see to that, my lady. May it be that on your return we have some definite news of the master."

When Lady Avay came again she had a short, hurried note written by her husband at the Earl of Mar's London house. It said that my lord was not to be expected at Avay, since he was for Mar's country house but knew not the exact time of taking the journey.

"What think you of that ? asked my lady.

"Mar's country house ? " I repeated. "That can have only one meaning."

" A rising ?" asked my lady.

" Yes, a rising , and , pray God , a restoration."

July dragged on. The country was in a state of ferment. Then towards the middle of August tidings came that Mar , with some friends, was for Scotland by sea. Shortly after this the master's brother in

Edinburgh, Charles Erskine , sent my lady word that certain Scottish noblemen were soon to be in Fife.

On receipt of this intelligence my lady requested me to consult with her brother, the Master of Sinclair, at Dysart, and to act in the best interests of Sir John.

The fisherfolks of Kirkcaldy were industriously mending their nets and seeing to their boats as I rode towards Dysart. When I arrived there it was to find the Sinclair household much excited. The Master himself was on the point of setting out for Elie, where he had heard, but an hour before, that Mar was about to land. I asked permission to accompany him, which he graciously granted.

About a mile from the little fishing village of Elie we sighted a small boat, with a party of men, rowing away from a larger vessel. Soon it came near to some rocks and, a plank being thrown betwixt the boat and a great boulder, four gentlemen followed by two servants sprang to the firm land.

"'Tis Mar. I know his gait - the slight stoop of the shoulders," cried the Master of Sinclair, spurring his horse forward.

I did likewise and shortly we were upon the small group, who were watching our approach somewhat uneasily. Then I heard the voice of my dear master, Sir John Erskine of Avay.

"All is well, my lord. The horsemen are none other than my brother-in-law, the Master of Sinclair, and my trusted factor, Mr. Lindsay." '

Being met, the Earl of Mar was very affable to us, expressing his joy that he had so early a manifestation of support for his coming hither on behalf of the King over the water.

After a hurried consultation it was agreed that the Master of Sinclair should return home to prepare the Fife gentlemen for the call to arms that soon would come. I do not propose to tell the story of the 'Fifteen (as it is now termed) in every detail but simply to narrate what I saw or heard that will make an account of the affair.

From Elie we rode to Strath Ardle and then to the Spittal of Glenshee, resting there overnight . Next morning we crossed the mountains to Mar's country. At the clachan of Braemar we were lodged with one of the Earl's vassals, Farquharson of Invercauld, who, being not willing to join Mar unless he were shown the King's commission, departed secretly by night taking many weapons so that Mar was much vexed.

About the 27th of the month - August 1715 - Mar held a hunt at which eight hundred Highland gentlemen with servants were present.

All day the deer were hunted in the Glen of Quoich. At sunset the company was called together by the sounding of horns at a spot where the burn of Quoich runs into the river Dee. Here the course of the stream is broken by massive slabs of shelving rock that lie athwart the river bed, so that the water is forced to one side, where it leaps high and froths. Now it chanced that in the middle of one huge slab Nature had hollowed the rock so that it formed a depression like a cup or as the Highlanders say, a quaich or quoich

When Sir John and I drew near to this Quoich great was my astonishment to see Mar's servants busily engaged stirring the hollow with long sticks of pine.

"What are these fellows about ?" I asked Sir John.

"Brewing of punch, " laughed my master.

As I write I can taste again the Earl of Mar's punch and feel it trickle down my throat but the strongest memory is the sight of countless drinking horns upraised to the toast:

"Success to King James and our arms."

Yet of all the events in the North the grandest was the Raising of the Standard on the sixth day of September. It was a warm autumn day, with a gentle breeze blowing. My lord Mar had chosen to take up his position on rising ground a little below the village. The hills were purple with heather as was the moor on which we stood , a band of some five hundred persons . Above was a blue, cloudless sky.

Close to Mar was Inverey and beside him the Laird of Aboyne and my own dear master, Sir John Erskine. About them were others whose names resound in Scotland's story - Huntly, Seaforth, Rollo, Nairne, Glenbucket.

On this occasion Mar spoke most eloquently, setting out the evils that had befallen the country from the signing of the Treaty of Union, in which he regretted he had once placed so much trust, and speaking also of the mischief done" since the accession of the Hanoverian.

Then came the memorable moment. A mighty silence fell upon the assembly so that the only sounds to be heard were the distant murmuring of the river and the snap of a heather twig beneath some foot shod in deerskin.

A loosening of silken cords; a flutter of blue in the air; a sight of the arms of Scotland in gold; a glimpse of the thistle; a straining of eyes to read the mottos - *"Nemo me impune lacessit"* and *"No Union"* - a streaming of two pendants of white ribbon, bearing the inscriptions - *"For our wronged king and oppressed country"* and *"For ourselves and liberties."*

All this in a matter of seconds: all in the unfurling of a banner.

For a moment the crowd remained silent, overcome with awe and emotion. Then, with one accord, from five hundred throats came the cry - "Long live the King." James VIII and III had been acclaimed by his loyal Highlanders.

Somewhere in the throng a piper began to play. I knew not the air but the melody caught at my heart and for a time the blue and the gold and the white were blurred: the blue and the gold and the white that Lady Mar had sewn to be our flag.

When my eyes cleared of the tears I raised my head. There it was streaming bravely in the September breeze — the standard on the Braes 0' Mar.

SHERIFFMUIR

November 1715 was heralded in with bitter cold and keen frost. Mar was still at Perth. Argyll was still at Stirling. The king had not left France. Everywhere the soldiery were searching the cottages, forcing the inhabitants to deliver up their grain at the point of the bayonet. Even the scraggiest of hens disappeared from the farm yards.

Then about the 9th November we left Perth. Sir John was in personal attendance on my lord Mar. I and Sandy Stewart were with the Master of Sinclair under the command of General Gordon.

Sandy in the time of William of Orange's ill years had been caught stealing meal ('twas for his starving mother) and had been given by the justiciary to Sir John as a perpetual servant: the poor fellow wore the brass collar of bondage.

Next day at Auchterarder Moor we were instructed to advance to Dunblane. Towards three in the afternoon, riding ahead of our party with the master of Sinclair, I caught sight, some way ahead , of the thatched roofs of Kinbuck. Suddenly the master reined his horse to a halt and I did likewise.

"What is amiss, Sir?" I cried.

"Look yonder," he answered, pointing to the rising ground on our left. "what see you?" »

"Merciful Heavens!" I exclaimed. "'Tis a lame child, running as if Satan were at his heels."

"The bairn leaps and hops like a wounded hare. Quick he has sighted us and is waving. Let us forward to see what ails him."

When we came up to him the lad was like to burst for shortness of breath but managed to gasp:

"Are ye from Perth, Sirs?"

"We are, lad," replied the Master gently, "but what concern of yours is that?"

Pushing his matted hair from his eyes and brushing the sweat from his face with the palm of his hand the boy burst forth:

"I'm frae Ledy Kippendavie tae warn ye Argyll's in Dunblane."

"Nonsense," exclaimed Sinclair, greatly taken aback. "Argyll is at Stirling."

"No no, Sir," retorted the lad. "It's the Stirlin'shire militia an' the Glesca' volunteers under Provost Aird that's keepin' the town. Argyll mairched across the Brig o' Stirlin' this mornin'. I saw the sodgers wi' my ain een comin' across the Corntoun fur I wis up on the hillside at Blawlowan whaur my grannie bides. My Faither's herd tae Kippendavie sae I ran hame tae tell him fur I ken the Laird's ledy disna like King Geordie's men."

"How came you out to meet us?" asked the Master.

"I'm tellin' ye – Kippendavie's ledy sent me,"declared the child stubbornly. "When I tellt my faither the sodgers were comin' he gaed tae the Big Hoose an' the mistress bade him gang doon tae Dunblane tee speir if I wis richt. An' so I wis," declared the lad with dour satisfaction.

"But why did Lady Kippendavie send you rather than your father?" pressed the Master.

Scorn for the gentleman's lack of understanding was writ plain on the boy's face as he replied:

"Argyll's close.ahint an' he'll be lookin' oot fur spies. A lame laddie like me's no likely tae be peyed muckle attention. Forbye," he added proudly, "I can hirple as quick's my faither can rin."

During the time of our speaking with this lad the main body of our horse had ridden upon us among whom chanced to be Kippendavie himself. The lame boy, seeing his master, shouted:

"Yonder's the Laird himsel'," upon which Kippendavie came up to us.

"This is Neil Graham, my herd's son. What does the bairn hereabouts?"

"Laird," cried the lad, "I'm lettin' them ken Argyll is ayont Dunblane but they think I'm tellin' lees. Ye can hing me on the gallows gin ye prove I bring fause news."

Seeing the lad's anxiety and earnestness I took it upon myself to address him.

"Be comforted, lad. These gentlemen believe you and are grateful to you for hastening hither. Your rightful king, too, were he here would be pleased indeed with your loyalty to his cause. 'Tis the unexpectedness of your news that makes it so strange to our ears."

At this the lad, somewhat mollified, muttered:

"Grown folk dinna aye ken better than bairns fur a' they think they dae, but I'm no muckle carin' aboot what ye think o' me as lang as I can tell my ledy I've gien ye her message. Noo ye've got it ye can mak' a kirk or a mill o't."

Kippendavie, having given the boy a silver coin for his service, which made the lad's eyes to open wide with very wonder, bade him return to his mistress. As General Gordon, Sinclair, and the others fell to discussing what was now to be done I watched our lame informant depart till he became but a speck in the distance.

Gordon decided to send straightwith an express with the news of Argyll's being in the neighbourhood to Mar, who had gone that day to Drummond Castel; while the Master of Sinclair sent forward some horse to find out more exactly what was happening.

Sandy Stewart and I went with this reconnoitring party, meeting about a mile ahead with some country folks, bringing peats from their stacks on the moor. They were decent bodies who told us all they knew , which was that they believed Argyll to have marched through Dunblane and to be halted on high ground near about.

When we reported what we had heard General Gordon decided to go no further that night. About nine o'clock we heard the approach of horsemen and waited with baited breath till it was made known that it was Mar himself. I afterwards was told by the Master of Sinclair that Mar, disbelieving the nearness of Argyll, had come to rebuke Gordon for not having advanced to Dunblane.

That night as we huddled together in the straw at Kinbuck, we slept ill for a bitter wind blew off the Ochils. By six o'clock next morning we had started moving up to the plain at the foot slopes of the Ochils. At the rising of the sun, we saw clearly a body of horse about a mile southwards. Then only did Mar credit the report of Argyll's nearness, but it was not till eleven in the morning that he resolved to act.

Mar, having consulted with the Commanders of Corps and with the clan chiefs announced that battle was about to be joined and a loud huzza filled the air. Hats and bonnets were tossed high and, Sir John, turning to me, exclaimed:

"No man who has the least drop of Scots blood in his veins, can feel other than exalted in such an hour, Mr. Lindsay. Behold those gallant Highlanders who count life but a cheap price to bring their King home again!"

"I saw the clansmen charge at Killiecrankie, Sir. Their courage is second to none. The Ochils this day shall witness a brave sight: of that I am certain."

All further conversation was stopped for the sound of the bagpipes began to fill the plain that was called Sheriffmuir. Then Mar, pulling off his hat, waved it aloft with a loud cheer.

162

At that sign, the Highlanders, two thousand strong, charged. The enemy fired. The clansmen threw themselves to the frozen ground. Argyll's firing slackened. Uprose the Highlanders to meet a fresh outburst of shot. The Captain of Clanranald pitched forward, mortally wounded. His men faltered. On came Glengarry, waving his feathered bonnet and crying:

"Revenge! revenge! to-day for revenge, and to-morrow for mourning."

With deep-throated cries the clansmen uttered their battle slogans, flung off their tartans as was their custom,and rushed into the very midst of the foot and horse forming Argyll's left flank.

Useless were the bayonets and muskets of the Hanoverian troops for the infuriated Highlanders, brushing them aside with their targes of bull-hide, struck right and left with their claymores. Screams of men ripped from chap to belly and the terrified snickering of wounded horses, mingled with the fierce strains of the pipes.

"Wightman is retreating," shouted Sir John. "Forward and let us chase him to Stirling."

And so with the victorious Highlanders we pressed on at full gallop, hot in pursuit of Carpenter's, Kerr's, and Stair's dragoons. Like a whirlwind we thundered across the Sheriffmuir, the boggy parts being frozen hard, and down into Bridge of Allan, past Ogilvy's tavern.

Still before us fled the dragoons and foot, straining to reach the Bridge of Stirling. We were about the Lang Causeway when a fugitive, concealed behind a rock, made to shoot at Sir John.

Fortunately Sandy, catching a glimpse of the red uniform, called out a warning so that the bullet missing its aim went clean through my lord's hat, only singeing his hair a little. Then, incensed at the peril in which his master had stood, Sandy made off uphill after the fellow, crying:

"Ye Hanoverian blackguaird, I'll tak yer gizzard."

Sandy fulfilled his threat, for re-appearing in a short time he said to Sir John: '

"Yon yin'll no hairm ye again, Sir."

"Sandy," declared the Laird, laying his hand on Stewart's shoulder, "I owe my life to you and for your faithfulness you shall never again wear the collar of serfdom. Come, we shall go even now to the smiddy at the head of the Lang Causeway."

When I heard this I was truly overjoyed for Sandy's crime to my way of thinking had been no more than the outburst of a man tormented by the sight of one he loved starving to death and in all the years he had served my master and mistress he had proved himself a good and loyal servant. So it was that the smith at the Causewayhead filed Sandy's collar from off his neck while he, poor soul, in his jubilation, running out to the Forth that flowed nearby, cast it far into the waters, there to lie for evermore.

Certain that our victorious charge would have been equalled, if not surpassed, by the left wing where the Master of Sinclair was positioned, we rode back towards Sheriffmuir in high spirits. Alas, our confidence was short-lived, for coming to the Allan Water about Dunblane we discovered to our dismay that Argyll's heavy cavalry under Cathcart, advancing across the frozen marshes of Sheriffmuir, had driven our men into the river itself, now flowing crimson with the blood of the slain. More horrible still was the sight of the starving cottars plundering the corpses of the dead clansmen for their pokes of meal. And foremost of the blood-stained tartans on the battlefield was that of clan Macrae, who had paid dearly in the cause of their prince.

Owing to the hilly nature of the ground over which we fought and the pursuit of the one wing of Hanoverians almost to Stirling, our leader was unaware of the disaster to the left till a gory messenger brought him word in the afternoon.

Thereupon orders were given for us to reform on the Sheriffmuir where we remained inactive till dusk, at which time we drew off to Ardoch.

As we rode away from the battlefield that grey Sunday afternoon, November thirteenth, 1715, I glanced up towards the Ochils. There I could see little groups of Hillfoots folks, who doubtless had come over from Logie and Menstrie and Avay to watch the struggle, turning and wending their way homewards.

But lower down, amid the blighted heather lay many a brave Soot - foe and friend, noble and common, all alike, for death is no respecter of persons - who would return no more to his ain ingle neuk.

Sheriffmuir was the end of our venture, though we realised it not at the time, for we looked upon it as a victory. Of all those who have written of our attempt, now called the Fifteen, Peter Rae of Dumfries has summed the situation best.

This I admit, though I detest his History of the Late Rebellion, raised against His Majesty King George by the friends of the Popish Pretender, published at Dumfries, 1718.

Herein he writes of Sheriffmuir:

"By this battle the heart of the Rebellion was broke, the Earl of Mar was baulked of his design,his undertaking for a March to the South was laid aside and never attempted afterwards, and his numbers daily decreased, so that he could never gather such an army again."

From Ardoch we retired to Perth, whence Mar dispatched an express to King James in France wherein he recounted our success

165

at Sheriffmuir and the emissary to whom this important letter was entrusted was none other than Sir John Erskine of Avay.

Some days after our master's departure Sandy came to me agog with news:

"Hech, Mr. Lindsay, but there's ill tidings in Perth this day. The English hae beaten and taen Borlum."

"Borlum captured? Where?"

"At a place ca'd Preston. Whaur exactly wid it be?"

"In the north-west of England, Sandy. Do you know of any others named prisoners there?"

"I've heard mentioned Kenmure an' Nithsdale an' an English lord cried Derwentwater."

"When did this engagement take place?"

"It's fair byordinar, but they're sayin' this battle o' Preston was ficht on that verra same Sunday as we were racin' aboot on Shirramuir."

Then, seeing me cast down at this melancholy event, the ever kindly Sandy did his best to hearten me, saying:

"Dinna be vext, Sir. It's a lang lane that has nae turnin'. A'thing'll be richt when the King comes."

"When the King comes ----- --" - but the King came not till December 22nd, landing in the north-east at Peterhead and coming to Perth on Monday, the ninth day of January, 1716.

I got my first sight of James XIII as he rode to the South Inch to view certain of our troops. His person was tall and thin and his face pale, showing as I thought the strain of the ague that had racked his body since coming ashore in Scotland.

When he spoke to the soldiers he was exceeding grave in manner, saying but few words. In general he appeared most solemn. Yet when I looked into his eyes I caught there a glow of kindliness that put me in remembrance of his father's graciousness to myself.

All this while we had heard nought of Sir John since his going into France in mid-November. Great, therefore, was my joy when a few day's after the King's coming to Perth a seamen sought me out with the news that Sir John was landed at Dundee and wished Sandy to take a letter to my lady at Avay.

While Sandy was away Argyll was joined by General Cadogan sent especially to Scotland by the English who thought Argyll not effective in suppressing the rebels (as they termed us).

Then Cadogan and Argyll rode out as far as Dunblane, viewing the highway and calculating how soon they might come upon us. Each fresh dispatch of Cadogan's road activities sent my lord Mar into such alarm that he influenced the King against his better judgement to sign an order for burning the villages of Auchterarder, Muthill, Crieff, Blackford, Dalreoch and Dunning.

The full horror of this deed was made plain to me at the end of the month when Sandy, returning from Avay, gave me an eyewitness account of what was done in Strath Earn.

"Eh, Sir, I maun tell ye whit I saw at Blackford. I left Avay House yester mornin' whiles it wis still grey an travellin' by the Broich Burn I cam oot on the hillside aboon Blackford. I wis standin' lookin' doon on the cottages whaun I saw the Hielanders rise up frae the bushes and rin throughoot the place flingin' lichted brands intae the hooses an' the cornyairds. The hale o' Blackford wis bleezin' frae ae end tae the ither. The puir folk gaithered roon the kirk lamentin'. Syne the Hielanders mairched awa'."

King James , liking not this business, shortly after ordered relief to be given to those who had lost their homes.

On the 30th day of January we withdrew from Perth to Montrose. There early in February Sir John came to me.

"The king leaves Scotland: all is over. Sandy and you must go with all speed and secrecy back to Avay. Tell my lady that I know not when I shall be able to get a letter to her,but I will not omit any chance to write."

Sandy and I got ourselves a passage in a boat that was leaving Montrose for the Forth. Being put ashore at Culross we went on foot to the Ochils and were heartily glad when coming in by the Devon Tower we saw , perched high on the hillside and surrounded by the saplings not long since planted, the House of Avay.

A curl of reek rose from the chimney at the south gable so that I pictured my lady sitting before the fire in that spacious west room, where Sir Charles and I had decided to ride forth to Killiecrankie to fight for James VII in 1689; where the dowager Lady Avay had given me the Ochil Eye ring I ever wear that had inspired me to serve James VIII in 1708 and now again in 1715-16; and where, even at that moment as I stood watching, my mistress would be awaiting her husband anxiously.

But Sir John was in France and much was to happen ere he came again to his wife and bairns and the House of Avay.

THE SILVER MINE

Spring came again to the Ochils with the bleat of new-born lambs on the hillside and the cawing of rooks nesting in the trees beside the Mill of Avay. At the Big House Sir John's lady kept outwardly a cheerful countenance for the sake of Master Charles and Master Henry, who bairnlike were forever asking how many years it was since their Papa had gone away and when would he be back.

Deep in my lady's heart, howbeit, I knew there was a grief, the ache of separation from a loved one and the gnaw of uncertainty, since we were still without news of my lord's whereabouts, knowing only he had gone to France.

Of my lady's sorrow I became increasingly sensible as we conversed daily anent the affairs of the estate. I recollect very clearly a fine March morning in that year of 1716, with a blink of sunshine filling the valley and a blue sky overhead. I had walked down to Braefoot - the cottar houses betwixt Avay House and the kirk - to see how the tenants were progressing with the ploughing, for I had been expounding to them earnestly upon the necessity to start early to that work.

When I got there I found my mistress already before me wrapped in a warm scarlet "Cardinal" cloak. As I came towards her I could not help but thinking how very lovely she was even in all the desolation of her heart, which gave her a more sober look than was her wont.

At this time my lady would be nigh on thirty. She was of medium stature and very slender, with a pale hue of pink in her cheeks. .From her hood some strands of her chestnut hair had escaped and were blowing in the slight breeze. When she heard me approach she turned, her lips parting in characteristic gentle smile, (that revealed teeth of such whiteness and perfection as I have never seen equalled) and her eyes lighting up, so that for the moment, the shadow of care lifting, she became the happy girl that had won my master's heart.

"You are scanning the fields, my lady."

"Ah, Mr. Lindsay, you, too, have come hither for the same purpose, I think."

"That is even so and I rejoice to see it has not been a fruitless errand. At long last the tenants are following Sir John's good advice and turning over the soil betimes."

"And he is not present to see it," sighed my lady.

Oh, Mr. Lindsay! if I could but hear from him I should be easier in my mind."

"Be not downcast. It cannot be long now till we get certain word of Sir John for Mr. Charles Erskine at Edinburgh does all he can to discover the master's whereabouts."

"Charles indeed makes all kind offers for which I am truly grateful, yet I cannot help but look to the dark side of the cloud."

"We must submit with patience to Our Merciful Father. Having hitherto preserved Sir John from so imminent dangers He will in His own good time restore him to Avay."

"Patience, alas, is a quality I fear I possess not. Many a time in our walks about these policies Sir John has talked to me of the virtue of resignation but, troth to tell, I find it hard to practise."

"Remember, my lady, you are not alone in your tribulation. The failure of our last rising, and the sad consequences thereof, is a hard calamity, which all of us, even from King James himself to his meanest follower, must learn to bear."

"'Tis not for myself I weep but for Sir John, who, for aught I know, may be in bitter pinches at this very moment. Here there is bread enough for the boys and myself."

Laying a hand upon my arm, she added, "Thanks to your diligence in overseeing the land, Mr. Lindsay."

"Nay, my lady," I protested, "my part is small.

"Avay estate owes much to your own industry. Yonder hedges that enclose the fields are your doing, as also are these new ditches. Few places, if any at all, in this shire have such improvements." »

"I had these things done because I knew Sir John intended them himself. He was particularly anxious about the ditches, considering the soil hereabouts to be inclined to rot the seed."

I was about to comment on the Laird's plans to reclaim the marsh ground about Avay when the silence of the fields about us was broken by the clear trill of a mavis, piping from a nearby tree.

"Hearken to that bird, Mr. Lindsay. He has been singing from our roof top each evening this week bypast."

Then, with a stifled sob, she whispered:

"Its note has much increased my sorrow."

Upon which touching confession I thought to myself that truly "*haec sunt lachrymae rerum*"; and said aloud to my lady,

"Weeping may endure for a night, but joy cometh in the morning."

And so indeed it was. About three weeks later, in mid April, word came from the master.

"A letter at last!" cried my lady, coming into the west laigh room, where I was busy calculating how much would have to be paid out in annual rents, Sir John having certain bonds that had to be maintained.

"From where?" I asked, starting from my chair in joy.

"From a French town called Beaune, whither he came but a week ago from Paris."

"I trust he is well, madam."

"In excellent health, thank God, though he finds French travel unpleasant. You will be amused by his account of his journey."

"I should be most happy to hear it."

In her pleasant, quiet voice, Lady Avay began to read:

'Last Saturday we parted from Paris by the coche d'eau where we passed one night most cursedly with a pack of nasty jades. Our cabin in a few hours stunk like the devil. To be quit of that we took at Montereau the very next worse voiture in the world - a cariole or

in broad Scots a covered cart, in which we came to Sens and from that to Auxerre. From that we came alongst on hired horses with a gentleman of this place.'

"So there are worse places than Scotland for travellers," I laughed.

"But there is something good of France that Sir John has to say. A moment till I find it."

Hastily scanning the folded sheet my lady went on:

"Sir John says it will interest you, Mr. Lindsay, and all the members of the Tilliebody Club."

"Indeed, my lady, then it must be some mention of wine."

"You are right. Here it is -

'Pray tell my good friend, Mr. Lindsay, that here is the place to have Burgundy both very good and as cheap as anywhere for the Pomar and what is particularly called Vin de Beaune grow both within half a league of here. I long to crack a bottle with the Tilliebody Club. '" .

"Pray God the Laird may do so very soon. Is he to stay some time at this place?"

"No. He says he sets out shortly for Lyons and thence he is to journey down the Rhone to Avignon."

"Avignon? Then he goes to join the King's court?"

"'Tis so. He writes that King James and our kinsman Mar have some use for him there."

"We must inform Mr. Charles in Edinburgh of this."

"'Twill not be necessary. You surely forget that he comes hither to-morrow, bringing his mother, who is to stay some weeks." '

"Your pardon, my lady. I had, indeed, forgotten."

Next day, when my old mistress and Charles Erskine arrived there was much excitement with the bairns, who knew full well that somewhere in their grandam's many trunks would be a parcel of sweetmeats for them. Nor were they disappointed and, moreover, Uncle Charles had brought the boys a fine new hunting crop each.

Later that night over a bottle of wine Charles spoke to me of the Laird.

"You will be happy to hear, Mr. Lindsay, that I have hopes my brother may be allowed to return hither this year."

"This year? That would indeed be most pleasing. But how, Sir, is it to be accomplished? I hear the Parliament is very violent against our party, sending many of the prisoners overseas to the plantations. Moreover, since Cadogan has replaced Argyll here in Scotland as army commander little mercy has been shown or may be expected."

"The Erskines are not without influence. Sister Nell's husband may do much for us."

Mrs. Haldane of Gleneagles?"

"The very same. He and sister Cath's husband, Patrick Campbell of Monzie, are both in London and have the ear of many about the court. I look to both of them to do all they may to preserve the family."

"Has Sir John's name been mentioned at all in Parliament?"

"Not so far, thank God, though several of his friends have already been attainted." d A

"What of Dr. Robert?" I asked, for Robert Erskine, having been appointed physician to Peter the Great was a man of some consequence abroad, to whom several gentlemen, including the Earl of Loudon, Keeper of the Great Seal of Scotland, had applied to favour friends and relations, seeking preferment at the Russian Court.

"Meantime I think Gleneagles and Monzie may do all that is needful. Should they fail I shall not hesitate to apply to Robert on John's behalf. Tell me, how think you my sister-in-law bears these trials? She says little, though at times I fear she grieves a deal."

"At first my lady was much overwhelmed but since hearing from my lord she has been more cheerful and does all she can to be useful in the present circumstances. Her thoughts are ever of what the Laird would have done to the estate. She bids me continue the planting of trees and thinks of setting up our own lime-kiln."

"What of the land you cultivate yourselves? Do you not find it overmuch?"

"My lady has been considering that and is of a mind to set some of it out in tenandry as long as Sir John is absent."

"I agree most heartily."

"There is, Sir, a matter on which Lady Avay would have your advice. Now that we know Sir John is with the court at Avignon she would

174

have a sum of money set aside at London upon which he or his agent may draw."

"That I can arrange with no great trouble. Well, Mr. Lindsay, provided our friends can circumvent the seizure of the estate, all will yet go well with the Erskines of Avay, despite John's rash adventure with Mar."

Seeing my look of displeasure at this last remark he went on,

"Aye, you may frown as you will, King James's man that you are, but a foolhardy business it was to my way of thinking. Howbeit 'tis past. Let's drink a last dram to the future - to my brother's homecoming."

As we raised our glasses I said with all my heart:

"To Sir John's speedy return." _

Matters in London, however, did not progress as swiftly as Charles had hoped. The clansmen were still defiant in the north whither Cadogan had gone to harry them so that the government continued vehement in their oppression of all those who had been out the previous year.

My lady's father, the old lord Sinclair, would have had her and the children stay with him at Dysart for (the Master of Sinclair like Sir John being in exile) there was much to be attended to there. Howbeit my lady rejected this proposal, feeling that her first duty lay in Avay.

About this time, too, we had news of Rob Roy's house being burnt and his cattle carried off, but he was not without his revenge, for waiting some way off in a wood he fell upon the attacking soldiers, killing several. Young Charles and young Henry both had severe attacks of the chincough, recovering but slowly despite the mild, pleasant weather.

Sir John's sister, Catherine, Monzie's spouse, gave birth to a fine son whom she called Charles after her father, the old Laird, which thing pleasured me greatly. Gleneagle's lady went off to Bath to partake of the waters there. Still no word came of a pardon for Sir John, which I could see was causing my lady dispeace. Strange and inscrutable indeed are the workings of Divine Providence for the business of Sir John's pardon was hastened on, not so much by the efforts of his kinsmen as by a circumstance which, at its first happening, seemed to us most calamitous.

It was the 4th of May when the blow fell. I was just coming up to the House from watching the last of the barley being sown at Braefoot as Master Charles came running to tell me his mother would speak with me at once.

When I entered the familiar laigh room I could see that my mistress was overwrought.

"Oh, Mr. Lindsay, troubles never come singly. James Hamilton has left us."

"Hamilton?" I repeated in astonishment. "What has happened?"

"That I know not. He came hither an hour ago, burst into this room, where I was sitting at my needlework and began straightway to abuse me in the roundest of terms , saying he was not paid enough for his labour and that he was going where his services would be more thought of. Then he dashed from the room. "

"Did you send anyone after him?"

"Sandy followed him but found he was gone from the village, riding hard towards Stirling. All his belongings have been taken from his lodging at the Strude. He knows too much of Mr Nebit. I like it not."

Nor did I. Hamilton possessed information about the estate that my lady and I had till then successfully concealed from the government. Mr Nebit was our privy name for Sir John's silver mine. Aye, you may well be surprised to hear that at Avay there was a mine of silver, lying to the west of the House in the glen betwixt the Wood

176

Hill and that other hill , called the Nebit , whence our manner of speaking of the mine and the silver as Mr Nebit.

Of that mine James Hamilton was overseer so that his going hence and his wild talk of being more thought of elsewhere was not to be taken lightly. Both my lady and I knew, though we hesitated to say it openly to one another that Hamilton had departed to inform the Government, hoping, no doubt, to gain some advancement from the Hanoverian.

This vein of silver Sir John had stumbled upon some years previously when searching for prettily coloured quartzes with which the hills abound. About one hundred and thirty four ounces of silver had been refined when Mar called the Laird to rise for James Stewart.

During all the time of our following Lord Mar, my Lady Avay continued this work, being still busy with it when I returned to the estate. The crude ore she had buried in casks about the face of the hill to the north west of the House. At first my Lady had thought the silver might support the King's cause, and then, this hope being blasted, she looked to it to maintain the family if Sir John were attainted and the estate forfeited, as was very possible.

Six weeks later, mid July, Charles Erskine brought us confirmation of our worst fears anent Hamilton.

"An express came to me yestreen from Gleneagles at London. Hamilton has made an affidavit there to the Lord Mayor regarding the silver mine."

" Alas! alas!" cried my lady , " what has the wretched man said, Charles ?"

Drawing forth Gleneagle's letter Charles read aloud:

" *The mine , say the informant, is just opened within about two or two and a half fathoms from the grass which grows on the surface of the earth. In it are two veins of ore running horizontally, the one above the other. The upper vein about 22 inches thick from top to bottom and about 18 inches wide or thereabout; the other about 14 inches thick and 18 inches wide."*

At the setting forth of the mine in such detail I could not forbear exclaiming:

"The villain has it exact. 'Tis a perfect description!

"What else has he said?" asked my lady wearily.

Charles, glancing again at Haldane's letter, replied:

"Hamilton says he was at first employed in smelting the ore but that on John going off with Mar, you gave him oversight of the mine and four workmen employed therein."

"'Tis true. I thought I could trust him."

"Hamilton also estimates that you have hidden about forty tons of ore in casks or barrels behind the House."

"There is a goodly amount, Sir," I observed, "but it is far from easy to reckon how much, the whole business having been carried out, as you know, in piecemeal fashion."

"This is the end of us," cried out my lady, bursting into tears.

"Nay, Catherine," said Charles, laying a hand about her shoulders to comfort her, "out of this villainy may yet come good. I have more to tell you."

"What, Charles, oh what?"

"Sister Cath's husband, Monzie, has also written me. His tidings are most heartening."

"Quickly, dear brother! What says Monzie?"

"He has conferred with the Master of the King's Mint."

"With the great Sir Isaac Newton?" I asked.

"None other, Mr. Lindsay. Sir Isaac listened most attentively to Monzie and interested in the prospect of opening up a new source of silver sent Monzie with his recommendation to Lord Townshend."

"Was Gleneagles also concerned in this?" inquired Lady Avay.

"He was. Indeed he visited my Lord Townshend with Monzie at which meeting they discussed the business most thoroughly. There being some difficulties about the laws of Scotland with regard to the mines our friends proposed Sir John's remission, since it would put an end to all controversies as to the law and right to the mines. They pointed out that if Sir John returned to work the silver, whereof he has more knowledge than anyone else, then by the Scots Act of Parliament of 1592 one tenth part would be given over to the Public Treasury."

"How was this proposal received, Sir?" I asked.

"Readily, Mr. Lindsay. The Cabinet agreed to it last Thursday and our nephew, Sir Harry Stirling, is to go abroad to prevail upon Sir John to comply with the terms proposed."

"Stirling of Ardoch's son!" I exclaimed. "Well do I recall marrying his father and mother in Avay Kirk away back in 1685. A liberal gift of money Sir William made that day to the poor of the parish."

"Ardoch was ever a kindly man," commented Charles, "and his son will use all energy to bring this affair to a happy conclusion."

"Where is Harry to meet John?" asked my lady.

"Probably at Copenhagen for John is, at present, in Norway and returns to Paris by way of Denmark. Robert also comes there shortly with his master the Czar. Young Harry is especially deSirous of talking with Robert, being eager to enter the service of the Moscovite: so he may at Copenhagen accomplish both purposes." _

"Sir John in Norway?" I cried, bewildered. "What business has he so far North?"

"You astound me also, Charles," broke in my lady. "When last I heard from Sir John he was in Paris, but 'tis several weeks ago and I have had no other letter since. Doubtless this journey to so distant a part accounts for his silence."

At these expressions of surprise from Lady Avay and myself, Charles looked much disconcerted, his sallow features flushing and his tendency to look glum, almost exasperated, becoming marked. I saw he was unwilling to reply, though at length he answered in hesitant fashion, his long, thin fingers drumming on the arm of his chair.

"There is much gossip and little certainty, which only time may prove or disprove. You are aware as I am that Charles of Sweden likes not George of Hanover. James Stewart likes not George of Hanover. I leave you to your own deductions. What concerns us, however, is the silver mine. There are commissioners to come, appointed by Sir Isaac Newton, to survey the ground."

"When?" asked my lady.

"That," replied Charles, "depends upon when John's pardon is granted."

Summer 1716 wore on. That year there was much sunshine which along with our having fields ditch-drained gave us an abundant harvest. The kirk of Avay having again fallen vacant Mr. William Campbell was inducted therein on the 14th day of August, being also appointed chaplain to the military at the castel of Stirling. I found him very pleasant in his conversation being a man without narrow prejudices.

Slowly news trickled through.to my mistress of what was happening abroad. First she heard that Sir John was to meet Robert incognito at Copenhagen, passing himself off as a materialist from

Amsterdam seeking the Doctor about medicines for the Russian army.

Then word was got from Harry Stirling, who had travelled to Copenhagen from Hamburg by post wagon, that Robert had cancelled this meeting , for having heard of the affair of the silver mine he expected that would be sufficient to obtain Sir John's pardon without the help of the Czar. Which indeed it was. In his letter Stirling also recounted how the Czar did honour Robert by dining with him on his birthday , September 8th.

My lady. still being without communication from Sir John, wrote continually , hoping that one letter at least might reach him. I know not how it has happened but in going over my papers when I first thought to write this tale, I found one of these letters which I see did succeed in coming into my master's hands for he had written on the back thereof :

Received at Paris, Sep. 1716.

I set it down here for it shows better than I can ever describe in words how fine a lady and how devoted a wife , my mistress was.

" To Sir John Erskine.

My Dearest Life,

It is now a month since I had the pleasure of hearing from you. I pray God you may be well. You will now know of the discovery James Hamilton made of Mr. Nebit's affair. It has grieved me very much, but it is no small satisfaction that it has not been by any neglect of mine. He

certainly designed to commit the villainy and went away with that view for nothing I could do could make him stay.God in His wise providence has ordered it and I must submit.

My being absent from you is the bitterest part of all. Your boys are well and my health is better now than it used to be. Accept the offer of pardon made as Harry Stirling will explain to you. There are people soon to be sent down in quest of Mr. Nebit and if it were possible you could be here its more in your power to manage than any one else. I recommend you

to read Monsieur Pascal's thoughts which I doubt not you will like.

Wishing my Dear Soul all manner of happiness I am in all sincerity.

Yours Catherine Avay, August 1716.'

It was late autumn when Sir John wrote to tell my lady he might be expected home shortly. With the same post came a letter from Charles Erskine announcing that the Commissioners appointed to examine the silver mine had left London, the order to do so having been given by the Prince of Wales, Guardian of the Kingdom, at Hampton Court, September, 1716.

"And who have been chosen to carry out the survey, my lady?" I enquired.

"Hamilton and a German, by the name of Dr. Justus Brandshagen."

"Hamilton!" I exclaimed. "The villain should be ashamed to set his foot in Avay. Who, pray, is this German?

I had expected Sir Isaac Newton himself would be present."

"Charles says Newton declined to come, representing he was unacquainted with the mining science. The German comes from King George's silver mines in the Hartz mountains."

"'Tis a long way from the Hartz to the Ochils but he will find much here to interest him. Does Mr. Charles say if they come by land or by sea?"

"By sea, Mr,Lindsay, to Leith, and Charles proposes they await Sir John in Edinburgh that they may all come together to Avay. I think I shall send Sandy Stewart to Edinburgh now, that he may attend upon Sir John when he gets thither. "

"Nothing, my lady, could give Sandy greater pleasure."

"Or Sir John either," rejoined my mistress, "for he has mentioned several times since his going into France how much he has missed the faithful fellow." -

Three weeks later the Master of Avay came riding up the hillside from Braefoot, followed by Sandy and the silver mine commissioners. The bairns were frenzied with excitement, running to clasp their Papa about the neck when he had gotten down from his horse. Nor would they stand aside when he came forward to take my lady into his arms and she, her heart too full for words, was able to murmur naught but, "John, John, at last, my dearest life."

"Gentlemen," I said, turning to the Commissioners,"with your leave I shall take you into the house where we may partake of some refreshment, for in the reunion of man and wife there is no place for strangers like ourselves."

After a while Sir John joined us in the west laigh parlour.

"Now, Mr. Lindsay, where are these gentlemen to stay? I presume you have made arrangements for their lodging."

"'Everything is settled, Sir John. Mr. Campbell, the minister, has agreed to house them in the manse. They will be near enough to the mine. Moreover, Mr. Campbell is not altogether unacquainted with the German tongue, which will doubtless be a comfort to Dr. Brandshagen."

Whereupon the gentleman referred to cried out:

"Good, good. And have you made all things ready for the survey and trial, dear Sir?"

"That I have. I shall come with you myself, tomorrow, and show you the tools and workmen that await you."

"Excellent", commented Sir John."If when the work begins anything else is found necessary I shall provide it willingly. Now, Mr. Lindsay, perhaps it would be best if you would conduct these gentlemen to the manse without further delay."

"Yes, yes," said Dr. Brandshagen eagerly, "if you please. I am so tired. The journey by sea was terrible schrecklich! For three weeks and two days I have not slept. Two storms have I suffered and twice were we driven on to sandbanks."

"You are not a sailor, then," laughed Sir John.

"Ach, no, Sir. ' I shall be very glad to be rested in your pastor's house if this gentleman will so kindly take us."'

Here James Hamilton interposed.

"Trouble not, Mr. Lindsay. I know the way."

"Doubtless you do, Sir," I answered very coolly, for I could not forgive the fellow his disloyalty to the Erskines, even though it had been the means of bringing Sir John home, but since I have arranged this matter with Mr. Campbell 'twould be mighty uncivil not to introduce Dr. Brandshagen to him myself."

The trial of the ores took several weeks during which two of the principal officers of the Edinburgh Mint -one of whom was the Master's brother-in-law, Gleneagles – came to witness what was done. In order to carry the work out thoroughly Sir John gave over to the Commissioners the Braefoot barn, built of stone that stood near to the burnside at the silver mine.

In it they built their furnaces for the smelting and there they made their assays of metals.

Dr. Brandshagen I soon discovered was a man of much scientific learning, who, seeing my interest in all that was being done, spoke freely to me of his work.

"Mr. Lindsay, I find this Scottish ore to be not ordinary."

"But surely, Sir, you have seen its equal somewhere," I replied, thinking the German to be flattering.

"Nein, nein. Not to my knowledge has the like ever been seen in Europe."

"What makes it so different from other ores?"

"Look, my dear Sir," and here he pointed to various crucibles set out on the long bench at the window.

"This Avay ore consists of sulphur, arsenic, copper, iron, lead and silver, good silver." -

"'Tis hardly to be believed, Dr. Brandshagen. Tell me, would it be profitable for Sir John to separate these other parts?"

"Ach, no, dear Sir. They are very interesting to us who study the mineral science: that is all. Only the silver is it worth Sir John's labour to get."

"The colouring of the ore is unusual, is it not?" I asked, fingering some specimens that lay before us.

"You are observant. Yes - notice it is darkish brown but near the edge it is white, like spar, with the colour of darker metallic ore mixed through it. You will find the dark-coloured ore in the middle of the vein is best."

"Is there no gold present? '

Brandshagen shook his head. "Alas, no! with gold in this ore your master would have been a rich man. But," he added with a smile, "you are a scholar. You have of the philosopher's stone heard ?"

"Yes: but what of it?"

The German chuckled.

"Sir Isaac Newton has commanded us to search the water near to this mine."

"The burn?" I exclaimed.

"So. And we are to report to him on the minerals we find therein. Maybe we find the philosopher;s stone and your master's silver become gold!"

"If that happens be sure to bring it to me," I replied joining in his jest.

Then becoming serious I went on, "Yet, here is something you may well find," and I held out for his inspection my ring.

"An agate, so. Is it from these hills gotten?"

"From none other and hence its name in these parts is the Ochil Eye."

The doctor then read aloud the inscription on the bezel, whereafter he looked at me, saying:

"An affair of the heart, my friend?" '

"Yes, indeed," I answered but refrained from further explanation, thinking it would be hardly proper to enter into a discussion of the Stewart cause with a Hanoverian scientist, and Sir John, coming upon the scene at the same time, the conversation returned to the mineral wealth of the estate.

Dr. Brandshagen, having in his short acquaintance with Sir John realised that the Laird was a man of invention and progress, spoke to him at some length of the presence of cobalt in the Silver Glen, as we now called the valley betwixt the Woodhill and the Nebit.

This cobalt he explained was of value in the manufacture of porcelain, declaring that the deep blue colouring that could be obtained from it to tint china and glass was as fine as that gotten from the mines of Saxony. Howbeit Sir John made no venture into the potter's realm but someday, mayhap, Avay cobalt may come into its own; for I am told that a manufacture of pottery recently set up at Prestonpans near Edinburgh is likely to create a demand for cobalt.

In all the trial of the mine lasted about 129 days, for which the German was paid twenty shillings a day. With James Hamilton I had little dealing, despising him heartily as I did all who sought to ingratiate themselves with the Hanoverian George, whom the cottar folk with their wonted shrewdness and humour spoke of as "the wee, wee German Lairdie!"

Oddly enough it was from Hamilton on the day the commission left Avay that I had a second indication of a plot being prepared in Northern Europe to restore the Chevalier.

It was a crisp December morning, with a sprinkling of rime on the hillside when I came down to the manse to bid Dr. Brandshagen farewell. He was inside with Mr. Campbell but without, at the gate, astride his mount and ready to depart was Hamilton.

As I came up the fellow called out:

"Why, Mr. Lindsay,'tis mighty civil of you to come to speed us on our way."

Swallowing my deSire to reply sharply I said: "I came to seek Dr. Brandshagen."

"He will be here presently. I await him also."

Then his face drawn into a sneer he went on:

"The Erskines have come well out of this business and you too, Mr. Jacobite."

At this last I could feel the flush of wrath suffuse my cheeks. '

"Have a care, Sir," I cried.

"Have a care," he mocked. "You would be better employed giving that advice to your precious Sir John's brother and his master, the Russian bear."

Being wholly unaware of what he hinted at I exclaimed:

"Dr. Robert!"

"Aye, Dr. Robert and his Swedish friends. Play not the innocent, Lindsay."

Then bending down towards me he spat out with evident venom.

"And once I have sufficient evidence, watch out, for the next time I shall take care to get more than the beggarly ten shillings a day I have had here."

Before I could think of any answer to this tirade Hamilton had straightened up in the saddle and from behind me came a guttural voice.

"Ach, so, it is Mr. Lindsay. You have come to say good-bye."

"And a safe journey," I added, shaking the German by the hand heartily.

"You have to me been very kind and also your master,Sir John Erskine. I have much enjoyed my stay here."

Looking towards the hills he went on earnestly.

"Your mountains here are not so large as my beloved Hartz but they have given to me pleasure and I forget them never. In my own tongue, Mr. Lindsay, I say to our meeting again – auf wiedersehen"

He bowed and then swiftly sprang to the saddle.

James Hamilton sat forward. Dr. Brandshagen turned to Mr. Campbell and myself, repeating once more:

" Auf wiedersehen."

To which we both replied: "God speed."

Mr. Campbell would have had me into the manse to drink a stoup of ale but I declined, saying I had business to attend to at Avay House. The truth, howbeit, was I deSired to be alone.

James Hamilton had given me much to think about, for, like a piece in a mosaic pattern, his embittered words fitted into Charles Erskine's comment on Sir John's visit to Norway.

In the days that followed there kept ringing in my ears:

"Charles of Sweden likes not George of Hanover - Dr. Robert and his Swedish friends."

And though I knew no more, of this I was certain – something was brewing in the Baltic, something connected with the Jacobite cause, and Robert Erskine.

THE CZAR'S PHYSICIAN

Handsel Monday dawned dry and frosty. Silent was the great bell that hung on the north-east wall of the house for that day , according to custom , the tenants and servants were freed from labour and made holiday , giving to one another gifts - a ribbon , a pipe , some meal, some ale, - in token of goodwill for the new year that was entered upon.

In the alehouses the weavers sang and drank and cast an eye upon the lasses so that many a summer marriage in the parish had its beginning on that first Monday of January. Being myself free from the tasks of the estate I turned my steps towards the Knapp to spend an hour or two with my kindly parents-in-law. John, despite his advanced years, was still lively in mind: Mrs Burns, much enfeebled , scarce ever stirred from her caff bed by the kitchen fire.

It was late when I left these good old people. The moon had risen so that the frost on the highway glistened and the cottages stood in dark outlines against the starry sky. Preoccupied with thoughts of the household I had left I was aware, but unheeding , of the sound of a horseman advancing upon me by the highroad from Stirling.

The rider came nearer , the frozen ground resounding harshly to the regular striking of the horse's hooves. I drew in closer to the dyke bounding the Longbank and the horseman passed me, but I raised not my head. A little space further on I realised the traveller had come to a standstill, opposite to the tavern adjoining the Butterha'. When I came abreast of the unknown rider, he called out softly:

"Mr. Lindsay, if I am not mistaken."

Something in the speaker's tone of voice sounded familiar, yet I could not name him for certain. I was about to open my mouth to ask who recognised me when, the door of the Butterha' changehouse being violently pushed open and a drunken fellow came stumbling forth, the rider's face was revealed in the shaft of light streaming form the ale-house interior.

A moment later and the door had banged close again, but in that fraction of time I had caught a glimpse of the inherited long features and dignified bearing of the Erskines.

"Dr. Robert!"

"Hush, no names, if you please. Can you mount behind me?"

"Easily "

In a trice I had swung myself up and so we came together - the Czar's physician and the rabbled curate - to the House of Avay on the night of Handsel Monday, 1717.

We sat, the four of us - Dr. Robert (his top boots mud bespattered) Sir John, my lady, and myself - late into the night talking. Dr. Robert spoke eagerly of what had brought him hither in secret fashion.

"My master, the Czar, is at present at Amsterdam, for he makes a grand visit of the rulers of Europe. From there I found it not difficult to slip over to Leith in a merchant ship. I had to come because an important pack of letters from London awaited me there. Moreover, I want to hear from those on whose account I can rely, how matters stand in Scotland now regarding King James. We, of the Jacobite party abroad, purpose to try again to set the Stewart on the throne. This time there must be no mistakes."

"Is it the affair of the North?" asked Sir John.

"It is. You know of the first movements made in that direction." _

"Aye, in troth. I came near to seeing you at that time in Copenhagen, had not Harry Stirling sent me word you thought it wiser that I take the Hanoverian's pardon than apply for the Czar's help."

"What thought you of the Swedish affair then?"

"I had little hope of it coming to aught for though Charles promised much I could not help wondering if, when it came to action, he could do all he undertook."

"Charles?" broke in Lady Avay. "Is it of our Charles you speak?"

"Nay, my dear," replied Sir John. "Robert and I speak of my journey to Charles, King of Sweden, last summer. I have not talked of it to you for it was a matter of the closest secrecy at Avignon and since my homecoming I have still considered myself bound to my oath of silence."

"Things are now so advanced," Dr. Robert hastened to say, "that we may take our Jacobite friends into our confidence.

Recount your part, John, to Catherine and Mr. Lindsay. I ventured to observe

"Your brother, Charles, hinted, Sir, that your Swedish journey might be connected with another attempt to restore King James."

"Therein he was not wrong," answered my master. "When I left the court at Avignon the situation was briefly as follows. The Regent of France, unlike old King Louis, gives not the Stewarts his support and King James has had to look elsewhere for allies. Charles of Sweden wants to take from George of Hanover the Duchies of Bremen and Verden which he has gotten from Denmark as an outlet to the sea, for Charles is distrustful of this Hanoverian expansion in the Baltic. In these circumstances it seemed a wise policy for Charles of Sweden to ally with James Stewart and give King James troops and weapons to destroy the Hanoverian here in Britain. My mission was to point all this out to the Swedish King."

"And," broke in Robert leaning towards us earnestly, "after John had gone from France our party decided to strengthen the scheme by drawing into it my master, Czar Peter. That is how I have become involved in these affairs."

"But, Sir," I interposed, "I believed the Czar and Charles of Sweden were sworn enemies, because Russia seized the Baltic provinces when the Swede was defeated at Puliowa back in 1709."

"You're right," replied Robert. "That was why my intervention was sought for it was no light task to reconcile Russia and Sweden."

"And have you succeeded, Robert?" enquired Sir John eagerly. '

"Yes, thank God. The Czar also dislikes the Hanoverian's interest in the Baltic."

"Then the united power of Sweden and Russia must surely break the Hanoverian," cried my lady, greatly delighted.

"But that is not all," declared Robert. "A third monarch has joined us - Philip of Spain."

"Spain!" exclaimed my master. "What interests him in the cause of James Stewart?"

"Trade, brother. Spain has long disliked English rivalry in the New World and anything that will embarrass England has Philip's support.

"'Tis a mighty project," I stammered forth, greatly taken aback at the thought of the powerful forces marshalling themselves in Europe for our King against George of Hanover.

"Mighty indeed, Mr. Lindsay. It must be all or nothing. ' This Grand Alliance, with Sweden the pivot, will chase the Hanoverian mongrel back across the Channel. Now that you all know what is afoot, tell me to what degree the dismal affair of last year has weakened the ranks of Scottish Jacobites?"

"Our people have suffered," answered Sir John, "and many, as you know, are in exile or tranported to the West. Of those who remain I can truly say their loyalty is in no wise diminished. If sufficient auxiliaries are sent the clansmen will come again from the glens and the lowlands from their farm crofts."

Fife, too, Joined in Lady Avay. my father tells me that the kingdom laments bitterly Mar's failure."

I too gave my opinion. "Presbyterianism, Dr. Robert, has imposed itself throughout the land, but everyhwere Episcopalians await the chance to fling off the yoke."

"These are good tidings," replied Dr. Robert. "Be assured that sufficient aid will be forthcoming. Charles of Sweden has ready 890 foot and 4000 horse. The Spaniard, too, promises men and weapons."

Sir John caught up in his brother's enthusiasm asked eagerly:

"Who is responsible for the conduct of affairs here?

Since my home-coming I have been fully engaged with the silver mine commissioners, hearing nought of the furtherance of this scheme."

"Our kinsman, Mar, has been very active. He wrote in the autumn to the Bishop of Edinburgh and to George Lockhart asking the Scottish Jacobites to send six thousand bolls of meal to Sweden, where there was much scarcity, thinking thereby to bind the Scots and Swedes ever closer."

"Six thousand bolls of meal! No word of this reached me."

"I am not surprised, John, for Lockhart replied at once saying it was not possible, many of the king's supporters being in straits and the shipping of such a quantity beingcertain to create suspicion with the government. The chief negotiators, howbeit, are the Swedish ministers at the Hague and in London, the Barons Gortz and Gyllenborg."

"Gyllenborg," echoed my master. "In troth I have heard from my London friends that such a one is a friend of our cause."

"Since November I have had much correspondence with both gentlemen. Gortz says that Gyllenborg declares ten thousand men transported hither will do the business amply."

"How is he so certain?"

"The Swedish minister says that those dissatisfied with George of Hanover (who leaves the affairs of the country in the hands of a few politicians) need but a body of regular troops to resist openly."

"What arms does he consider needed?"

"Sweden is to send weapons for fifteen thousand men.'Tis said there are sufficient horses here."

"Aye, that is right. When is it proposed to land?"

"Gyllenborg suggests March, being the period of easterly winds, a time the Government will not readily think of."

"And money? Are the English Jacobites willing to open their purses?"

"It seems so, brother. The Swede says he is certain of £60,000. Moreover the English Jacobites have offered to furnish sea officers to assist in the transport of the Swedish forces."

"Have you met Count Gyllenborg?" asked my lady.

"No, sister. I can tell you nought personally of him, but I am confident our affairs are safe in his hands. It is his caution that has brought me to Scotland just now. Being afraid to risk his last letters to the post he sent me word that if I could get over to Leith from Amsterdam his agent would meet me."

"So he suspects his postbag is watched?"

"Aye, John. His agent told me that his master's recent communications with Gortz at the Hague have all been tampered with. Hence his hesitancy to communicate with me by the ordinary channels. I am to meet Gortz at the Hague at the end of this month to make final plans."

"Pray God, nothing miscarry," breathed my lady fervently.

"Amen," we all responded solemnly.

Then Sir John went on."Once the Swedes set foot in Scotland, Robert, you may depend on my help."

"And mine too," I hastened to add.

"May it not be long ere King James thanks you in person here in Scotland," answered Robert.

"That," observed my lady, "will be a happy, happy day. Now,since you have done with politics, I would know how long you stay with us."

"I must leave to-morrow, though by my faith I think I should say to-day, for I see we have talked one day out and another in."

"So soon!" exclaimed my lady, disappointed.

"A boat returning to Amsterdam leaves the pier of Leith a little after midnight. Whenever the dusk of evening begins to fall I must set out for Edinburgh.

"Do you intend to call upon our mother?" asked Sir John.

"A brief visit, though brother Charles will not approve of the business that has brought me hither."

"For all that he will rejoice to see you," my lady assured Dr. Robert. "When John was abroad Charles was very kind to me and the bairns. Come, now, take what rest you may"

A little after four in the afternoon Dr. Robert took his farewell of us all and hardly had he gone when a ploughman from the Knapp came to tell me that Mrs. Burns was no more, having slept peacefully away.

February was heralded in with a great fall of snow that drifted against the dykes and hedges and hindered travel along the Hillfoots. But the bairns both at Avay House and about the village had much entertainment there from, fashioning images they called snowmen, using stones for eyes and nose and teeth, and capping the effigy with a tattered bonnet.

A thaw coming towards the middle of the month Sir John rode into Stirling anent some business. When he returned the mistress gave him but one look and then cried out very frightened.

"John, what ails you? What is amiss?"

The master spread his hands over the fire that crackled on the hearth as if to bring himself back to life, yet for all the heat of the leaping flames his face retained its ashen hue.

"Sir," I said, "will I get you a dram?"

He nodded. My lady took his hands and sought to warm them in hers. When he had swallowed the spirits he seemed to revive. Then looking first at my lady and next at myself for a space, he at length spoke.

"Gyllenborg has been arrested in London and Gortz taken into custody at Arnheim in the Low Countries at the instance of the British Cabinet. The Swedish plan is at an end."

"God have mercy on us all," whispered my lady.

"And the King," I added, "for again he has been disappointed in his hopes."

"What happened, John? When did all this take place?"

Sir John heaved a sigh and drew his chair nearer the fire as if to drive out the chill in his heart with the warmth from the blaze.

"I had it all to-day in Stirling from the Governor of the castel. It seems that at the end of last month the government were informed by one of their agents that the Swedish ambassador was encouraging the English Jacobites.

Accordingly a detachment of the Guards was detailed to surround the Swede's lodgings on the night of January 29th. Gyllenborg suspected nothing and when his room was entered he had no chance to conceal his papers which were seized and taken away."

"Who was in charge of the arrest, Sir John?"

"General Wade"

"Wade? I have heard he is come to Scotland to garrison the Highlands and to open up the country by making roads and bridges."

"Aye there is some proposal of the sort. Meantime, however, he has wrecked our hopes of rising "

"Is it known who informed the government of Gyllenborg's association with the Jacobites?"

"No name is definitely mentioned, but 'tis strange there is a rumour of one Hamilton being concerned"

Sir John saw me start.

"This interest you Mr Lindsay?"

"It does my lord" and thereupon I told my master of James Hamilton's threatening talk of Dr. Robert the day he went from Avay with Dr Brandshagen.

"There is no mention of Robert's name as yet but I cannot think he will escape being brought into this business for he was in closest contact with the Swedes" sighed the Laird

In the weeks and months that followed a great uproar was raised by the body of foreign diplomats in London, for those who represented their countries at the court of St James, considering they held a privileged position, objected to the ministry's invasion of Gyllenborg's chambers and the confiscation of his papers.

It was said (and with this opinion Sir John agreed heartily) that if the Government had cause to complain of the Swede's activity the correct course was to order him to leave the country. Whatever the right or the wrong in this matter of diplomatic privilege, what did concern us at Avay was the news that Secretary Stanhope had written to Czar Peter declaring that in Gyllenborg's papers they had found reference to Dr. Erskine's work in influencing His Czarish majesty to support the Stewarts.

Without delay the Czar sent a memorial to King George protesting his own innocence of the Swedish plot and vouchsafing for the honesty of his physician. Concerning which the Hanoverian could do nothing more than to answer Czar Peter that he was satisfied the Russian designed no evil towards him.

So in the course of time the agitation settled and the arrested ministers were released.

The last we heard of it in Avay was late in the Spring when, at divine service one Sunday Mr. Campbell announced that, by order of the General Assembly, he would hold a service of fast the week following "for the deliverance of the nation from the designed invasion by the Swedes in favour of the Popish Pretender."

And that Sunday the Laird's loft was empty.

At this time also Sir John got word from Mar that the King had been obliged to leave Avignon, seeking refuge in Italy. For a while James

Stewart was in Rome, where he celebrated his twenty ninth birthday.

In July 1717, he removed to the castle of Urbino, a medieval mountain fortress that the Pope had given our King for his use. Of this place we first heard from my lord Mar, who wrote to my master saying "there was more snow there than in all Lochaber or Badenoch and that life was very dull one day being as like another as two eggs and them eaten without pepper or salt."

More news of Urbino came the next year when King James himself wrote to Sir John, with which communication my master was much delighted. That those who come after me may witness for themselves the affability betwixt the King and Sir John, I have gotten His Majesty's permission to include this letter in my writings.

Here I must record how graciously His Majesty acceded to my request, coming to me in person in the library and talking for a considerable time of the Fifteen, asking me to recount my own part therein and praising the services of Sir John now, alas, departed this life eight years ago.

January 1, 1718.

My friend and comrade,

John's good luck since he left me hath made me some amends for the being deprived of his good company. To assure you none shall ever undermine you with me is a great truth, but a phrase that wants a bottle of Burgundy to make it pass. I am still in hopes it will not be long ere we meet when we wish. It will not be my fault if I continue long a single man, which I believe will not displease you.

I am now writing to you in the middle of hills, frost and snow and not like to see the ground these two months. Pray let me hear sometimes from you and present my service to your good lady, whose goodwill for me I can never forget. Were I vain enough for it, I should think myself now a perfect man, being cured of the only fault you were pleased to find in me. But I hope we shall be enough together yet to shew an opinion of me, though in one point I think I deserve yours and that is, in being true to those who are it to me. I include you in that number and shall be so to you I assure, que l'on ponde que l'on crie, que l'on ponde and so adieu, with the same words we used to conclude many a bottle.

You know my hand and so need not sign, being ever sincerely your most obedient humble servant."

Though written at the beginning of the new year this letter did not reach Avay till the Spring by which time my worthy father-in-law John Burns at the Knapp had followed his spouse to rest beneath the green grass of the kirkyaird.

The thread of life in country places changes not from one generation to another: it is in the

pattern woven that the difference is found. During my ministry in Avay there had been Sabbath breakers and so it continued in the time of Mr. Campbell's ministry. Four of the village lassies went gathering berries on the hill that summer of 1718 when they should have been sitting doucely in the kirk and the miller, who well knew better, set the mill to grind on the Sabbath night. All of this I heard from Mr. Campbell himself, who was much exercised on the question of discipline. The time of the minister and the Session being often taken up with cases of libel that in the end could not be proven, the kirk decided to demand a security of 13/4 Scots from anyone bringing a libel to the Session, which sum was to be forfeit for the use of the poor if the case failed.

At Avay House Mr. Campbell found some of the servants without testimonials from their former parishes so that the Session made special intimation that all servants were to have ready their certificates from the ministers under whose inspection they formerly had been.

There was also some trouble anent William Morris, recently employed in the Avay House stables. Morris had like Sir John, myself and Sandy Stewart, been out in what Mr. Campbell called "the late rebellion" though he joined not with us. Now the fellow was seeking baptism for his child but not having attended public worship since the rising he had to make repentance before the bairn was christened.

Later in the year news came that the King was to marry the Polish Princess, Clementina, daughter of Prince James Sobieski, but that by the evil machinations of the English King she was hindered in her journey to Rome.

Sometime in the autumn, I remember not exactly when, the postmaster at Stirling sent two of his servants out to Avay House with a great wooden chest that we saw from the outer coverings had come from Russia. My lady was much excited and the boys crowded round it wide-eyed.

"Is it from Uncle Robert, Mama?" asked Henry.

"'Tis from Russia, so from whom else could it come?" observed Charles scornfully.

"Mayhap from Czar Peter," retorted his brother, whereupon Master Charles rudely put forth his tongue at his brother, receiving from Sir John a friendly cuff about the head for his trouble.

"Open it quickly, Catherine, or your sons must die of anticipation," laughed my master. "Here is the key which the shipmaster who brought it from Archangel to Leith also sent care of the postmaster."

With trembling fingers my lady lifted the lid and, on sighting what lay on the top, she gasped:

"Silken hangings."

Then she held up for our inspection rich crimson curtains. My lady looked to Sir John.

"Where will Robert have gotten such lovely stuffs?"

"By their appearance I would say they were the hangings of some Tartar tent."

"'Twill be so. You remember Robert visited some Tartar princes this summer for his master.

"Is there nought for us?" demanded the boys anxiously.

"Have patience," answered their mother, bending over the chest. "There are many things yet to be brought forth. Why, what is here? Help me, John, to lift this forth.",

And out came a long, low wooden item with curved metal runners at the end thereof which I saw was like to the sleds the countryfolks use for carrying burdens of peats and meal and so on.

"'Tis a small Russian ice sledge," said Sir John.

"In Sweden and Russia, larger ones, drawn by'animals, are the ordinary means of travel. This is a little one that the boys may use on the hills when the snow comes."

But the young gentlemen could not wait till winter came so went forthwith to the grassy bank at the side of the House to try out their new plaything and very pleased they were with it.

But they were more delighted when the year ended and December snows lay thick and frozen hard on the Ochils. Then indeed did young Charles and Henry discover the pleasures of ice sledging, cascading down into the village to join the cottar bairns in rapping upon doors and reciting the customary rhymes:

Rise up, gudewife, an' shake yir feathers,

Ye neednae think that ye are beggars.

We're only bairns come oot tae play,

Rise up, an gie's oor Hogmanay."

January 1719 saw the calmness of our country ways at Avay, being broken in upon by tidings that were ill and tidings that were good.

First came the unhappy news that Doctor Robert had died in Russia, having reached only his forty first year. This sad news was sent by Henry Stirling who had gotten a position at the Czar's court through the favours of Robert. Sir John commented to us from Stirling's letter.

"Robert was at a place called Koucheserski, about 100 miles north east of the capital, taking the mineral waters there, when he died.

Is he buried there?" asked my lady.

"Nay, Catherine. His body was brought to St.Petersburg and buried in the churchyard of the Alexander Nevski monastery."

"Did the Czar attend, Sir?" I asked.

In troth he did, Mr. Lindsay, taking his place in the funeral procession and bearing a lighted torch according to their wont

My lady dried a tear from her eye.

"Does Harry say if there were many there to do,poor Robert, a last service?"

"He went not down unto the grave unhonoured, my love.Two hundred mourners followed his corpse."

Whereat my lady's grief welled up anew and I sought to bring her solace. -

"My lady, Doctor Robert once wrote to me of the kindness he received in Russia and I was struck by his words for he said that were it not he was so far from his kin and friends he would be well content to leave his bones in that cold climate. And so he has done in the hinder end. Grieve not but rather be glad he sleeps in a land he loved well."

Second came the unhappy intelligence that Charles of Sweden, whilst besieging the fortress of Frederickshall in Norway, had been mortally injured, a musket ball entering his right temple, (and having passed through his skull), coming out at his left eye. Thus was the Stewart cause robbed of all possibility of Swedish aid for his successor favoured not King James.

Yet to counterbalance this the third message that January 1719 brought us was that England had declared war on Spain and the Spanish minister, Cardinal Alberoni, had invited the Chevalier to Madrid. So throughout the opening months of the year the occupants of the House of Avay awaited eagerly the outcome of Alberoni's schemes.

In hidden places of the glen, where the rocks give shelter, the primrose was unfolding when Sir John became acquaint with what was passing overseas.

"The Earl Marischal and his brother, James Keith, are reported to be on their way hither. If they weather the storm, the first thrust in this new venture must, of a surety, come from the Highlands," the Laird informed me.

"Is there any indication of what forces these gentlemen have?"

"Marischal's detachment is small,Mr. Lindsay: in all there can be no more than three hundred Spaniards in two frigates. Keith comes with several gentlemen who hope to raise their own people - Tullibardine, Seaforth, Glendaruel, Brigadier Macintosh."

"Macintosh how happily I recall being with him in 1715. Had all our leaders possessed his energy things might have been very different to-day."

"Therein you speak the truth. Borlum is a good Jacobite and, more important, a good soldier."

"Pray God we have speedy news of them."

At last, towards the third week in April, every Jacobite howff in Scotland buzzed with the intelligence that Keith and his friends, having sailed from Le Havre, were ashore in Lewis and Marischal's frigates were at Stornaway. Next we heard that the Jacobites of the north-west were hurrying to Loch Alsh.

Thereafter events moved quickly. Government warships, under a Captain Boyle, appeared in Loch Alsh, where the Spaniards and Jacobites had made the ancient, square keep of Eilean Donan their powder and provision magazine.

The report of our party being defeated there was confirmed some time later when Charles Erskine wrote from Edinburgh saying, among other things, that an English warship with Spanish prisoners from the north had anchored in Leith and he had seen.the men taken to the castle of Edinburgh.

A sorry sight they were, the freshness of their white and yellow uniforms gone, and the men, themselves, ill at ease in a strange land.

The time of our receiving this account of the Spanish prisoners must have been the middle of May for it was about the third week of that month when the summons came for me.

It is strange how oft times coming events, casting their shadow before them, cause a heaviness of disposition in the human soul and a sultriness in Nature as if the creation sympathised with the created. Certainly it was so in May 1719.

Not a breath of wind stirred the grasses on the Ochils; heavy clouds, charged we knew not whether with rain or heat, hung low on the hill tops; and everywhere a clamminess and closeness made life a burden. And all the time I felt as if some leaden weight were crushing me down, down, ever down. I was labouring in this Slough of Despond - to take a phrase from that lively writer John Bunyan - when suddenly, like a hand stretched out to draw me from the quagmire, came a messenger from Archibald Ogilvy at Bridge of Allan seeking me.

One glance at the note the lad brought was enough to send the blood coursing through my veins.

"A gentleman from the Braes o' Balquhidder is going into the north and west and is of the opinion that Mr. Lindsay of Avay might care to join him. If Mr. Lindsay so chooses let him meet the gentleman at Ogilvy's changehouse two nights hence: if not, let it be as if he had never looked upon this."

When I had shown the parchment to my master, he asked:

"What purpose you to do?"

"Ride forth, Sir."

"You go with my blessing. I, too, would gladly take up arms but, for the meantime, I must let discretion be the better part of valour. There is the estate to be thought of and the boys' inheritance."

"That I understand full well," I hastened to assure Sir John. "The man that has a wife and child truly has given hostages to fortune. I have neither. If this business succeed and we come south then 'twill be time enough for you to act."

Sir John took me by the hand.

"Pray God it will succeed but we have been disappointed so often I fear even to think of what may hap this time. Before you set off is there anything I can do for you, Mr. Lindsay?"

"There is, Sir John. Sandy Stewart, like myself, ever hopes to bring the King home some day. Will you let him come with me?"

"Gladly," replied Sir John, "if that be Sandy's will and yours."

Two nights later we tied our horses to the rings on the wall of the changehouse at Bridge of Allan and there we met the gentleman from the Braes o' Balquhidder, who was mustering the Stirlingshire Jacobites. He wasted no time in explaining the situation. We were to set forward at once. ,Lord George Murray with the men of Perthshire would join us on the way. Marischall and Tullibardine were in need of our assistance. Our destination was Glenshiel. If we were still willing to go we would have a dram and be off.

Archibald Ogilvy brought in his finest liquor. We drank: "To the King." 'We went outside, untied the horses, and rode far into the night and far into the Highlands.

The light of the moon fell upon my plain brown suit and upon Sandy's grey cloth and it also fell upon our companion wrapped tightly in his Highlander's plaid. His tartan had but two colours arranged in bold squares of each hue - blackand red. Those who saw it and knew of such matters had no need to ask his name. But you, who were not there, will be wondering with whom we travelled. He was called Macgregor -son to Rob Roy.

GLENSHIEL.

From Bridge of Allan we made our way by Doune and the Braes o' Balquhidder, where some Macgregors and Maclarens joined us, to Strath Fillan and Bridge of Orchy. Thence we crossed a great expanse of heather and rock which my companions told me was the Moor of Rannoch. It now being the first week in June the purple buds were beginning to swell, giving promise of that regal colouring ever associated with the hills and glens of Scotland.

As we rode through Glencoe I noticed mounds of tumbled house stones which, though now grown over with the hill grass, were still dread memorials of the rule of William of Orange and that black night in February 1692 when the treacherous Campbells fell upon the unsuspecting Macdonalds. The Government had thought then to crush the Jacobite cause I reflected but here we were twenty seven years later, still fighting and hoping.

Thereafter our road seemed ever to wind by some loch whether it were a stretch of inland water or an arm of the sea Loch Leven, Linnhe, Lochy, Garry, Cluanie.

By the time we reached this last body of water several of the Camerons through whose country we had come, joined us so that all told we were a force of about eighty men.

On the evening of June 8th, we halted at the inn at Cluanie Bridge, which was far from comfortable.

No oats were to be got for the horses. The principal room was both damp and dirty and the smell of peat reek was scarce able to triumph over the other ill smells that filled the air. On a roughly hewn fir table was an ashet of meat, the grease from which had spilled over on to the boards, mingling with the dregs of an over-turned ale stoup.

Despite his poor place and his half savage appearance the landlord was an obliging fellow. His flaming red hair hung in tangles about his face that plainly had but a nodding acquaintance with the cleansing power of water. He was dressed in the tartan of the Camerons and his deerskin brogues were sadly worn and his saffron shirt much rent.

"Yes, indeed. I have been hearing that there are men come from Spain to Loch Duich," he replied in answer to the young Macgregor's questioning.

"Have you seen any wearing my cloth?"

"Some gentlemen passed this way several days since."

"That would be my father," said Macgregor to me.

"Can you name any of those already at Loch Duich?" I demanded.

The landlord thought a moment.

"The leader is said to be Tullibardine and the people are saying Seaforth, Lochiel and Borlum are with him."

"What of King George's.soldiers?" asked Macgregor.

"They are at Inverness under a major-general called Wightman," our host answered.

"Wightman of Sheriffmuir," I heard Sandy mutter.

"Is there any information about these troops leaving Inverness?" I asked.

The Highlander shook his head and no further information forthcoming the gentlemen of our party betook themselves to the squalid sleeping accommodation upstairs.

Next morning the landlord came to us agog with news:

"The English soldiers have left Inverness. They are advancing by Glenmoriston on Glenshiel," he cried.

"We must on at once and warn Tullibardine," exclaimed Macgregor.

So it was that on the ninth we were with the entire Jacobite force in lonely Glenshiel. Sandy and I were attached to the Perthshire men with Lord George Murray, whose company was detailed for duty as outposts.

A great sun had beat all day upon the earth so that the June night was pleasantly warm as we watched from a massive boulder, high upon the hillside looking east to Cluanie Bridge.

The only sounds to break the silence of this quiet Highlandland landscape were the noises of men in the camp below sharpening their claymores and laughing and talking, heedless of what the the morrow might bring forth.

Sandy and I were silent, each occupied with his own thoughts. Then, on a sudden, I sensed my fellow sentry had become rigid and was staring into the distance, shading his eyes with his hands.

"What is it, Sandy?"

"Quick, Maister Lindsay, yir glass. Awa' yonder whaur thon bit water lies."

I directed my glass towards Loch Cluanie.

"Soldiers."

"I thocht as muckle - redcoats."

"Run to the camp and warn my lord Murray. Tell him they appear to be pitching their tents by the loohside."

When Sandy returned the forces under Wightman were preparing to pass that night at Loch Cluanie. The dragoons had set their horses to grass and the commander's tent was being erected. The rising of smoke followed by blazes of red betokened the camp fires over which the evening meal would soon be cooking.

Gradually night closed over the nearby hills and the distant loch. Then Sandy and I, being relieved of our duty, lay down in the shelter of the rock from which we had been watching and snatched an hour or two of sleep.

A little before daylight we were again on the watch. The sun rose and the bright morning hours began to slip by so that we wondered if Wightman were to move that day or not.

Then a little after ten I caught sight of the enemy beginning to strike camp.

"What dae ye think they hae wi' them, Sir?" asked Sandy. "There's a fearfu' glint o' the sun on metal."

"Some pieces of mortar, no doubt."

"They're no iron by the gleam."

"Probably they are Cohorn mortars."

"Cohorn mortars? I've ne'er heard o' them afore."

"They were designed about fifty years ago by the Dutch military engineer Baron van Cohorn," I replied.

"Hae a keek at the foot, Sir."

"Forming line! Aye, the advance is beginning. Come, we must report this to my lord."

Quickly we retired towards the main body of our force stationed in the Pass of Glenshiel and, meeting with Tullibardine we took up our position on the south bank of the River Shiel, being the right of our army. Our leaders were in good spirits, a fact upon which, to my surprise, Sandy commented in somewhat disapproving fashion.

"Tullibardine an' a' the ither gentry are gey gleg the day."

"And why not?" I asked.

"It'll be time enough tae craw when the fechtin's ower."

"But, Sandy, know you not what day this is?"

"The 10th o' June. Whit o' it?"

"King James's birthday! A victory for our arms would be a gift beyond price for His majesty."

The dour look on Sandy's face changed to a smile.

"Eh Sir, I didna ken that. Joy tae the King ----"

Here he paused, his glance becoming fixed on something in the distance - "an' confusion tae yon band o' rogues."

I followed his gaze. Wightman had come in sight and had halted to deploy his troops for attack.

Glenshiel is one of those Highland Valleys seldom trod by the foot of man so that its grandeur is the grandeur of solitude. It runs inland south easterly from Loch Duich. Tullibardine had chosen to engage in battle in the pass of the Little Glen which he deemed properest for defence.At this spot a southern shoulder of that great mountain Scour Ouran projects onto the northern side of the glen, which itself narrows into a dreadful gorge.

"Yon's a fearsome fa' o' water " observed Sandy.

"What say you?" I cried, for the roaring torrent of the Shiel over its rocky bed and through its narrow passage drowned my companion's words.

"I'm sayin' thon water's gey frichtenin'," shouted Sandy

"The power of Nature," I replied.

"Mair like the power o' the Deil," commented Sandy.

"I see Tullibardine's been busy flingin' a barricade across the road."

"Not only there has he been at work. Observe the entrenchments on the hill face."

"Eh, but a' this gars me think o' Shirramuir."

"It takes me further back than that, Sandy. This place is not unlike Killiecrankie."

"Killiecrankie, Mr. Lindsay? I wisna lang born then."

"I was twenty nine and had never drawn a sword in battle," I laughed.

"Ye've been a bonnie fechter fur the Stewarts -Killiecrankie, the 1708 stramash, Shirramuir an' noo Glenshiel

"Well, Sandy," I replied very soberly, "if we succeed not this time I fear I shall not march for the King again. My sixty years begin to lie heavily on me. The spirit is willing but the flesh indeed weak." '

"Hoots," cried Sandy, "ye're a gey birkie, Sir, fur a' yir hair's as white as Sir Johns siller."

"As you will, my friend, yet this I can say. When the day comes that I am no longer able to lift the sword for the Stewarts I shall get some other means of serving them. Not till death comes seeking me shall I cease to serve my earthly King, truly and wholeheartedly, even as I have also sought to serve my heavenly King."

The rest of our force began taking up positions so that for a time we ceased to speak. On the north side of the Shiel river was the main body - the Spaniards under Don Nicolas Bolano, Borlum, Lochiel, Glengarry, McKinnon and Mackenzie. Seaforth was on the extreme left high up on the slopes of Scour Duran, with the Earl Marischal and Brigadier Campbell. We, as I have said, were on the left with Murray. Tullibardine and Glendaruel were in the centre.

Meantime the enemy had been setting themselves out in battle formation. On their right were a body of grenadiers, Montagu's regiment, and Huffel's Dutch regiment, all under General Clayton. Their left, which like ourselves, were on the south side of the river, was Clayton's regiment and the Munroes. Wightman himself was in the centre. The roadway through the glen was being held by the dragoons and the mortars.

The afternoon wore on so that Sandy began to be impatient.

"Deil tak' them" he burst out - and then remembering with whom he was, he hastily added, "Yir pardon, Mr. Lindsay, but I'm ettlin' tae be on wi' this wark."

"I also, Sandy. Tullibardine and Wightman, however will be waiting till the air is cooler. At Killiecrankie we moved not an inch till sundown."

"I canna see it maks muckle odds, Sir, fur gin it were freezin' cauld aince ye hear the Highlanders blaw their pipes and skriegh in the Erse tongue, the blude gaes leapin' sae in yir veins that ye feel as het's a Culross girdle hingin'on a swee."

"Well, Sandy, whenever it begins I am certain we shall have the first taste."

"Hoo that?"

"Our wing is on the lower ground where 'twill be easier to attack. Moreover their cannon can be brought along the road to dominate our position."

"Sae let it be," replied Sandy, with a certain air of grim satisfaction. "As my mither was gey fond o' sayin',Mr. Lindsay, "the hetter war, the suner peace.""

Scarcely had he uttered this example of proverbial wisdom when, as I had foreseen, the dragoons gave cover to the mortar battery, which, having moved forward, opened fire upon us. Then Clayton's men and the Munroes attacked. This we repelled, but the foe came on again reinforced.

I caught a glimpse of Sandy laying low a redcoat that had made to slash him about the face. For myself I seemed to be ever parrying and thrusting and wiping the sweat from my brow. Then, out of the corner of my eye, I saw a fellow slip from the rear and come towards my right. I scarce had time to think what he purposed when with a mighty rush, I saw him bearing down upon me.

All I can remember now of his appearance is that his face was as red as his uniform. I stepped back, half turning at the same time to raise my sword in defence. He lunged forward, his sword's point missing my body by a hair's breadth.

Carried onwards by his own momentum he fell heavily against my shoulder so that for a moment, I thought we were to fall together. My sword went flying from my hand. The fellow's hot breath filled my nostrils and in a wave of repulsion and battle fury I instinctively struck out with my clenched fist, hitting him full in the belly so that he fell to the ground as one dead.

I picked up my sword and re-entered the general struggle. We fought like wild mountain cats but all in vain.

Behind us was a stream descending from a mountain corrie and over its steep banks we had perforce to retreat.From there we saw our left wing up on the hillside being brought into action by Wightman's right. On them, too, cannon were directed. The Spaniards resisted valiantly and long, but a general feeling of despair overcoming the Highlanders our army began to flee up over the shoulder of Scour Ouran.

I have heard since that the natives in these parts have named one of the clefts in the mountain Bealach na- Spainnteach which translated from the Gaelic means the Pass of the Spaniards.

Seeing the collapse of our army I turned to Sandy.

"Three hours and it is all over. Each is shifting for himself so we may do likewise."

"Whaur dae ye aim tae gaun, Sir? I dinna think we sud try the hill," replied my companion, pointing to the rocky height of Scour Ouran over which our men were still toiling.

"No, Sandy. we'll follow the stream to the West. Wightman will not advance over far this night. If we leave now and keep going through the hours of darkness we may well get beyond the enemy's clutches."

"As ye say, Sir."_

Swiftly we left the field, keeping close to the water's edge. Several of our fellow Jacobites were ahead of us. A short distance ahead the river, falling over a high ledge of rock, formed a deep pool into which we saw some of our party casting their arms, so that if apprehended the Government would not benefit by the seizure of their weapons. Not knowing, however, what dangerous situations we might find ourselves in ere we saw the Ochils again, Sandy and I kept our pistols and dirks, but tossed deep into that swirling, frothing pit our long swords.

By that hour the grey shadows of night were filling the valley and darkening the hill peaks which stood out very black and very distant. The air, chill upon our sweat-soaked bodies, congealed the blood that trickled from a cheek wound on Sandy's face.

It must have been midnight when we came to a clachan of cottages near to the shore of Loch Duich, where a kindly old man gave us a bite to eat and a couch of bracken by his peat fire, whereon to rest.

Next day we were up by first light. Fortunately for us our host knew a little English whereby we got some indications of the land about us.

"There are two ways you can be after choosing," he said.

"Tell us carefully about both," I replied. "Remember we are ignorant of these parts."

217

"Come," he answered and took us to the door. "Yonder you will be going east and north by the loch till you come to the place called Dornie."

"Through whose country will we pass?"

The old man smiled."Through my country, Sir, the country of the Mackenzies.

Then as an afterthought he added, "And of the Macraes, too. They are a wild people, but kindly in their own way and will not be harming you if they know you have been fighting for the King."

"Where may we go from this place called Dornie?"

"You can be going by boat to Skye or if you are the ones for walking you will find your way by Glen Carron and Strath Bran to the Cromarty Water. I cannot be telling you of that though for I have never gone myself." ,

"And this other way?" I asked, pointing westwards.

"From here it is not far to Glenelg. There you will see the mountains of Skye and many islands."

Sandy and I had a few words on these two ways, both in the end agreeing to go westwards to Glenelg in the hope that we might manage thence by the sea and the western isles to the Clyde.

Our pockets bulging with a gift of cheese and oatmeal we took our leave of the hospitable Mackenzie and followed the track that led ever upwards. We seemed to climb and ever climb again. We spoke only when was necessary, saving our breath for the toil of the ascent.

Afterwards I discovered we had traversed what is called the Pass of Mam Ratachan. When we reached the topmost part we sat down upon the heather for a little space. There before us lay the high mountains of the Isle of Skye and down at the mainland's edge, our present objective, the village of Glenelg.

The descent we found as arduous as the ascent, our feet ever slipping on loose stones and the pain behind my knees causing me much discomfort so that I was sharply reminded of the sad fact that the years had, indeed, taken their toll of my agility.

When we came within hail of the clachan the only person to be seen about the place was a fisherman busy with his nets at the water. As we got nearer I saw he was a small, sturdy man of about thirty years of age, black of visage with the look of one who would fear no storm at sea.

I spoke to him, slowly and clearly, for I was uncertain if he would speak the Lowland English.

"Goodmorrow to you, fisher."

The man looked up from his work.

"Goodmorrow to you, Sir, and to your friend. Perchance you are from the Shiel?"

I breathed more easily for here was one in the land of the Erse speech with whom I could speak easily. Moreover, I thought I caught a note of interest in his inquiry concerning whence we had come, but at first I answered with caution;

"We have been the Shiel way. You have an interest there?"

The fisherman gave Sandy's scarred brow and my rent clothing a long look.

"I am hearing that there are many pretty fellows thereabouts," he continued. -

Acting on an impulse within that urged me to trust this stranger I answered.

"There were."

"Were?" he cried in horror. "Were?"

Then abruptly he demanded, "on which side fought you, gentlemen?"

Looking him straight in the eyes I said very quietly,"James Stewart."

"Sirs, you are very welcome. My name is Stewart McIver and I would know what has happened in Glenshiel."

Quickly we told our story and at the end the fisherman of Glenelg shook his head sadly:

"Always we are thinking the King will come again and always we are being disappointed.

"We must go on hoping," I cried, "till we are rewarded with success."

Sandy joined in.

"This is no oor first fecht fur King Jamie an' God willin', it'll no be oor last."

To this the Highlander made no reply but I could see he was glad to hear us speak so and I am certain his next words were the outcome of his esteeming our opinions.

"You will be wanting to get away from here?"

"That is what we seek," I replied.

"My brither and I have often thought of letting down the nets in Loch Nan Uamh that lies southward. This will be a good time to try our fortune there. Come, we will go into the house and talk with my brither."

Now the name Loch Nan Uamh meant nothing whatsoever to me when the fisherman first spoke of it but an hour later, having discussed the matter at length with our benefactors -

Stewart and Hector McIver I knew it was an arm of the sea from whence we might journey across country back to Glencoe and so to Loch Earn and Perthshire. I had also instructions how we were to take the road from Loch Nan Uamh to Loch Linnhe and to avoid the military garrison at Fort William.

The McIvers being of a mind to depart at once, believing Wightman would follow quickly to Glenelg in the expectation of arresting fugitives seeking to get to Skye, we were only too glad to signify our approval. Accordingly, the brothers rowing in front, and Sandy and I seated behind them, we drew away from Glenelg a little after noon.

For once Fortune was with us. The wind blowing southwards filled the sail of the little fishing boat, speeding us on our way. The Highlanders talked but little to each other and when they did so it was in their own language.

Sandy and I watched the strange landscape with avid interest. Always there were the mountains, rising range upon range on either side of the sound through which we passed betwixt the mainland and the Isle of Skye. Towards evening we came close to the shore at a point where the sands stretched for some considerable distance and were, to our amazement, not golden but silver. This we learnt was Morar.

The sun had gone down behind the hills when we rounded a rocky point into the peaceful waters of Loch Nan Uamh.

Here the wind dropping somewhat and our course changing Sandy and I took to the rowing along with the brothers, till the head of the loch was reached. That night, after a meal of fish broiled on a fine fire that the McIvers were not long in getting going, we slept in the bield of the rocks beside that part of the shore where the trees grew thickest.

With the coming of the dawn next day Sandy and I prepared to depart. The country around us was exceedingly beautiful, the mountain slopes being covered with many, fine tall oak trees that were then thick in leaf.

"What call you this part?" I enquired of Stewart McIver.

"In our speech it is Cuildarach."

"And in my tongue what signifies the name?"

The Highlander reflected and then replied, "The place of oaks is what I am thinking the Sassenachs would be calling it." ~

"It's weel called," observed Sandy, "fur there's a deal o' aik timmer aboot. An' I'm thinkin' there'll be a wheen deer amang the trees."

When I had translated Sandy's Lowland Scots into a more English mode of expression the McIver brothers agreed most heartily, observing that we would assuredly see many of the beasts on our journey.

When we expressed our farewell thanks to the brothers they replied with one accord:

"We serve gladly those who serve King James."

And that spirit of honest loyalty Sandy and I found at every door betwixt Loch Nan Uamh and the Corran Narrows, where we crossed the Linnhe Loch, aye, even in Campbell country.

Of that journey I propose not to write narrowly. Suffice it to record we travelled by Loch Ailort and Loch Eilt over mountain paths that wound up and down and up and down till the bones of our bodies ached interminably.

I remember coming down the brae to the head of a great sheet of water on which the June sun so sparkled that the blue was of a hue I had never seen before and never saw again till I came to this foreign place, where the sun blazes down the live-long summer day:

(but,oh, it is in my heart for a day of mist in the Ochils and the sting of rain driving along the Hillfootsl).

At a cottage where we stopped to ask for a night's shelter we were told that this sapphire gem of Nature's was Loch Shiel and the clachan Glenfinnan.

Glenfinnan was it only two years ago that name rang throughout this city of Rome, causing the thin blood of my eighty seven years to stir again with hopes of a Stewart restoration?

Little thought I in June 1719 to hear ever again of that lovely spot at the head of Loch Shiel.

When we reached Loch Eil we continued east along its southern shore till we came within sight of William's fortress behind which rose the bulk of Ben Nevis that was even at that time of year snow-capped. Then we sought the shelter of the wooded hill slopes and turned south to Ardgour, from where the ferryman, whatever he thought, asked no questions but landed us before sunrise one morning on the opposite coast at Onich in Nether Lochaber.

From thence we travelled slowly in unfrequented paths and, for the greater part, by night, fearing to walk openly by daylight, lest we chanced upon Government troops proceeding north by Glencoe to reinforce Wightman.

The month of June was ended when we pushed back the yett and paused a moment before crossing the courtyard and coming to the great front door of Avay House.

"Eh, Mr. Lindsay," said Sandy, "yon muckle Hielan' hills are dootless sweeter nor life itsel' tae the billies that wear the tartan but gie me the laigh, kindly Ochils an' a' this couthie carse o' Stirlin'."

I followed my companion's glance as it swept the valley from the ford at Kerseypow over which a lass was passing, her coats kilted high, to the castel on the rock, standing bright and clear in the July sunshine.

"Eight and thirty years have I dwelt here," I observed uttering my thoughts aloud.

"An' mony mair tae come, if God spares ye, Sir."

To which that summer day in 1719 I answered "Amen"and concerning which I can now say this summer day of 1747 that God has indeed spared me, though not to dwell in my native land.

Little thought I, as we stood viewing the carse, that my eight and thirtieth year at the Hillfoots was to be my last in Avay. Soon I was to arise and go into a far country.

EXILE,

Youth is the age of blind confidence. When I was a young man in the ministry I had a fondness for preaching on the faith of Abraham, holding forth to my people with all the confidence of my twenty odd summers that the merit of the patriarch's setting out from Ur of the Chaldees lay going, knowing not whither he travelled. Now with the years that have brought me to view all things through the eye of experience I believe that Abraham's true valour is shown, not in his disregard of his unknown destination, but in his acceptance of a new way of life at an age when he might well have thought to sit before his tent and rest.

This truth I began to realise in the Spring of 1720. By that time I had managed to hear what had befallen those alongside of whom I had fought in Glenshiel the previous summer, Tullibardine, Seaforth, the Keiths, and George Murray eventually got away to France. The Spanish prisoners in Edinburgh castel were sent home in October. As for Alberoni, the instigator of our rising, he was cast off by Philip of Spain and retired to Italy.

For myself I returned to my duties on the estate of Avay, to which Sir John gave all his energy, becoming keenly interested in the opening up of rich coal seams in the neighbourhood. We spent much time surveying the countryside about the River Devon, as Sir John planned to cut a canal along its banks to convey his coal more quickly and more easily to the Forth

Thus busily engaged I took little heed of the passing days so that Spring 1720 came upon me swiftly and unexpectedly. On the last Monday in March news came of the death of Cousin Davie, who since the Presbyterian revolution of 1689 had laboured quietly in his little grey stone kirk on the cliffs at Muchalls near to Stonehaven. With David's passing I was now the last of my race.

My mind was engaged with this melancholy reflection when Sir John sought me out with intelligence new arrived from Harry Stirling in St. Petersburg.

"At last, we have word of Robert's estate, Mr. Lindsay All the money he has in this country, at London, is to go to our mother. What money there is in St. Petersburg is to be given to the poor."

"Ah, Sir John, that is indeed like Dr. Robert. As he had many occasions of beneficence and generosity I truly believe he never let one of them slip."

"That," reflected my master, "makes his memory lovely to all who knew him."

"What of Dr. Robert's books?"

"These, along with his house, the value whereof is 16,000 rix dollars, are bequeathed to the hospital at Edinburgh."

"So he forgot not the city that taught him his art."

"He forgot no one. The Czaritsa is to have all his lace which is entire and not torn and all his porcelain ware.

The Czar is to be allowed to purchase his curiosities and surgical instruments, the money received going to Scottish orphanages and almshouses."

"What of yourself, Sir John?"

"Robert has given me the gold snuff box presented to him by the Czar when they were at The Hague in 1716."

Here my master broke down a little saying, "Poor Robert, to die so early."

"Sir," I answered, "grieve not, for Doctor Robert was a good man, ever thinking of others as even at this moment his testament proves. Moreover, as Christians we have sufficient ground to judge him now infinitely happier than any he had left behind."

"None deserved it more," replied my master. Then reverting to the letter in his hand he went on, "I purpose to journey to Edinbrugh to-day to consult with Charles anent some matters concerning Robert's estate, in particular his East India bonds. I leave you to deal with the notar from Stirling who is to come to-morrow regarding the feus in the Strude which I intend granting. I hope to return two nights hence."

But Sir John was away from Avay longer than he expected - a week, not two days - and when he came again he sent at once for my lady to speak with him in the laigh parlour.

I mind it was a day of alternate sunshine and storm. The rain with hail and snow through it came driving along the hillside from the west in sudden bursts of fury. Then the blue would appear in the sky and a gleam of sunlight fill the house. And as swiftly as it had come the brightness would pass into gloom and the snowflakes would rest lightly on the hills. It being April the country folks called these vagaries of the elements Gowk Storms.

Sir John and my lady were closeted for almost an hour at the end of which I was requested to join them. It was plain from their looks that whatever it was they had to say to me it would not be pleasant hearing. And that premonition was borne out in the very first words Sir John spoke.

"Mr. Lindsay, I have ill tidings for you."

He hesitated.

"Proceed, Sir," I replied. "In my life I have endured much. Whatever this may be that you have to tell me I shall meet it as well as a man may."

"God give you courage," murmured my lady.

"Briefly, it is this. The Government, baulked in their designs to capture the Jacobite leaders of 1719 have set about ferretting out the King's supporters of lesser rank. Among their agents is one who hates the Erskines of Avay and all connected with them."

In a flash I saw what my master was about to say and exclaimed aloud,

"James Hamilton has betrayed me."

"Aye, indeed, Sir. That is what delayed me at Edinburgh. Charles had but got wind of it when I arrived. I did all I could with those of influence whom I know but 'twas of no avail. The warrant for your arrest is expected any day now."

My lady spoke. "You must flee straightway."

"Flee? Whither?" I cried ponfusedly.

"Overseas," replied Sir John.

"Leave Scotland?"

"Alas," said my lady, well understanding my bewilderment, "there is no other help for it. Scotland is no longer safe for you."

While I sat, stunned with this unexpected and overwhelming turn of events, Sir John went on:

"I have arranged what I could for you. You will go from here to Leith to-morrow. Charles has gotten a trading vessel to take you to Dieppe. Thence you will travel to Paris with this letter of introduction I have written for you to our kinsman Mar."

Sir John went over to his writing tables I saw the folded paper my master held out to me with his great red seal upon it. I saw the familiar taper holder with its roll of wax candle that had stood there in old Sir Charles' time for the sealing of documents. I saw the two folio volumes of the Cambridge Bible with Ogleby's cuts and the calf-bound Acts of Parliament that ever rested on my lord's table. I saw and yet did not see. I was overwhelmed and could say naught.

My lady hastened to comfort me.

"You need not worry for money. Sir John and I have arranged to give you a small pension from the estate. This you will have as long as you live"

To which I could only answer brokenly:

"My lady, you and Sir John are too kind. I deserve it not."

"Nay, Mr. Lindsay," replied Lady Avay, "our only regret is we cannot grant more. You have served us well."

"I know not what Mar will do for you," continued Sir John, "but I have told him of your services here to me and of your loyalty to the cause since 1689. I am certain he will not fail to find you a place."

"In Paris?"

"Not there, I think: more probably at our Jacobite court at Rome. Now we must prepare against your departure."

The rest of that day I spent in a veritable whirlwind of activity. Matters of the estate had to be gone over with the master and my personal belongings sorted out. I packed my small trunk (the one I had in my college days) with things I wanted not to part with, Sir John promising to send it to me once I was settled. And so he did. It is here in this very room, standing over yonder in the shadow beside the fireplace in the exact same spot where I placed it myself when it was delivered to me twenty seven years ago.

What I could not keep I gave to Sandy Stewart who was much grieved at what had befallen me.

"I'm rale sorry it's had tae come tae this. Yon Hamilton wis aye a scoondrel, but he'll get nae guid o' this day's wark."

"Aye, Sandy, it is indeed a sad day for me to be preparing to leave the Hillfoots; yet, whatever we feel we must remember that vengeance is not given to us. Hamilton will get his deserts: if not in this world, then in the next. The wicked like the green bay tree may flourish, but only for a season. I know not whether you and I shall ever meet again in the flesh. Tis certain you and all the goodfolks of Avay will never be far from my thoughts."

"Weel, Sir, it's no likely I'll be in furrin' pairts but gin I e'er traivel ower the seas I'll seek ye oot. Noo, is there ony wee bit service I can dae ye afore ye gang awa'?"

I thought a moment. '

"There is nothing you can do at present, Sandy, but when I am gone, there is something I would be happy to know you did for me."

,"E'en tell me, Sir, an' it sall be dune."

"Sandy, keep my burial place in the kirkyaird neat and free from dockens and if you see the through stone begin to sink, raise it up."
-

"Dinna fash yirsel' aboot that. I'll see that it's aye as braw as ye keepit it a' the years I've kent ye, Sir."

And the faithful Sandy has kept his promise as I learnt only a week or two ago but that is something yet to come in this tale.

The day following, being a Wednesday in the first week of April, I took my leave of the Erskines. with difficulty I kept a tear from my eye. Sir John would have accompanied me part of the way but I declined his kind offer, saying I wanted my last remembrance of the House of Avay to be of my lord and my lady at their ain door cheek with the bairns about them.

The April sun shone through the budding trees as I rode down the long avenue to the kirk. At the north side I reined in my horse to have a last look at the earthly resting place of my loved ones and to take a last farewell of the kirk in which I had ministered. The wind blew gently over the grasses and all was silent save for the creaking of the bell above the west doorway.

A moment or two later I was setting forward at an easy pace along the highroad to Stirling. Few folks were at their doors so that I left the village almost unseen.

When I came to the Kaverkie Burn that bounds the parish on the west I halted to look about me. Alone I had come into Avay in April 1681: alone I was going forth from it in April 1720. I

Twenty one I had been when I had first ridden by the Hillfoots to this place. Here I had spent my life: here I had loved and been loved: here I had sorrowed almost beyond bearing: here I had chosen to be a Jacobite.

Now at three score years I was to go into a strange land to begin a new life, in no wise an easy undertaking. If only I were a younger man, I thought, my spirit would not be so bruised with this forced parting from familiar ways, for youth is not bound about with the cords of habit. So it was as I pondered thus that I came to a new understanding of Abraham's courage in departing out of Haran at three score and ten years.

I stood awhile watching the white fleeced clouds,drifting across the carse, and listening to the birds whistling from the nearby oak trees, the bonnie oaks o' Kaverkie. I could have stood for ever, for I belonged not to this world, being caught up in that eternity of thought created by the contemplation of past scenes and the ensuing recollection of past events. Yet, at last, with a great effort of will I turned my back on Avay and splashed across the burn.My long exile had begun.

I met my lord Mar at Paris in his lodging within the shadow of the ancient cathedral of Notre Dame. His lordship straightway gave me a letter of recommendation to His Majesty's chief secretary at Rome and arranged for me to sail thither from Marseilles.

My first impression of Rome was disappointing. I had expected colour and gaiety. Instead I found filth and squalor. With the exception of the principal highways the streets were narrow and straggling with old, decaying buildings on either side and labyrinths of alleys down which no stranger dared walk.

Dark-skinned men with long, untrimmed beards sat at dirty doorsteps idly smoking. Dark-eyed women with half naked children, clinging to their skirts gossiped volubly. Out and in these groups of unwashed Romans went an unending stream of religious - priests, monks, nuns - their long flowing habits brushing aside the egg-shells and fruit skins that lay where they had been flung from nearby windows. The smell of garlic stunk in my nostrils.

When, after some little difficulty, I found myself in the Via degli Artisti where Mar's serving-man had recommended me to lodge, I was relieved to observe it had some semblance of cleanliness and decency. At the second house from the end I lifted the great brass knocker, the face of which doubtless represented some classical goddess and heard its mighty clang go echoing through the building.

I was hastily formulating my speech of introduction in the Italian tongue when the door opened. A tall, thinly built man of about fifty with keen, piercing, grey eyes scanned me from head to toe without uttering a word. Then,as I was about to say:"Buon giorno, Signore," there fell upon my ears, to my amazement and joy, the well known accents of the Hillfoots. .

"An' whaur micht ye be frae?"

Seeing my look of utter astonishment the man laughed."I ken fine ye're a Scot like mysel'. It's written 'a' ower yir face. Forbye," he added, coming a little nearer and looking more closely at my cloak, "there's only ae place that maks that plaidin' - Avay. Sae come awa' ben an' ye can tell me yir business ower a dram. My name's Henderson."

So on that June afternoon in 1720 began my friendship with Jamie Henderson, which, in the years that have slipped by, has grown ever stronger and which to-day is one of my greatest sources of happiness.

"Ay, ye'd be expectin' tae be coupit wi' a jaw o' Italian whaun the door opened. Were ye no?"

"Indeed, I was. My lord Mar's servant gave me no hint that this was a Scottish household."

"No likely. He'd be thinkin' it wid be a grand surprise fur ye."

"To what part of the Hillfoots do you belong?"

"Afore the '15 I had a' croft wi' my brither at the Banchrie Brae. Ye'll ken the place."

"Abercrombie's land - between Tullibody and Menstrie, on the rising ground?"

"The verra same, Mr. Lindsay. Weel tae mak a langstory short I hadna muckle time for the Orangeman or Queen Anne that thocht they cud mak a better job o' rulin' the land than auld King Jamie. An' I had less time fur the German so whaun Mar cam tae Shirramuir I up an' jined him, alang wi' ane o'Laird Abercrombie's freends, that's a doctor body."

"Doctor Abercrombie!" I exclaimed. "My master, Sir John Erskine, knew him at the court at Avignon."

"An' I kent yir Sir John fur I gaed wi' the doctor as his servant tae France an' then last simmer we cam here. There bein' a wheen Scots fowk needin' ludgin's in this toon my maister took this big hoose fur he disna mak muckle at his medicine."

"Can you accommodate me?"

"Ye're rale fortunate, Sir. There's a braw room tae the front empty. Frae it ye can hae a keek at a' that gauns on in the street."

233

And here it is in Jamie's "braw room tae the front" that I sit penning my memoirs.

Early next day I betook myself to the Palazzo Muti at the far end of Piazzo degli Apostoli, lately restored by Pope Clement XI. Having presented Mar's letter I was brought before one of the King's secretaries, Mr. James Edgar, who promised to do what he could for me. A month later I was informed that I had been appointed to keep the King's papers.

At first this was a formidable task, no previous attempt having been made to preserve the court correspondence in regular fashion. Great bundles of letters, some tied but the majority being single, lay in boxes and chests in the room that is now called the palace library.

Gradually, however, I made order where previously there had been chaos and, this done, my work became lighter the daily additions being not over many to handle. And though this work is now carried out by my assistant I still manage to go twice or thrice in the week to see that all is done as

I would have it.

These documents - the Stewart Papers I have titled them - present a very vivid picture of our struggle since 1689. Future generations who pause to turn over their pages, that some day will be yellow with age, will learn from them not the mere facts of history alone. There they will read of men who, like Stirling of Keir, counting loyalty to king more than worldly comfort, gave their all in the Jacobite cause.

They will meet women who, like Lady Nithsdale, faced danger fearlessly to save the men they loved, that they might live to fight again for the House of Stewart. There, too, they will see mention of Sir John Erskine of Avay for I was interested to observe his name appear in several letters dealing with the Fifteen

The year 1720 closed with a happy event. Jamie Henderson had bid me return early from the palace on the evening of December 31st for he intended to keep Hogmanay in customary Scots manner, but it was close on twelve when I stepped into his room.

"Whit news?" he cried. "Ye're gey late. Has the bairn come?"

"Aye, it has, Jamie: at five minutes to ten."

"A lad or a lass?"

"A lad."

"God be thankit an' may He restore the bairn tae Scotland. Dae ye ken whit he's tae be named?"

"He has been named and baptised. Our Prince is Charles Edward Louis John Casimir Silvester Severino Mario."

So year succeeded year and life went its wonted way in Stewart circles in Rome. George of Hanover died and though Jacobite hopes rose for a while the time was judged not fitting for King James to travel again to Scotland. Prince Charles grew into youth , showing a military spirit and marked personal charm . When the Queen died at thirty three years of age and was buried in St Peter's the

King withdrew much from public life.

In 1739 yet another link was severed in the chain of human ties betwixt myself and Scotland with the death of Sir John Erskine. The new Laird, Master Charles, wrote to me very kindly , telling me that he had recently gotten a commission in the Scots Royals and that he would continue the pension his father had granted me.

With the beginning of the new decade, 1740 , the smouldering fire of Jacobitism began to show — faintly , yet it was there – a red glow of life. Frederick of Prussia and Maria Theresa of Austria went to war and Jacobites at home and abroad speculated upon how this might be turned to their account when England and France were drawn into the struggle. There was a constant coming and going betwixt Scotland and Rome and Paris.Then, at last , in January 1744, hope became reality.

I hastened from the palace to tell Henderson.

" Prince Charles has gone to Paris , at the request of the French minister."

Jamie remained unmoved.

" An' whit wid that signify syne ?"

" Jamie, " I exclaimed, " in your own way of speech you are a thrawn auld deil."

The beginning of a smile appeared on Henderson's face.

" Losh, Sir, but I didna think ye cud sweir. Were ye thinkin' the Prince micht be steppin' over free Paris tae a place we baith ken weel ?"

" Fine you know I mean that Paris is but a halting place on the road to Scotland."

" Then, " replied Jamie , ever ready to seize upon any opportunity for lawful recourse to the wine bottle, " come awa ben an' we'll wish an end tae the long exile the Stewarts hae tholed."

"And to our own, I added, for even at four score and four years deSire fails not in the human heart and I longed for my ain countrie.

THE WHITE ROSE.

Spring of 1745 gave way to summer and the Prince was still in Paris awaiting the French assistance he had been led to expect the year before. It looked as if this were to be yet another disappointment for his father, King James, and so hoped the English Hanoverian party.

But neither they nor we, for that matter, had calculated upon the fervour of a young man determined to "try his own destiny" (as Charles informed Louis of France) and "to conquer or to die" (as he wrote to his father). These sentiments the Prince turned into fact when on June 22nd with nothing more than seven friends and his own personal charm to recommend him he sailed from France for Scotland aboard the "Du Teillay."

Every evening Jamie eagerly awaited my return from the Palazzo Muti, avid for the latest intelligence from Scotland.

At first news came slowly so that it was not till October I was able to bring home the tidings my friend longed to hear. That night he knew from my face I had something to tell.

"News at last. Dinna deny it. I can see the glint in yir e'e."

"Aye," I cried, rubbing my hands for warmth and happiness, "good news indeed. The standard has been raised."

"Whaur?"

"Glenfinnan. Know you the place?" '

"I canna say I dae. I dinna ken muckle aboot the North."

" Life is strange, Jamie, for it was by Glenfinnan that I returned from Glenshiel in 1719. The report says the Prince touched Scottish soil first at the island of Eriskay , from where he sailed to Loch Nan Uamh, landing on the mainland near to Arisaig."

" An' whaun wis the Standard set up ?"

" On Monday the 19th of August . When he got there he had only fifty of Macdonald of Clanranald's men and the seven who had come with him from France. Tullibardine unfurled the flag - white, blue and red - and then pronounced the King's commission appointing the Prince as regent of Great Britain and Ireland."

" Eh, Hr Lindsay, gin you and I had been there!."

" Aye , indeed: but this is the affair of another generation.'

All we can do is to wait and pray that they succeed where we failed."

From Glenfinnan Charles came south to Edinburgh, where at Gray's Mill , close to the village of Slateford, the baillies tried in vain to delay the Prince's entry to the city. But, at last, a Stewart had come again to the Royal Palace of Holyroodhouse: on September seventeenth Charles appeared before his people, the Star of St Andrew gleaming on the breast of his tartan short coat , and a white cockade - emblem of the Jacobite cause - in his bonnet.

Soon after came the defeat of the Hanoverian troops under Cope at Prestonpans and the march on England.

Here in Rome we could scarce wait with patience the arrival of each succeeding post. Carlisle was taken, the Prince entering that city on a splendid, white horse with the skirl of a hundred pipers heralding his coming.

Thence the victorious army marched by Kendal, Preston, Manchester, to Derby. On receipt of this last intelligence Jamie Henderson and I began to speculate upon how soon we would hear of the Jacobite entry into London. That the English were in a state of great alarum we, at the Court of Rome, knew full well, certain letters written by one-time Prime Minister Walpole's son, Horace, to the British Minister (Mann) at Florence having been intercepted. From this correspondence it was clear that many citizens were leaving London for the country, that Cope was in disgrace and General Wade very popular, and that the banks were having difficulties, the people being inclined to make a run on them at every fresh rumour of a Jacobite advance.

Moreover, 'twas said George ll had a vessel at Tower Quay, ready to depart at a moment's warning.

Then one day in mid-December as I was discussing with my assistant the advisability of preserving some maps and plans of the fords across the River Forth that had been used in the campaign of 1715, the King himself came into the library. I thought he looked paler than usual but gave the matter no particular attention.

" What charts are these, Mr Lindsay ?"

" Your Majesty, they are of the fords of the Fo'rth. Once you are restored and the plan that Lord Mar has for a canal betwixt the Clyde and the Forth is carried out, these will not be needed."

Slowly the King laid down a chart.

" Mr Lindsay , it grieves me to tell you that within the last hour word has reached me that my son has been forced by his advisers to retreat from Derby."

Soon on the heels of that black news came the intelligence that King George's son, the Duke of Cumberland, was harrying the retreat north. Early in the new year, that is last year - 1746 -the scene of the struggle shifted to Falkirk where the Jacobites overcame the Hanoverians under Hawley.

Yet, despite the victory at Falkirk, the Prince was forced into the Highlands: and all the while Cumberland and his Hessians were making for Aberdeen.

Wednesday, April 16th, 1746, was the end.

Twenty five minutes of shattering fire and merciless bayonet attack from the fresh, well-fed government troops brought the utter collapse of the weary, hungry, dispirited Highland army at Culloden moor.

Charles became a hunted man with a price of thirty thousand pounds on his head. Thirty thousand pounds - you who perchance are sitting by a warm fire, with a full belly, reading this tale, may feel no temptation, but pause to consider the people who for three months hid our Prince and got him safely to France at last. Think of their poverty and their misery. Think of how thirty thousand pounds - aye, of how even one thousandth part of that figure -would have made them rich beyond all their dreams: and then thank God that not one Highlander filed his hands with Hanoverian lucre.

Not till September did Charles get aboard the French vessel awaiting him in the waters of Loch Nan Uamh so that his venture ended where it had begun. Being indisposed with a slight chill I was not at the palace library when at the beginning of November it became known that the Prince had gotten safe to France: my assistant, however, kindly sent a messenger to advise me of the tidings.

When I had perused the note I called Jamie Henderson to my chamber.

"Jamie, 'tis all over for certain. I have word here the Prince is back in France."

"Puir laddie, Mr. Lindsay, tae hae got sae near an' then tae be sae cast doon. He maun hae a gey sair hert the day."

"And his father, too, though at times I feel King James has become resigned to exile."

"Maybe it's jist as weel if that's the wey o't fur I'm beginnin' tae think mysel' there's no muckle hope fur ony o' us e'er winnin' hame noo." '

On the small gilt and carved table by my chair was a bowl of white roses, the season's last. Jamie would have no other bloom indoors save this flower of the House of Stewart.

Some petals from a full-blown rose lay scattered on the floor. Jamie placed his fingers beneath the blossom.

"The white rose of the Stewarts," I commented.

"Charles wore it in his bonnet, they say, when he rode into England"

"Aye, Sir, but God help us, noo, it's wede awa'."

As he spoke it fell before my eyes, exposing to view a fresh bud that had been concealed behind the blown flower.

'"Look, Jamie - a rosebud. As one flower dies another is born. Life and the hope of fulfilment go on. So it is in Nature and so it is in our human existence."

Whilk truth I see proven before my eyes this present year of grace 1747; for, still hoping that they live to fight another day, many a pretty lad has come to fling in his lot with our exiled court rather than bend the knee to George II. Some are Lairds whose lands are now forfeit to the government and who have scarce a shirt to their back, having lost all in their fealty to the Prince. Some are poor ordinary fellows that have followed their masters into banishment. Here in the streets of the Eternal City you may hear the accents of all Scotland.

Indeed, so accustomed had I become to hear the Scots tongue mingle with the Italian that, on returning home one evening in April past and hearing Jamie conversing with another who sounded a fellow countryman I gave the matter no particular attention.

Accordingly, not wishing to disturb them at their talk, I slipped quietly into my own room sitting down before the bright fire with my old and battered Horace wherein I ever find consolation and company. About ten minutes thereafter,a knock coming to the door which I presumed to be Henderson, I called out:

"Come in, Jamie."

The door opened and a voice I had thought never to hear again said:

"It's no Jamie, Mr. Lindsay. It's Sandy Stewart o' Avay."

"Sandy!" I exclaimed, rising to my feet. "Can it truly be you?"

"Nae ither Sir. I've been crackin' wi' Jamie Henderson till ye wud win hame."

At that moment Jamie himself appeared in the doorway.

"Weel, Sir, this'll be a happy nicht fur ye."

"Happy indeed. Come, draw the chairs to the warmth and tell me what has brought about this joyful occasion."

"Weel, Sir," started Sandy, "as ye ken, efter ye left Avay, I steyed on wi' Sir John, workin' awa' aboot the place ' an' then Sir John deed an' my lady an' the young Laird keepit me on. I'm no needin' tae tell ye what gaed on in Avay a' thae years fur it wis jist the same as in yir ain time."

"That I can well believe, Sandy, but ere you proceed further, tell me, how is my lady and the Laird and the other members of the family?"

"Daein' awa' brawly; Maister Charles, the Laird, is a gran' sodger, e'en tho' he fechts fur King George."

"History repeats itself. His Uncle James was a William of Orange's man. But what of yourself, Sandy? Are you still loyal to the cause?"

Stewart laughed.

242

"If I hadna been leal tae the Prince I widna been here the nicht. I wis oot wi' him at Falkirk."

"You fought last year?" I cried, much excited.

"Dae ye think I cud sit in Avay an' ken the Stewart wis near aboot an' no gaun oot tae gie his enemies a clout?"

"No, indeed, Sandy: you bear the name yourself."

"Aye," observed Jamie, with a smile, "but a' Stewarts are no sib tae the King."

"Maybe no," retorted Sandy, spiritedly, "but they are a' ready tae draw the sword fur him."

"Come then, tell us of Falkirk."

" Eh, but it wis cauld on Falkirk muir. We gaed forrit tae the risin' grund south an' west o' Falkirk. I wis in the first line. We heard that Hawley's dragoons were hurryin' tae occupy the ridge o' the hill afore us."

"Was Hawley with the dragoons ?"

" Deed no. He wia claverin' awa' at Callender Hoose wi' Ledy Kilmarnock. The puir fule didna ken she wis keepin' him gabbin' there tae gie us time tae get the advantage o' him."

" An' did ye get there afore the dragoons ?" asked Jamie.

" That we did an' nae suner were we there whaun doon cam' the rain soakin' us tae the skin. As fur Hawley's men their hands wir freezin' tae their muskets."

" Who led you into action ?"

" Lord George Murray. Ne'er a shot did the enemy fire till my lord was gey near face tae face wi' the dragoons. Then the hale Hielan' airmy rushed on the English an' them that fell struck up wi' their dirks, rippin' the bellies o' the dragoons' horses."

"And what of you ?" I asked.

" I dinna richtly ken whit happened neist but I must hae got a knock fur whaun I cam tae mysel' I was sittin' on a rock. Thinkin' some men approachin' were Macdonnells I gied a shout. Before I kent richt whit wis happenin' I was a prisoner."

" Where did they take you ?"

" That nicht we slept at Linlithgow."

"Linlithgow! I heard Hawley's men fired the palace there."

"I saw it wi' my ain e'en, tho' later they tried to say it wis a mischance. Frae Linlithgow they brocht me tae the Tolbooth 0' Edinburgh. "

"The Tolbooth," I cried, "the last time I was 'inside that place was in 1708 when visiting the Stirlingshire Lairds at their'trial for High Treason."

"Weary on the Tolbooth o' Edinburgh. I lay there frae Januar till September afore they gied me my dischairge."

"Your discharge?" I asked.

"Jist a bit paper tae tell a' the world I've lain in the jail a wheen months," laughed Sandy. "Hae a keek at it."

From the depth of an inside pocket the good fellow produced the following written roughly on a half sheet of paper much thumbed.

"These are certifying that the bearer hereof, Alexander Stewart in Avay, was made prisoner the 19th day of Januar 1746 years in the Tolbooth of Edinburgh till the 30th September which day George Drummond Esq., Lord Provost of the place dismissed him from the said prison.

Dated at Edinburgh this second day of October 1746.

Signed. Robert Rennie.

"But how came you to Rome?" I enquired next.

"Wi' a Hieland gentleman that lay in the Tolbooth wi' me an' wis set free some months syne. He wis some freend o' Lochiel's that wis brocht tae Edinburgh efter Culloden. Puir man, he wis sair woundit aboot the kist an' troubled in consequence wi' a kittle hoast. Bein' a Jacobite he thocht he'd like tae come tae the coort at Rome an' bein' a Catholic had a notion tae veesit the Paip."

Here Sandy paused and then went on, a little upset with painful recollections.

"He didna see the King nor the Paip, but he saw Rome an' it gied him pleesur'. We cam hither on horseback an' had only gotten within sicht o' St. Peter's whaun Mr. Cameron suddenly cried oot an' slippit frae his beast. I wis doon aside him in a meenute: there wis naethin' I cud dae but steek his e'en."

"When was all this Sandy?" S

"Three days ago."

Jamie added some wood to the fire and asked:

"Whit are ye gaun tae dae noo?"

Sandy sighed.

"I'm sure I dinna ken."

I leant forward to my old friend.

"Sandy, is there aught to take you back to Avay?"

"I hae nae kin binna my sister's son an' he's thrang wi' his wife an' bairns. But I dearly loe the hills. I widna like tae be awa' frae Craigleith or the Nebit fur aye. An' mair nor that, Sir, I'd like tae sleep my last sleep in the auld kirkyaird."

"Sandy, well do I understand your feelings. I am an old man. My time cannot be much longer. Will you stay with me here in Rome and when the hour of death comes, take my heart back to Avay to rest beside my wife and bairns?"

"Mr. Lindsay, ye've been a gude freend tae me an' I'll dae as ye ask me gladly."

Then Jamie spoke.

"It disna aye gae by years yet gin the course o' Nature tak its wey Sandy an' I sud be left thegither. If that happens I'll gae back wi' him tae the Hillfits."

When Sandy and Jamie went from my room that night and I was left alone with my memories there came into my mind the idea to write them all down. Next morning I sent out for a new quill and a paper book vellum bound.

When I looked in the calendar to date the beginning of my tale I found it was April twentieth - the anniversary of my entry into the Kirk of Avay and also my eighty seventh birthday.

VOUS Y REGNEZ SEUL.

Now my story is almost at an end. It only remains for me to acquaint you with what has passed since the night in April when Sandy Stewart came to join me here in Rome and to write Finis and so close these memoirs.

Early in May we were both cast down in spirit for I had a melancholy letter written from Edinburgh by Charles Erskine, who is now known as Lord Tinwald. It was to tell me that the young Laird, his nephew, Sir Charles 4th baronet of Avay, Major in the first battalion of the Scots Royals had fallen in battle near Hulst in the country of Axel.

Of Charles' death his uncle wrote:

"He died in defence of liberty and property and all that is dear and valuable unto us as men and Christians, on Friday the 24th April 1747 betwixt nine and twelve at night."

"Aye," declared Sandy when I read this to him,"there'll be changes at Avay afore lang."

"What mean you?"

"Jist this. maister Henry, wha'll noo get the estate has nae likin' tae settle doon tae the life o' a country Laird an' I hae a feelin' that whaun the auld Lady Avay slips awa' he'll sell the place."

"Sell Avay?" I cried out in astonishment. "To whom?"

"His uncle Tinwald. He's fell important in Edinburgh. Deed they were sayin' whaun I left that he'd be Lord Justice Clerk by anither year. I've heard tae a wheen times that he has the notion tae be Laird o'Avay. Forby his son James is makin' a grand wey fur himsel' as an advocate sae they're lookin' roond fur a bit land."

"Well, Sandy, I'm glad to hear the estate is to remain in the Erskine family - at least in my time."

"Maister Henry's a' fur the sodgerin'. It's no sae verra lang sin he tellt me he wis gaun tae write a fine sang aboot hoo the Scottish sodger cud fecht fur freedom."

"Henry turned poet!" I exclaimed. I

"Aye, he recited a line or twa but he said it wisna feenished yet."

"Can you recall any of it?"

Sandy thought a while.

"Eh, Sir, a' I can mind is somethin' aboot 'in the garb of old Gaul" an' the "heath covered mountains of Scotia."

The rest o' it's clean awa' frae my mind."

"A song of Scotland - 'twould have delighted his grandfather, old Sir Charles. If Henry's mind is not on the estate mayhap it will be as well for Tinwald to have it. He was ever anxious about its well-being."

"I dinna think I tellt ye that Lord Tinwald was veesitin at Avay whaun Prince Chairlie an' his men mairched intae Edinburgh last autumn. Rale worrit he wis aboot his gear in the toun lyin' at the mercy o' the Hielanders. Hooever, a freend o' his, a banker by the name o' Campbell, pit his mind at ease by sendin' word tae Avay that though his hoose had been searched baith inside an' oot by a son o Powhoose, wha wis huntin' fur weapons, naethin' wis fund an' naethin' taen." I smiled.

"Poor Charles Erskine. He never did like the Jacobites!"

When I wrote to console Lord Tinwald on the loss of his dear nephew I took the opportunity to ask him to arrange that on my death all I should be possessed of and, in particular, the legacy his mother had left me, be shared betwixt Jamie Henderson and Sandy

248

Stewart. Moreover I begged him to forward a letter to the new Laird, Henry, in which I requested him as a last favour to settle these two old faithful friends upon the estate in some way suitable to their age. Only last week I had a long letter in reply, assuring me that all would be done as I wished, adding for the further peace of my mind that Jamie and Sandy would be housed at the Strude near to the kirk. All of which has much comforted me in this the twilight of my earthly day.

The blood of an old man is thin so that as I sit writing I have thrown a plaid of the Stewart tartan over my shoulders for the sun has set and I feel a chill. Such is the contrariness of life that here in exile I may wear the tartan freely yet in Scotland this very day - Lammas 1747 - the wearing of the tartan has been proscribed.

Strange it is that a cloth should mean so much. To the Highlander it is the symbol of freedom , worth living for, worth dying for. And this truth the Hanoverian king recognises for, in the same breath as he forbids the people to wear the tartan, he permits it as military uniform, knowing that his highland armies will bravely answer the call: " Bring on the tartan."

Soon Sandy will bring in the candles and Jamie will set the tinder to the wood fire in the grate. Then I shall leave my desk, drawing my chair close to the bright blaze. There I shall sit till supper-time dreaming the dreams of an old man and gazing on the Ochil Eye as my hands lie resting in my lap.

The stone is as fresh and gleaming as it was when I got it nigh on sixty years ago, but the silver bezel bears the rubbing of time. Howbeit the engraved heart and motto are still decipherable.

" Vous Y regnez seul — Jean, my beloved wife, you alone of womankind have reigned in my heart and I know and am glad it will not be long now till we are re-united and the bairns too.

"Vous Y regnez seul" - House of Stewart, you, of all other worldly interests, have reigned alone in my heart. I can say truly and without any tincture of vainglorious boast that in my time I have done as James Stewart commanded me that June afternoon so long ago at the manse of Avay -

"Continue to serve the House of Stewart, as you have done this day, Mr. Lindsay, with affection and loyalty."

Many a time I have thought to see our royal family come again to their own but now I begin to ask if it will ever be so. Nevertheless, whatever the future has in store for the Stewarts, of this at least I am certain - though he never wear the golden crown that lies hidden away in the castel of Edinburgh, this last champion of the cause, Bonnie Prince Charlie (as I hear the country folks call him) will reign for ever in the hearts of all who are proud to call themselves Scots, -

One last thing I have to record. My Ochil Eye is to rest with my heart beneath the green grass of Avay kirkyaird This morning when I took up my pen I knew I would end my tale by night and I wondered how I might take my leave of my readers. My Bible chanced to be lying open where I had been reading of Judas Macabeus who fought valiantly and long for the rights of Israel and there I found my farewell to those who have followed with patience the story of one man's life:

" And here I will make an end.

If I have done well , and as the

story required , it is the thing

that I desired; but if I have

spoken slenderly and barely

I have done that I could."

II Maccabees. XV. 39

Printed in Great Britain
by Amazon